CHiFF CHaFF

CHiFF CHaFF

DAVID BARNARD

Matador
9 Priory Business Park,
Wistow Road, Kibworth Beauchamp,
Leicestershire. LE8 0RX
Tel: 0116 279 2299
Email: books@troubador.co.uk
Web: www.troubador.co.uk/matador
Twitter: @matadorbooks

ISBN 978 1788039 536

British Library Cataloguing in Publication Data.
A catalogue record for this book is available from the British Library.

Printed and bound in Great Britain by 4edge Limited
Typeset in 11pt Book Antiqua by Troubador Publishing Ltd, Leicester, UK

Matador is an imprint of Troubador Publishing Ltd

For Harry and Irene

"It was not, I thought, entirely unreasonable that the son of a man who had no name should have no name also."

The Third Policeman by Flann O' Brien,

"Now the problem I'll be discussing today may not be yours but they could be someday."

Frankie Byrne, Woman's Page, RTE Radio
Courtesy of RTE Archives.

CHiFF

CHAPTER I

ME AND THE WORLD-FAMOUS

JUNe 1952

A hypnotist takes a white handkerchief (free of snot) from one jacket pocket, and then from the other.

A hypnotist holds, face-high, the two white handkerchiefs (free of snot) and then crumples them together. He uses both hands to do so. He is wearing white gloves.

A hypnotist then puffs into the side of what is now one very large white handkerchief and sort of makes a spell, and out comes many white birds that go, 'coo-coo, coo-coo'.

A hypnotist can 'coo-coo, coo-coo' as well, if he chooses to.

A hypnotist is a very clever person… I know. I know.

I am onstage. This tall man standing next to me is a hypnotist. No… he… is… *the…* hypnotist. I recognise him from the poster on the noticeboard outside the shop. He has a thin line of hair between his nose and lips, and eyes that follow you.

I am standing next to Mister Edwin Heath. I am.

The Most Electrifying Personality of Modern Times. The World-Famous Hypnotist.

That's what it says on the poster.

3

My hands are held tight over my head. I am kept waiting. I am watching *his* hands, *his* gloves. I am waiting. Where are the white birds? 'Coo-coo, coo-coo.'

That's what hypnotists do. They produce coo-cooing white birds, and then and only then can you ask them about something that's bothering you.

I know. I know.

"Now, what's your name, young man?" He is speaking to me.

I know my name. I am Alexander Harvey Flett Alexander Clifton Thomson Alexander Seater. That's what it says on my birth certificate. It is a bit long, isn't it? In Orkney, people's names can be as long as baler twine. Folk here know me as Alexander A. Alexander, or Alexander for short.

I think about whether to tell him my full name or not. Then I think about whether to tell *him* my name at all. You know what? I don't see the point. I can't see how telling him my name will get these coo-cooing white birds to appear.

I say nothing.

"And how old are you, Alexander?" He is asking me another question.

I am sixteen. I am proud to be sixteen. I am a man. I am an adult. I will answer him. My mouth is wide open. I try to speak. No words come out. My mouth is wide open. No sound. Mouth open. No words. Hands held tight over my head; arms aching.

The world-famous hypnotist walks to the front of the stage and looks back over his shoulder at me. He looks worried. No, he is smiling. He is smiling at me. He clicks his fingers, and my hands above my head are released from the spell. I let them fall to my sides.

I like him.

The world-famous hypnotist turns to face the audience once more.

"Ladies and gentlemen, let me ask Alexander something a little easier.

"Young man, our United Kingdom has a new royal head. Our Orkney has a queen. What's the name of our new monarch? I'll give you a clue. *E*, then *L*."

There is laughter.

I do not like the laughing. I do not like the laughing.

Mister Heath joins in the laughter.

I do not like him.

"Alexander, what am I holding in front of you? I will tell you. It is a fob watch. Look."

Puzzled. Suspicious. Getting angry. I have no interest in this watch. It isn't meant to be like this. I want coo-cooing white birds. That's what hypnotists do. One large-white handkerchief; then the other. Both handkerchiefs (free of snot). Blow in the side. 'Coo-coo, coo-coo.' Proper hypnotists always look serious. They don't laugh.

"Alexander, look at me. Follow the watch as it swings from side to side, side to side. I will count to ten and then snap my fingers, and you will be fast asleep."

No. I won't. I am not sleepy. I do not like him.

I follow the movement of the watch with eyes and neck. Right to left and left to right. Right to left and left to right. I want him to bring out a white handkerchief (free of snot) from one jacket pocket, and then from the other.

I will play along with this stupid game. His game, not mine.

To be got out of the way. *His* warm-up for *his* main act.

The world-famous hypnotist is here in Orkney to take out both handkerchiefs and magic coo-cooing birds. That's what hypnotists do. Then and only then will I be able to…

"You will close your eyes."

I close my eyes. Pretendy.

This man standing next to me is a hypnotist. That's right,

but more than just a hypnotist. The World-Famous. He starts to count up to ten.

I know how to count up to ten as well. I know. I know.

"Three… four… five." Yes. *I* say the numbers out loud, even before *he* does. *This is a silly game.*

As for the rest, I don't know. I just don't know. I hear a snap of the fingers. A snap of the fingers. Eyes wide open, even though I've just shut them. I wasn't asleep. No. *I wasn't.*

"Three… four… five." Did I get to say 'six'?

The lights are bright. I am dazzled. I am blinded. I am awake. I can now see shapes in front of me. Two of them, adult-tall. Where did they come from? These two adults must be doing better than me in this contest. They are three steps in front of me. Cheats. All because of me following this watch. Eyes and neck. Right to left. Left to right. Tick-tock. Tick-tock. These adults have cheated.

They may be adults but they have no right. No right at all.

Just them and Mister Edwin Heath with me on-stage. I cannot see any others. Shall I check behind me? Safer not to. I cannot feel anyone's breath on the back of my neck. Phew.

I count up to ten from the start, slowly, to myself. Keep looking in front. Adults. Both of them.

Not fair. Not fair.

Shall I join them out in front? No.

I stay put.

I play statues.

I play invisible.

No one will notice me.

Mister Edwin Heath is now to the side of the stage. I am there to see him because he is a very clever man. Anyone who can magic white birds out of large white handkerchiefs (free of snot) has all the answers. He will give me the best advice going.

I will tell him my problem. Now.

He will tell me what I should do. Now.

But where are the coo-cooing birds?

'Coo-coo, coo-coo.'

Mister Edwin Heath walks towards me. He is smiling. I am confused.

"Ladies and gentlemen, Alexander has been a good sport. Let's give this young man a big hand."

I am in shock. Cannot move. In the spotlight. He is smiling at me, and then as quick as a click of the fingers, has stopped smiling. He wants me to do something but I do not know what. What does he want me to do?

A tug. Mister Edwin Heath leads me towards the steps at the side of the stage.

I stop. I am going to ask him my question. I am so. Mister Edwin Heath gives me a wink. A broad grin. Fixed.

A second tug, followed by a push in the back. I am to return to my seat. Now.

My time has come and gone. My performance is over.

Everyone in the audience is clapping and cheering. *Not* laughing at me. Good. I like the fact that everyone likes me. But deep down, I am very disappointed. I have gone to receive the word, but Mister Edwin Heath hasn't even allowed me to ask the question.

After that night, I was famous. Entertainment-famous.

Me. Entertainment.

Outside the shop. Some younger than me, others older. Lounging about. Passing the time. On seeing me they would shout, "Alexander…Alexander." Over and over again.

Me. Entertainment.

I didn't mind the 'Alexander…Alexander' chant. I *did* mind them doing the dance.

7

First, they would clasp their hands just in front of their chests. Then they would go 'cluck-cluck-cluck', pumping their elbows out like they were laying an egg.

Then they would shout out, over and over again, "Alexander has got big ears... Alexander has got big ears." The 'Alexander has got big ears' didn't get to me. But the dance always did. Making me look really stupid.

That one time, I saw my sweetheart Gail joining in. Her hands clasped together in front of her chest. Elbows out. 'Cluck-cluck-cluck.' The girl of my dreams, doing the dance.

I wanted to die. There and then. Then and there.

Maybe this humiliation of all humiliations was my punishment. Punishment for going to see Mister Edwin Heath. Going against the Lord's will.

The Minister had warned us only last Sabbath.

"The world-famous hypnotist Mister Edwin Heath is appearing at the Garrison Theatre. Do not go.

"The poster in our parish gives us the date when he will be here. It is to be next Friday 13th June... and it says *1952*. We don't need to be told what year we're in. It has been 1952 from New Year's Day up to now. From now right up to the year end, it will stay at 1952. Why state the obvious? It is the Devil poking fun at us Orkney folk.

"Not even six months have passed since that fateful day when the Devil wrought destruction everywhere in our parish. He and those January winds of his.

"Brethren, there is always a price to pay. Do not be fooled by the poster into believing that this show will be harmless fun.

"Mister Edwin Heath is like that bad egg, no longer needing to seek cover. Wickedness rises to the surface and floats and swims like an egg gone bad. Do not swim alongside this agent of the Devil. Do... not... be... a... swimmer.

8

"The world-famous hypnotist Mister Edwin Heath will be amongst us before next Sabbath. Resist temptation.

"Do not put the Second Coming at risk.

"*Do not see him.*"

I did not know what to do for the best. I was like that pushme-pullyou animal.

Seeing the world-famous hypnotist would be going against the Minister's wishes and bring badness on us all, and put this Second Coming, this joyous occasion, at risk.

The Minister was the voice of the Lord.

But

Mither passed away less than six months back.

My duty was as clear as clear could be. I had to keep our farm going. Only the World-Famous would tell me how to do this. Anyone who could magic coo-cooing birds has all the right answers.

I couldn't make my mind up.

I would have to talk to Ephraim. He's been with us as our farmhand for five years now. I liked and trusted Ephraim like you'd trust a real faether. I wouldn't tell him everything though.

Ephraim was my pretendy faether. Ephraim was *not* my real faether.

There he was in our byre, our cowshed, busy working away. Putting down fresh straw bedding for Popeye. Popeye was our big cow. Popeye. Our big cow. One good eye. Pop-eye. Ephraim always found time for me. He put down his pitchfork and from behind his ear took a roll-your-own. Smoking. Puff-puff. A roll-your-own. Behind his ear. Adult.

"What's up, beuy?"

"Ephraim, I want to go and see Mister Edwin Heath, the world-famous hypnotist. He's here next week at the Garrison

Theatre but we heard the Minister say last Sabbath that to go and see him would be very, very bad."

"Beuy, the Lord can't be checking on everyone at the same time. He would need to have more eyes than an octopus has arms. The Lord is omnipotent but He has His work cut out in Orkney."

I nodded.

'Omnipotent.' The Minister had used that word last Sabbath.

Ephraim always spoke to me adult-like. And so he should. I was sixteen. When he used these big adult words with me, he knew I would understand them. Man-to-man talk. Big, adult words.

To try and remember a big new word, I would swill it round and round in my mouth and then would spit it out like I was cleaning my teeth. This remembering was hard but I would never let on.

'Omnipotent.' 'Omnipotent' was a big word. When I heard the Minister use this big word at the Sabbath service, it was like... like... a thunderbolt. 'Omnipotent.' What a big, beefy, adult word that was.

Up 'til then I had been daydreaming, sidestepping all of the Minister's words, like I was avoiding loads and loads of puddles. 'I saw Esau, sitting on the see-saw.' 'Esau... see-saw.' 'Esau... see-saw.' No room for anything else. This rhyme was going round and round in my head.

I needed to get to the bottom of this word, 'omnipotent'. I had to know. Now. This moment. Even before we went back indoors, inside our bu, I had to ask. I had to take that risk. I would be clever. I would not ask directly.

"Ephraim, why would the Lord have His work cut out in Orkney? Is Orkney difficult for the Lord? Him being omnipotent and that."

"Beuy, Orkney is just a small island off the north coast of Scotland. Too far away to receive the Lord's undivided attention.

"Banks of clouds mass together over Orkney to form a shield, making it easier for sinners to get away with badness. This shield is as black as the inside of a cow. Keeps things hidden from Him."

I was watching Ephraim closely as he said this. He kept on rubbing behind his ear where the roll-your-own had been.

"From these banks of clouds comes the rain. It rains a lot in Orkney. For the Lord, Orkney is *Sodden and Gomorrah.*"

I nodded.

Ephraim started to lift the barrow. It was full of dung-matted straw. Suddenly he stopped. He had a bit more to say.

"It's very important, Alexander, to be able to listen to people who can tell their arse from their elbow. Wise fellers have wisdom. Them hypnotists are wise fellers, holy men with an insight. Anyway, why is it so important for you to see this world-famous feller, this Mister Edwin Heath?" Ephraim winked at me. Friendly-like. Not faether-like. Pretendy-faether-like.

I wanted, there and then, to magic coo-cooing birds like the world-famous hypnotist does. I took out my handkerchief. Just the one. It was not free of snot. My nose had become itchy. I thought I was going to aaah-choo, but sneezed right loudly. Blew a large snotty bit into my handkerchief.

Ephraim took this snot-blowing as my reply.

"Well, beuy, that's your business, but if you don't go and see him, you'll be kicking yourself... Mister Edwin Heath wouldn't be calling himself 'world-famous', if he wasn't. World-famous people always have something very important to say. Someone that world-famous coming to Orkney is as rare a sight as an octopus using his arms to count up to ten."

I'd seen many puffins with their orangey beaks. I'd seen many fulmars, that bird that throws up all over you if you get too close. I had yet to see this octopus. I had yet to see a world-famous person.

"You go, beuy."

And I did. At the Garrison Theatre. In Stromness. Just down the road from where I live. It was on Friday 13th June 19... no, we'll just leave it at Friday the 13th. That says it all. A waste of time. Not even any 'coo-coo' birds.

The Minister never let on about me being there. If he ever had found out, I would have blamed Ephraim. I wasn't afraid of the Minister. I wasn't afraid of Ephraim.

I am sixteen years old. I know as much as any adult knows. I can read and write and do my sums and am in charge of Mither's farm.

Let them do the dance. I don't care.

I am Alexander A. Alexander.

I will never let on that I ever did something that did not turn out for the best.

I will never let on my secrets.

I will never let on that I am ever wrong.

I will never let on that there is something that I do not understand.

I will make sure that Mither will always be proud of her Alexander.

I am Alexander A. Alexander.

'Coo-coo, coo-coo.'

CHAPTER 2

MY BIG BU

February 1947

Our farm on the West Mainland of the island of Orkney was a big farm. Our farm was a big farm because the next-door neighbour's bu – farmhouse – was a long way away. The sea was very big also. Near. Not so far away. Big. Just a cow's spit away from our big bu. Between us and Scotland and the rest of the world was this big sea that could get very angry, as angry as the Minister could on Sabbath. The Minister was a big man. Big man.

Bu.

Sea.

Man.

Big.

Mind, I was only eleven years old and still growing up, and everything and everyone seemed big to me then. Big.

The parish where I lived was called Birsay. West Mainland of Orkney. At the top. Left-hand side. The Point. Then this island. The Brough. My parish was a big parish. I had lots of aunties and uncles there. They would always be popping in.

But I was different from the rest. No faether.

Others had a faether.

Why me with no faether? I would scrunch my eyes and try to will Faether to appear right in front of me. Now. This very moment. But Faether never came. I would count up to ten. No Faether. I never knew what Faether looked like, but I had no difficulty in making him appear in my head. No photographs of him in our bu. But this kind face before me – it was *him*.

No faether. Others have a faether. Why haven't I got a faether?

That's why the day Ephraim Isaac Mower came into my life was of such bigness to me. Ephraim wasn't Faether. Well, not at first.

Before that day of him being with us, there was just me and Mither in our big white bu.

Our bu had no upstairs, so didn't have a downstairs. It did have a lum, a hole in the roof. The centre of the room. Lum. Nowhere near the hearth. Lum. Peaty smoke from the hearth to be taken away. Lum. The rain to be stopped from coming in. That was the idea. Lum. Rain. More often than not in Orkney. The lum was only any good at getting rid of the smoke. Peaty smoke taken away. As for the rain. Well. Lum.

Useless lum.

Not much natural light in our bu. "The light that shines from the Lord is ever-present." That's what Mither said.

Without Faether there, Mither had lots to do. She was always busy, keeping the farm tickety-boo. Tickety-boo. I never went hungry. I did my bit. It was only right. I helped Mither a lot. I could do so. I wasn't now at school. Eleven years old. That was how old I was; soon to be twelve.

I remember exactly where I was the day Ephraim Isaac Mower came into my life.

Standing by the hearth in the in-by. The kitchen and front room all rolled into one. Lunchtime. Watching the eggs bubble away in the saucepan. Dangerous saucepan. *Dangerous*. Mither said I was not to touch the saucepan except by the handle. Only by the handle. Hot. Can burn me. Must be careful.

Lunchtime. The wireless turned on, lit up, giving out that yellow glow of goodness. Warm. Our in-by. Mither came through from the ben. Her bedroom.

"If only our Winston Churchill was still Prime Minister," she said. "He was there when the nation needed him and we need him now more than ever. It's been less than two years since the end of the war and life is harder. We miss our Prime Minister."

Mither had got this wrong. I knew who Winston Churchill was, but Mither had said this Churchill was *the Minister*. We have *our Minister* here in Birsay. He has never gone away. He has stayed with us all the time. Our Minister was not called Winston Churchill.

Mither had got this wrong.

It had been a stormy day. Black clouds and bad rain. I just knew that we would be getting lightning. Any minute. I stopped watching the saucepan on the hearth and went to the small window to get a good view. Quick as a flash.

Lightning did not scare me. After every flash, I would scrunch my fist and grin. Scrunch my fist. Lightning. Grin.

This time round I'm sure I heard the thunder. A long way off. No lightning. I counted up to ten on my fingers. No lightning. Thunder but no lightning. I must have missed it. Maybe the lightning was in a hurry or unwell. Maybe I had been too busy looking at the saucepan. I heard the thunder. I did so. It was a long way off. No lightning.

Then out of our window, there he was. A stranger at the top of our lane, a man on a bike. A man on a bike.

The stranger got closer and closer to our bu. There was something not right in the way he was riding his bike. Something not right. One minute on the saddle; the next out of the saddle. On and out. Out and on. Now outside our front door. I saw him clearly. He was blowing his cheeks. Outside our front door. He lifted the front wheel of his bike off the ground. He did so. Adults should not be doing this. The man was showing off. Wheelies. Him an adult as well.

"Close your mouth, Alexander, or you'll be swallowing midges." Mither joined me at the window, hand gentle on my shoulder. "It's Ephraim, and about time too. We'll be seeing a lot of him from now on because he'll be helping us round the farm. Ephraim is a troubled soul who is wrestling with his demons. We must pray for his redemption, and you, Alexander, must help."

"I will, Mither." My mouth wide open. "I will."

"Ephraim is from one of the isles of Orkney. He is from Egilsay. That's where our great Saint Magnus met his Maker."

Mither made Ephraim sound all mysterious and important.

Perhaps Faether also came from Egilsay. Perhaps Faether also knew this Saint Magnus and this Maker feller.

This stranger. Now. Inside *my* bu. Stood in front of me and Mither. Mither and me. Me and Mither. The stranger. In my home. He was wearing old clothes and his boots had split. I remember it all clearly, as if it was yesterday. I could see him. I could smell him. More sweet than stinky-muck-like. This man. Face to face. Big and strong. Magnificent. Like a bull. Like a bull that had won first prize at our West Mainland Farmers' Show. Ephraim.

"Well, missus, here I am reporting for duty, eleven o'clock as agreed, and who is this fine young man?" he boomed. He lifted his cap. Smiling at Mither and me. Me and Mither. Mither and me. In my home. My bu. My big bu.

I smiled back. Went red in the face. Looked down.

"Ephraim, you're an hour late." Mither pointed at our

grandfaether clock, which went tick-tock and chimed on the hour. "My name is Isabella, not Missus, and this fine young man is Alexander."

When Mither said nice things about me in front of adults, it always made me very happy. I liked this stranger.

And who is this fine young man? That's what he said about me... *me.*

Why, then, did he have to spoil everything by looking at his watch? Looking at his watch on his wrist. He nearly made me cry. He did so.

No watch. Others have a watch. Why haven't I got a watch? Even Phemie Sinclair has a watch and she is only nine years old.

I was not feeling so happy now.

"Well, you're late. What have you to say for yourself, Ephraim?"

"Well, it's a right mystery, missus... I mean Isabella. You say I'm an hour late. I must have lost this hour somewhere. Alexander, will you help me look for it? Sixpence for you if you find the hour before I do."

Ephraim had the broadest of smiles on his face, and gently pinched my cheeks.

"Alexander, we're going to be good friends. You are to call me Ephraim, because that's my name and both of us are equal in the eyes of the Lord." Ephraim winked at me.

Equal. He said I was his equal.

I was happy again. I was only eleven, but this stranger had said that I was important. *His equal.* Important. That's what *equal* means. He was an adult and taller and built like a prize-winning bull, but I was his equal. Important. Big. Yes, I was. The biggest in my class at school, when I used to go.

He spoke loud, but he was not dangerous.

He was going to give me money to buy sweets at the shop. Well, whatever our weekly ration-book allowance would let me buy. All I had to do was to help him find this hour which he'd lost.

Mither told me on that first day to leave Ephraim be. Not get in his way.

I did as I was told. I stayed indoors. From the window, I watched him wheeling the barrow from the byre and stables to the dung pit and back.

He wasn't walking normal. It was as if slippery-sliding stuff had been spread over the yard. His feet never really left the ground. Never really on the ground. All tiptoe. Bandy legs. At any moment, I thought he was going to end up on his arse, but I never saw him fall over. Not once. Slippery-slidey. Tiptoe. Bandy legs.

He never fetched me to help him look for the missing hour. Long before supper he left us to bike home. In and out of the saddle. The missing hour. Missing.

That was his first day with us.

Not dangerous. Ephraim.

Not my faether. Ephraim.

Not in my bu. Ephraim.

You stay outside. Ephraim.

I liked him. I think.

No sweets for me. He'd promised. I wasn't cross with him. Maybe tomorrow he would have more time. Maybe the missing hour would turn up without me having to look for it. He would give me a tanner. Chocolate and liquorice from the shop. I knew he would keep his promise. He was an adult. "Adults keep their promises." That's what Mither said.

Adults.

Promises.

Keep them.

After supper I said to Mither, "Why do we need Ephraim here? Can't I do his work?"

"We need Ephraim to do the heavy work round the farm. Every farm needs a strong man to do the heavy lifting. Alexander, you are not yet old enough to cut peat for the fire. You must be very kind towards Ephraim. He needs our help in fighting his demons. Now, young man, no more questions. Time for bed. Say your prayers."

I said a prayer for Ephraim before I got into bed. Ephraim needed help. Demons were dangerous. Red-hot. Saucepan. Red-hot.

The following day, I went with Mither to the shop. She spoke hushed-like to the lady behind the counter. Mither said this word 'dropsy' a lot. I'd heard talk about the dropsy before. Adult talk. Secret talk. Dropsy hushed talk. 'Dropsy' must be Birsay adult talk for 'the plague'. The plague.

That nice Missus Linklater took half a crown from Mither and handed over a bottle of medicine. That nice Missus Linklater did talk so. So that was it. Ephraim was ill with the plague. Poor Ephraim. That's why he rode his bike in a strange way and walked ungainly, and was always about to fall on his arse but never did so. The plague. Half a crown.

Half a crown was a lot of money. You could buy a month's worth of sweets for half a crown. Two and sixpence. Liquorice and chocolate. Why was Mither spending all this money on a stranger? I, and not medicine, would protect Mither from this dropsy should Ephraim try to pass it on.

I didn't want Mither and me to get the plague. Ephraim being here meant we were at risk. Dropsy. Danger. Mind. Should Ephraim die, that half a crown would be mine. Half a crown. Chocolate and liquorice. All for me.

The following day. Ephraim once again on his bike home before supper. I watched him. On the saddle. Out of the saddle. His cheeks. Puff-puffing. Ephraim walked odd. Ephraim also rode his bike odd. Ephraim said that I was his equal. Did I want to be his equal?

"You shouldn't have been staring so, Alexander. It's rude. We will say a special prayer for Ephraim tonight. The Power of the Lord. The Power of the Lord." Mither told me off, but in a nice, gentle way. Must stop staring. Must.

Poor Ephraim. I liked him, but he wasn't Faether. Ephraim was fun, but he wasn't Faether. Ephraim was going to give me sixpence for sweets, but he wasn't Faether. He was find-the-missing hour Ephraim. He was sixpence-for-sweets Ephraim.

We said our evening prayers. After supper. Me and Mither. Mither and me. Not for the first time, I asked Mither, "Where is Faether?"

"He was called home many years ago, Alexander." Mither hugged me. Her voice, soft and warm. "Called home."

"But this bu is his home." I was not happy with Mither's answer. I asked again. I wanted to know. "Where is Faether? Where… is… Faether?"

"Alexander, your faether has gone forth to His garden. You must understand," Mither replied in her soft voice. "Gone forth to His garden."

His garden? I didn't understand. It was unfair. I was eleven. It was unfair. Called home. Gone forth to his garden. I didn't understand. I did not like this not-understanding. I was eleven.

"Mither, why does Faether have his own garden? What's wrong with *our* garden?" Angry, then crying. *I am eleven, not a crybaby. I am eleven, not a hush-a-bye crybaby. Our garden. I am eleven. I will soon be twelve.*

Our…

Big…

Garden.

"Your faether," Mither's arms were round me, "is in the Garden of Eden. You will always be special to me, Alexander." Mither. Soft. Warm.

I stopped crying. I wiped away my tears. Both eyes. Same finger. Licked finger. Salty. Mither has said I was special. That made me feel proud. Both eyes. Salty. Special.

Everyone in Orkney was special anyway, with the wind and the sea and the Big Sky and the light that could be so bright and the Ancient Stones and the full moon and the sea and the Big Sky and… and…

Me. Alexander A. Alexander. Special. Once. Twice over.

Me. Alexander A. Alexander. From Orkney where the wind and the sea and the Big Sky always talked to each other.

Magic.

Special.

Extra special.

Big special.

Faether was never far away from my thoughts. You know what. Him not being there hurt even more than me not having a watch.

Every good beuy should have a mither, a faether and a watch, but especially a faether.

We needed Ephraim here. Digging. Heavy lifting. Mucking out. Peat-cutting for our smoky fire. Mither had said so. I knew I wasn't yet strong enough to do proper man's work, but I would be twelve soon. I'm nearly twelve.

I quickly got used to Ephraim being in our bu and on our farm. Arrived in the morning. Left before supper. Sometimes didn't turn up for work at all. I hoped when we next saw him our prayers would be answered and Ephraim would no longer have the dropsy. I was scared that the dropsy had got him. Dropsy. Plague. Demons.

Ephraim had been with us now for a few months. It was the middle of June. Never got dark in Orkney in June. I liked the light being with us from me waking up to going to bed. All the time. Comforting. Even in the middle of the night. Tried to catch the light out, but it was always there. The light. Peekaboo. Even when I was asleep. All the time. Comforting. The light didn't need to go home. In June. Sunrise. Sunset. Didn't matter. Didn't.

Same with Ephraim. Ephraim should stay here all the time. Didn't need to go home at the end of the day. All the time in our bu. Not just in June. No need for peekaboo. Ephraim with us. Here. All the time in our Bu. He would then have time to keep that promise. Sixpence for the missing hour. Ephraim.

Then things changed. When? I know, around and about. That's good enough.

When did summer start in Orkney? Always strong winds came and went, and then the winds went off on holiday. One day here. Next day gone. Vanished. No announcement on the noticeboard outside the shop. Wind. Here. Wind. Gone. Summer just happened.

Mind, I'm sure the wind would have told the Big Sky and the sea before going away. Tipped them off. They talked to each other. Only right to keep each other in the picture. All sang from the same hymn sheet. Sabbath-together.

That Mister Wind. Sort of shy. Didn't like a face to face. Didn't like you walking towards him. Always better having Mister Wind behind you. That Mister Wind. The wind.

What about me?

Don't forget me. I'm the Green Land. Gentle fields. A happy reel or two on my fiddle. The wind, the Big Sky and the sea talk to me as well. I play a tune back. Lush Green Land. Useful. Whatever you do, don't confuse me with lum.

Useless lum.

The Green Land. Gentle. But a bit *'look at me'*. Green. But sometimes with bumps in it, as if something was bubbling away underneath. Like the water in the saucepan covering the eggs. On the hearth. Bubbling away. This force. Erupting. Bubbling away. Below the surface. Forcing upwards. Bumps.

Like on my face. Spots. Yellow, not green. Eggy colour. Spots were there to be squeezed. Bumps in the ground, covered in grass. Popping up, waiting to be squeezed. More fun than picking your nose and eating the dried snot.

The wind. The Big Sky. The sea. The Green Land.

As for the lum, I agree. It was… it was… it was useless.

Useless lum.

Then things changed.

Ephraim no longer went home at the day's end. He joined us for supper – at first once in a while, and then more often than not, and then not at all, and then every night. And this was the oddest of things: Ephraim could have gone home even after eating supper with us, but chose not to. He must have heard my wishes.

I saw Ephraim's work clothes on the washing line.

I saw his bike outside the front door when I woke up in the morning.

I saw his Sabbath shoes in Mither's bedroom.

I saw his clothes there. Every day.

All in my big bu.

Then Ephraim went missing for days on end, and it must have been my fault, him not being here, and I must have said or done something bad to him. My fault. My fault.

When Ephraim turned up after going missing, Mither and

me were very happy. He would always smile at me and say, "What's up, beuy?" Gently pinch my cheeks. Would give me a threepenny bit to buy sweets in the shop. Sherbet dab. Fizzy. Would have preferred a tanner, a sixpenny bit but...

I must tell you something. That threepenny bit. Weighty. Heavy. Mither said on one side was His Majesty, the king. On the other side, a thrift plant. Mither was right. As always. And... and... outside our bu grew many thrift plants. Orkney was on my threepenny bit. Orkney was in my mouth. Sherbet dab. Fizzy. What a tasty threepenny bit. Orkney in my pocket. Pocket money. Orkney. Special.

I know... I know.

Ephraim never got worse, but never got better. He was still walking strange and rode his bike in that way of his. Here's another thing. His breath was ever so sweet, like too-fresh hay in Popeye's mouth. His hands did shake. Never got worse, but never better. Sweet breath. Shaky hands. Maybe the next stage of the dropsy.

Warm in my box bed at night. My bed in an open cupboard with sliding doors. Box bed. Orkney box bed.

From the ben to my left, I often heard Mither and Ephraim and what must have been bits of adult talk, and sometimes I heard strange adult noises as if Mither and Ephraim were in pain.

From the byre to my right, there was Popeye. 'Moo-moo.'

Smoky shapes appeared like magic and then disappeared. The peat fire in the in-by puff-puffed away, night and day. Puff-puff.

I was tucked up. Safe and special, like that wee one in his baby bed in Bethlehem. Protected from the outside. Tucked up. Safe. Angry noises. Outside. Scary.

Tucked up,

Safe and special,

In my big bu.

Ephraim's strange way of walking. His breath. Sometimes shaky hands. Here's another strange thing: Ephraim was always very red in the face. Very red in the face. He never looked as if he was working hard, so it wasn't that he was trying to do too much. Orkney winds blew strongly here, there and everywhere. The winds made this redness.

Magical Orkney winds. Fresh. Always brought with them air that can change the colour of your skin. Winds. Fresh with colour. Brought the red colour. Red. You have to look closely. Winds. Fresh with colour. Winds with no colour on the outside hid the blood-red on the inside. Blood-red.

I would follow Ephraim everywhere. He was never cross with me. I liked it when he ruffled my hair, and very much so when he pinched my cheeks. Playful.

"You're right, beuy. We are all equal in the eyes of the Lord, but Alexander, you are first among equals." He used to say that a lot to me.

He would sometimes use words I did not understand when we talked. Words. Big new words… like… like… like…I never let on that I didn't understand these words. I would make shapes of these words, to help me remember them. Words. Big new words, like those smoky shapes at night, first large and scary; soon to disappear and more often than not quickly forgotten. Those big new words. Difficult.

Big…

New…

Words.

Big new words. As big as the waves that the sea made.

Big…

New…

Waves.

Big and scary.

25

To disappear and be forgotten.

Only to be replaced by...

Big new waves.

These waves have the right to do big and scary things. As will I, when I become an adult.

Our big bu, no longer just Mither and me. Now there was Mither and Ephraim and me. Ephraim. Him, an adult. Make-do Ephraim. Ephraim in the way between me and Mither.

Ephraim would make do. I missed Faether, but Ephraim would make do. No Faether, but Ephraim. He would be my make-do faether. But you know what? I was in our bu before Ephraim came. Here in *my* bu. I was here first.

There's something I've learnt. I must tell you.

I have to share this special fact with someone. I don't go to school? No, not that I don't go to school. I've already told you that.

Everyone on Orkney has hens? No, not that everyone on Orkney has hens. That isn't the special thing I want to tell you. Don't rush me.

It's that hens are birds that don't fly, and that birds are hens that don't lay eggs? No, it's not even that.

It's that I know something that you don't.

So there.

Mither has said that I was to be in charge of the hens.

That made me not just ordinary special. It made me big special.

Someone told me that Orkney hens laid fifty million eggs a year. One day my hens will lay one million of those fifty million. That's a lot of eggs.

Imagine if there were fifty million hens and birdies in the Big Sky. All at the same time. We have chiffchaffs here. Chiffchaffs. Imagine there were fifty million chiffchaffs. All laying eggs. Dropping down on you like those bombs in the war. *Rrrrruuuughrrrr. Splat. Kerpow. Splat.*

Orkney's hens, the best layers in Great Britain. Orkney hens were happy hens. Eggs were very, very important to Orkney. Mind, we were a big island and Orkney was the tops. Doing my bit for Orkney. Mither said I was to be in charge of the hens. Ephraim would help me. Orkney hens. Happy hens.

There we are. I have shared this secret with you.

I was no fool when it came to eggs and made sure that Ephraim knew this. I quickly got the hang of being in charge of the eggs.

Each day I would pick up the eggs here, there and everywhere. I would wash them. One by one under the downpipe in the yard. Mither told me not to drown the eggs by washing them all together in a bucket. One by one. Not in one go. Mucky eggs. Clean eggs.

I had a question for Ephraim. I went to see him. I would ask him my question without letting on that I did not know the answer.

Ephraim was in the byre, milking Popeye. Hands underneath. Bucket there for the milk. Ephraim's hands on Popeye's udders. Udders. Underneath. Milk squirting out. Not drip-drip. More like an Orkney shower. Whoosh into the bucket. Whoosh. Ephraim was not using my egg bucket for milking. Moo-moo. Ephraim was not allowed to use *my* egg bucket. Whoosh. Whoosh.

Ephraim looked up. "What's up, beuy?" He raised his right hand to his ear. Behind his ear was a roll-your-own. He put his wet fingers round the roll-your-own; raised it just above the ear as if about to light up, but then put it back where it belonged. Adult. I wanted to do that. I wanted to always have a roll-your-own behind my ear. Even when I was in my box bed, fast asleep. Adult.

Ephraim's fingers were working away on Popeye's udders. Underneath. Udders. Whoosh. Whoosh. Not splish. Not splish. Lum. Useless lum.

Before I had even asked Ephraim my question, he was nodding. Nodding. As if he fully understood and had the answer. Before I had even asked my question. Nodding. Clever. Adult. This nodding was strange but clever.

Nod before. Nod after. Right clever. Noddy.

Don't know, but pretend I know. Nod-nod. Puff-puff. Nod-nod. Clever. Adult.

Whoosh. Whoosh. Not splish-splash. Clever. Popeye.

"Ephraim, why do hens make so many eggs, and what happens to all of the eggs that they make?" I had been saying this over and over again to make sure my question came out right first time. It did. It did. Right clever. I nodded. Pleased with myself.

I knew I'd got him here.

Ephraim nodded and said nothing for a long time. He was thinking. Then he spoke. His answer was very clever, adult-clever, and holy because he started talking about the Lord.

"Beuy, when was the last time you saw a hen pat itself on the back? Listen to what I am saying, beuy. If an egg is bad it rises to the surface of the pan. It swims. Badness is bad. The Lord does not like bad people."

I didn't understand his answer to my very clever question, but some of his words did stick. *Bad. Swim. Egg.* These were easy words. If I said these words over and over again, it would all make sense. If sometimes it didn't make sense, I would say the same words again and again but in a different order. *Swim. Egg. Bad. Egg. Bad. Swim. Swim. Bad. Egg.*

I was going to ask Ephraim about Faether, not his faether but my faether and the Garden of Eden.

Bad.

Swim.

Egg.

But that was enough for one day.

Badness and swimming and eggs.

Badness was bad. I will never do a bad thing in my life. That was a promise I would keep. If I did a bad thing, I would never be able to get into the Garden of Eden.

I wanted to visit Faether in his Garden of Eden.

I knew Faether's Garden of Eden would be special.

It would be in a special place.

This special place was just under the sea.

I don't know why it was there. I just knew that it was.

At the start of the year there was Mither and me and Popeye. By the end of the year there was Mither and me and Ephraim. And let's not forget dear Popeye and all those eggs.

At the start of the year I went to school. By the end of the year I did not go to school.

At the start of the year I was eleven. By the end of the year I was twelve. I must have had a birthday at some time during the year.

Between the age of eleven and twelve I said one very important thing to Ephraim. I did so. You know what it was?

"There are twelve pence in every shilling. Twelve."

I, Alexander A. Alexander, even at the age of eleven, knew that I was clever.

CHAPTER 3

DUCK'S ARSE

1951

And the days gave way to months and the months to years. I had grown out of many sets of clothes. I was now wearing long trousers. Long trousers. Soon I'll be growing out of my chubby cheeks, pointy ears and spots.

I still enjoyed squeezing my spots. The egg-yolky runny bit always popping out first. Whoosh. The rush. The egg-yolky bit of the spot. Squeeze. Pop. Exciting. Then the let-down. The I'm-so-sorry blood. Apologetic blood. Seeping out and surrounding the yellowy bit and swallowing it up. The let-down. The pretendy, I'm-so-sorry blood.

I was fifteen years old.

School?

"You are special and needed on the farm, what with Faether not being around because he is looking after his own garden and with Ephraim needing help, and how dare that headmistress accuse you of having nits in your hair, and have the cheek to say that my home is unclean."

Mither said that to me. It was ages ago.

School? It was for children.

I was fifteen years old.

I was *special*. I still needed Mither to say that I was.

In my box bed, I heard Mither whispering to Ephraim and Ephraim repeating back in his loud voice. Echo. First soft woman's voice; then loud, booming man's voice. Duet. Echo with a different voice.

"Feed payments."

"*Feed payments.*"

"Paying back the loan."

"*Paying back the loan.*"

"Makin' ends meet."

"*Makin' ends meet.*"

"Where's the money to come from?"

"*…money to come from?*"

First. Coughing. Then. Coughing. Mither coughing. No echo. No duet echoes. There was then a 'moo-moo' from Popeye.

I didn't have to go to school. I was fifteen. On the farm, I was doing man's work. Man's work. Adult work. I was an adult.

Indoors, Mither now trusted me to light the peaty fire on my own. Indoors was always safe. Bed. Mither. Food. Warmth.

Outdoors I helped to mend fences and trimmed hedges and counted sheep and did my bit to make the barley grow. Outdoors is where it all happened.

Outdoors is where it was noisy. The wind, the Big Sky and the sea; all doin' away.

I could also hear the birdies up in the sky, calling and chattering, chattering and calling. Tweet-tweet. Caw-caw. Chirp-chirp. Not one by one. All together now. Even the starlings, I could hear them. They always seemed to be singing other birdies' songs. Maybe they quickly got tired of their own.

My big bantams down on the ground, first thing in the morning. Waiting for the cock-a-doodle-do. Cock-a-doodle-do time. Time for them to start work. Eggs to be laid.

I gave them a bit of time to get going and then I started. Gathering and washing. Couldn't just leave it to the Big Sky to send down the rain to make clean the eggs. Couldn't just leave it to the wind to gather the eggs up in one place.

I was in charge of the eggs. In charge. Real in-charge. Proper in-charge. Not pretendy in-charge. Adult in-charge. Outdoors.

I rarely left the West Mainland of Orkney. I rarely left my parish. No need to. Birsay was my whole world. Birsay was special and will always be so.

The view from outside our bu was better than being at the pictures. The best seat in the house. The view was special. I was special. Birsay Bay and me…special.

To the left, the steep cliffs of Marwick, and the Memorial on top to that First World War leader. Lord Kitchener. He went down on a big ship there. He was a hero. The others who went down with him were heroes, too. There was a lot of hush-hush about it all.

To the right, the magical island just off the coast, the Brough of Birsay. We say 'brough' here as 'broch', like you're trying to clear your throat. At low tide, the Brough was just a hop, step and jump away from the Mainland, from the Point. The Point of Buckquoy. *Brochhhh. Buckweeeeee.* There was a lighthouse there.

I reckon the Kitchener Memorial and the lighthouse were the same height. Maybe they're twins.

Everyday our hero Kitchener would shout, "Cooee" and the lighthouse on the *Brochhhh* would give a wink back. They then would have a fine chat. A chat between twins.

"Cooee"…Wink-wink.

All around us, the sea. You could see, hear, smell, and yes, touch the sea. The sea was awake all the time. It didn't need supper. It didn't need sleep. It didn't need to wash behind its ears and keep its fingernails clean. The sea was a friend, when happy. Calm. Still. Alive. Breathing. Your best friend. Could get very angry, a bit like our Minister. You *didn't* mess with the sea when it was very angry.

And the wind. Didn't always see eye to eye with the sea, but they talked. Close friends and rivals. The wind had a temper. If the sea just went that one step too far – whoosh – the wind forced the sea to make wave after wave with that toothpaste-spit on top. Best not to annoy the wind. The wind had a temper; could bend you to its will.

Better not forget the Big Sky as well. Watchful. Majestic. Like our king. Looking down. Apart. Royal. Above it all. Wouldn't get involved in childish squabbles. Would only pick up the phone if necessary. From time to time, blew into its pipe. Side of the mouth. Puff-puff. White. Not smoky. Clear shapes. Clouds. Racing with each other. Playing. Up there. Big Sky.

Then the wind joined in the game. Would only pick up the phone if necessary. Our Big Sky.

You could take them in any order. The sea. The wind. The Big Sky. Let's try. The wind. The Big Sky. The sea. All together now. All friends and not friends. All talking to each other but doing their own thing. Weather. Orkney weather.

Never could make its mind up, Orkney weather. Fidgety. Sunshine, winds, winds, blue skies, misty skies, black clouds, rain, rain, sunshine again. Not one or the other. Never made its mind up. Fidgety. At night-time, it must get even naughtier. All sorts of mischief. Black skies. Us asleep.

That's why Orkney was so special. Nothing stands still. Not even those Ancient Stones.

You know what? I reckon the Big Sky and the sea and the wind not being able to keep still gave us the right to do things

33

that others shouldn't. We could do things that others who don't live on an island are not allowed.

This not being able to settle on one thing. This not staying still long enough. No fixed position. Right or wrong. Rain or shine. Sodden and Gomorrah. Everyone in Orkney free to do what they want.

Badness is only someone else's point of view.

Early summer before the midges. Morning. I was working away, almost bent double over the downpipe, removing the muck from the eggs. Ephraim joined me.

"You're doing important work there, beuy. You're doing Orkney's work, and Orkney eggs are the best in the world."

I said nothing. Didn't even look up. I was concentrating. Didn't want to drop and break any of the eggs. All that lovely yolk gone to waste. Broken eggshells meant witches getting up to badness. Evil spells. Less money for Mither and our farm. Mustn't break any eggs. We needed the money.

Ephraim tried again. "You're very quiet this morning, beuy. I can tell you've got something on your mind. Alexander? When I was your age there were lots of things that just didn't seem fair. You'll soon be sixteen. I still remember the beatings my faether gave me at your age… but I knew that things would work out for the best…"

I could not believe my ears. Washing the eggs could wait. "What did you do wrong, Ephraim, to be given beatings?" I never thought there could be a bad side to having a faether. Faether handing out beatings. A faether.

"Never you mind, Alexander. Why did I just say that? It was all such a long time ago. You seem a bit down, beuy. Let's take our break early. I've got the tea. Look, we'll sit in our usual place out of the way of the north-westerly."

We sat down on the nearside of the stone wall. I was not going to let the bucket out of sight. My morning's work. A full bucket of eggs. All those eggs. Money for the farm. Money for Mither.

My favourite view. The whole bay with the sandy, grassy bumps and the Kitchener Memorial. Most of the day the sea surrounded the Brough of Birsay. Winds or no winds. Big Sky had no say. Brough of Birsay was an island. Big Sky; important, but not that important.

The Big Sky. The sea. The wind. Talked to each other but did their own thing…I've missed out the Green Land. Sorry.

Black clouds only at special moments would open their curtains and show us something remarkable. Out would pop a rainbow. Yes, it would. It would pop out, not like egg-yolky spots waiting to be squeezed. It would pop out, not like those grassy bumps on the Green Land. It would pop out like magic but only at special moments. Yes, up there in the Big Sky. Rainbow. Magic. Rainbow. Up there. But only once in a while. Out it popped. The rainbow.

A rainbow over the the Bay of Birsay. Rain. Bow. Started up in the Big Sky. All the way down to the sea. All in one piece. I was always excited to see it. Must be magic. Watched it until it disappeared, to put on a show elsewhere. That's my secret. You mustn't tell.

That afternoon – sometime back, I couldn't say when; this year, definitely – the rainbow was there. Curtains opened. Out it popped. A special one.

Rain. Magic-special. Bright. Purple-blue-green-yellow-orange-red-bright. Shimmering. Playful. See-through. Different colours. Invited me to reach out and touch. The sea's spray. Shimmering. From the Big Sky right down to the sea and below. A ladder, bendy like Ephraim's legs. From the Big Sky all the way down to Faether's garden. Head to toe. Quick, it won't be here for long. *Bow.*

Yoo-hoo! I'm home. Come and see me, Alexander. My son. My dear son.

I knew this rainbow was a sign from Faether.

I'm home. Come and see me, Alexander.

So that one morning, I said to myself, *Let's go see him. Now.* That morning. I walked across the bumpy Green Land, across the powdery sand that gets in your boots, and right into the sea. The water was very cold. Arms out in front. Ready to touch it. The rainbow ladder. *Rain. Bow.* Only one or two steps down to Faether's Garden of Eden. A beautiful place. Just under the surface of the water. Water, waist-high. Water, chest-high. Water, neck-high. Rainbow. Colour purple on the outside. Colour purple and then…

I was going visiting. I was answering the call.

Yoo-hoo! I'm home. Your faether's waiting.

It was the right thing to do. I was not going to float on the surface of the water, so would not be going against the Minister's wishes. I was not going to be one of those swimmers tempted by the Devil. Badness and eggs gone off. Badness. Swimming. Eggs. Faether's garden was underwater. I would be just below the surface of the sea. I was not being bad. I was going visiting.

Gold top. Ephraim liked saying *gold top.* He said *gold top* when something pleased him. *Beuy, you've done well. You're like cream rising to the top. Gold top.* Ephraim would be proud of me. *Gold top, Alexander. You going to pay Faether a call. Gold top.*

I took in a deep breath. Made sure I did not swallow any water. The rainbow ladder. Purple was the first colour I saw. Purple was the last colour I remembered seeing.

Yoo-hoo! I'm home. Your faether's waiting.

I remember opening my eyes afterwards, back in the bu in front of the hearth with a large blanket wrapped round me and Mither and Ephraim looking very worried.

That afternoon. Nineteen fifty-one. All year.

The doctor was there as well. On his wrist, a watch. In his ears, metal pads with a long metal lead icy-cold, pressed against my chest, a stetho-something. Cold metal. Icy-cold. I was asked to take deep breaths and count up to ten. One. Two. Three…

Mither and Ephraim never told me off, but said that I had done a silly thing that I should never do again. No *gold top for Alexander.*

Anyway. Where was I? Oh yes. Morning tea with Ephraim. Today was a clear day. No rain so far. Let's snap out of this thinking about what took place.

"You listening to me, beuy?"

"Isn't this a grand spot, Ephraim?"

"Gold top, beuy. Gold top."

We sat on the nearside of the stone wall. A clear day. No chance of a popping out rainbow. I could feel something. We weren't on our own, even though we were… if you get my drift.

All around us. They were there. You couldn't see nor touch them. All around us. Neolithics. Them Vikings and Picts. Faeries. Them trowees and hobgoblins as well. Chock-full of ancient folk… and the little people.

Badness is only someone else's point of view.

Now driftwood. Nothing special about driftwood. You look out to sea and there's something bobbing away. Up and down. Too small at first to make sense of. Gets closer. You work out what it is. A piece of driftwood. Waves bring that piece ever closer and closer to the shore. Gets larger. A piece of wood, drifting on the water. Then under the water. Then on the surface of the water. Peekaboo. Driftwood.

Nothing special about driftwood. But where did it come from? Few trees and no forests in Orkney. That's why you get the Big Sky here. The wood wouldn't have come from the land. Maybe the wood fell out of the Big Sky. I knew that driftwood was bad. Swimming the waves of its own free will. *On the surface. A swimmer.* Driftwood. Badness.

I watched this piece of driftwood get larger and larger as it got nearer and nearer. On the water. Under the water. On the water. Swimming. Peekaboo. I'd be waiting for the moment. Driftwood surrounded by bundles of seaweed. Driftwood strangled. Driftwood dragged under, never to be seen again. I'd clench my fist in celebration when that happened. Clench. Fist. *Yes. Yes. Yes.*

Badness is only someone else's point of view.

Ephraim, roll-your-own behind his ear, took out his pipe. Filled it with baccy. Roll-your-own still behind his ear. Adult. Lit up and started to speak. Puff-puff. He could puff-puff and puff-puff. Smoked his pipe and talked out of the side of his mouth at one and the same time. Puff-puff and puff-puff. That's how hypnotists get white doves from white handkerchiefs (free of snot). Side of the mouth. Hypnotist-clever. I wanted to learn that trick.

"You've noticed over the years how your Ephraim walks in a contrary way, haven't you? I told you what happened when I was your age, and it changed me. You're a big lad now, I mean a man, and taller than even your Ephraim. Always walk tall and straight and upright and you'll be able to look the world in the eye." He emptied the contents of his pipe and started to whistle. I've heard that song that he's whistling on the wireless. It's called *Ghost Riders in the Sky.*

I wanted to whistle as good as Ephraim.

The hens were making an almighty racket. We got up and turned round to see what was going on. They had ganged up on one of their own. Ephraim whistling *Ghost Riders in the Sky.* Squawking got too loud for whistling. Ephraim shouting, his face contorted. Hens squawking. Ephraim was yelling to make himself heard.

"If you've a lot of money, your left side becomes stronger from head to toe. But if you've had some sadness in your life, your right side becomes weak. With money, you can transfer the extra strength from your left side to make good what your right side is short of. It's like giving blood."

I was looking at my hens hopping from one foot to the other. Left to right. Right to left. Wondering what side was their strong side.

My hens were going in for the kill. They weren't about to give blood for the good. They were going to kill one of their own for the bad. Spilling of the blood. Exciting. Wrong, but exciting. Maybe not wrong. Orkney. Exciting.

Badness is only someone else's point of view.

"It is a lucky man who has spare cash so can walk tall and help others."

His face, like Mister Punch. He leant over and picked up an egg from my bucket. He didn't ask me whether he could do so. Just went ahead. Better not drop one of *my* eggs. Better not. You dare. I was watching him. I was watching him closely. Hand open. Hand closed. Egg inside. Hand raised. Hand and egg in the air. Egg inside his hand, held securely, not crushed. Raised. In triumph. Not crushed.

"The more eggs them hens lay, the more upright a man… I… can… be…"

He lowered his hand. He opened his hand. He returned the egg to the bucket. The egg was placed on the top of the pile. Not broken. A pretendy faether would not have been so gentle.

Ephraim. *My faether.*

Ephraim had asked me for help. Man-to-man. He had asked *me* for *my* help. Ephraim needed *my* help. I was there for him as I would always be there for Mither. A pretendy faether would not have asked me for help.

Ephraim. *My faether.*

His cheeks like a red balloon about to go pop. Mouth wide open. Wide enough, I swear, to swallow a big birdie. Yelling. Making sure he would be heard above the squawking.

I must listen to my faether.

"The more eggs them hens lay, the happier you will make Mither. She is not in the best of health, as you know."

The noise. What was going on? I had to see. Looking elsewhere when someone's talking to you was rude, but I had to see. A hen was being pecked to death by one of its own. Both of us watching the killing. Like being at the pictures. Feathers everywhere with blood oozing out of the hen's side. I should be stopping this. I was not at the pictures. At the pictures, all you have to do is sit and watch.

I will wait for my faether to do something. He will stop this.

He just sat there. Said nothing. Whistled nothing. Stared at the dying hen. Ephraim went back to puffing his pipe as if everything was all right. It was not all right. It…was…not…all…right.

Ephraim had not behaved like Faether. Ephraim had done nothing to prevent this. Ephraim had let me down. Ephraim had behaved as if he was just a pretendy faether. I had to put a stop to this. I walked towards the hens. Ephraim was two steps behind. I could smell his sweet breath on my neck. Felt his hand on my shoulder, firm, not gentle like Mither's.

I turned around. Faether face-to-face. Faether's hand moved towards my face. Faether pinched my cheeks as he had done many a time. Pinch. Cheeks. Playful. But now. Did not let go. Hurt me. Sharp nails dug into my flesh. Now. Possessed. Grinned at me. Drew blood, my blood. Not now-you-see-it-now-you-don't blood. Not spot-pop-egg-yolky-fun blood. I could feel his nails. Blood. Pain blood.

"Stop. Stop. You're hurting me." I wanted the pain to go away. Couldn't move. Being punished. Burst into tears. Me, fifteen. Still a hush-a-bye crybaby. He was not my real faether. I wanted the pain to go away. I did not want this to happen. I wished it was all pretendy.

Ephraim let go of me and walked off. He was whistling *Ghost Riders in the Sky*.

I was shaking. Crying. Should have gone to Mither there and then. Didn't. Didn't want to. Not manly.

Ran to see Popeye. Popeye. Indoors. In the byre. I must have sinned. Badness. Punishment. Needed redemption. Popeye would make things better. 'Moo-moo, moo-moo.'

The next few days, I kept well clear of Ephraim.

Didn't have morning tea with him at our hidey-hole from the north-westerly. At meal times, I kept to 'yes' and 'no' when he tried to get me to talk. Ephraim was back to being normal Ephraim. Mither could tell there was something up.

I am not feeling very well, and that's just a scratch on my face.

By the time Sabbath came around, I knew what I had to do. The best way to get back into the Lord's good books. I knew what to do: pretend that it was all my fault. No – pretend that it didn't happen. Clever. It didn't happen. It didn't happen. I would be extra good from now on. What had taken place, hadn't. Make-believe. And if anyone did find out, it was my fault anyway.

That scratch on my face was done by the hens.

What had taken place, hadn't. Make-believe. It was my fault.

It was an accident. They didn't mean to. My hens wouldn't hurt me.

An accident. Clever. Sabbath was a few days away...

Was all my fault anyway.

Sabbath soon came round. It was Sabbath. We were outside our kirk. The Big Sky was light. Just before we went inside for the service, I looked up at the Big Sky. Eyes. Neck. Upwards. There was a bonxie bird; a skua. 'Bonxie' – Orkney-speak for skua. Ephraim/faether. Bonxie/skua. Swooping down. It had eyed its prey. That poor little chiffchaff on the ground. Flown all that way. Bonxie swooped down.

It had no chance. Bad bonxie. Bad skua. Poor chiffchaff. Good chiffchaff.

Badness. Goodness.

The chiffchaff didn't stand a chance. But the bonxie bird was hungry. Loads of its own chicks to feed. Chicks.

Goodness. Badness.

Badness is only someone else's point of view.

In kirk, I was going to sit still. Bolt upright. Not fidgety. Looking straight ahead. That was the plan. That would show the Lord how truly sorry I was. I sat next to Ephraim. Ephraim was back to normal Ephraim. Ephraim sat next to Mither. Ephraim/faether. Ephraim back to normal. We're in our usual seats, halfway back in the middle. The best seats in the house. Like being at the pictures.

Ephraim, with one of his loud whispers.

"Look at the Minister. Look at him, Alexander. Fine hairstyle he's got. It's called a Duck's Arse. DA."

"Why is it called a Duck's Arse?" I whispered back. Proper whisper. Hushed-like.

"The hair's greased, just like them Italian prisoners of war in our Orkney. Them Yanks who stayed on after the war had their greasy hair shaped at the back, making it look just like a Duck's Arse."

"When the service is over, just look at the back of our Minister's head. You'll see his DA. Shit comes out from his head, from his backside, and pours out of his mouth. That's our Minister for you." Ephraim winked. "Don't tell Mither what I've just said because I'll get into all sorts of trouble."

Mither gave Ephraim a look. People around us were sniggering.

"You can't say that about the Minister." I bit my upper lip to stop myself. Mustn't laugh in kirk. Had to keep a straight face to get back in the Lord's good books.

"It may be the Sabbath but even on the Sabbath things are not always gold top." He winks at me.

The Minister was angry. *The Minister was a big man. Big man.* Looking down from his pulpit. The Minister was telling us the Truth. It wasn't a nice Truth. *Big man.* Not telling; more like shouting.

"There are people living in our Holy Land who are agents of the Devil. They are no different to eggs that have turned bad. These bad people are swimmers. They do not swim in regret. They swim in sin. The agents of the Devil are here in our kirk. They live and swim in sin!" he roared, and looked at Mither, Ephraim and me. Stared, long and hard, at all of us, from left to right and right to left. Like me taking in my view from the Kitchener Memorial to the Brough of Birsay and back. The Minister. Staring. Unforgiving. Direct. Judgemental.

Badness is only someone else's point of view.

I did not like the Minister's stare. I broke my promise – *Bolt upright. Not fidgety. Looked straight ahead* – and I looked away. Left and right. Right and left. Forward. Sideways. Not backward. Anywhere but straight ahead. Across the pews. Not over my shoulder. Everyone was looking down at the floor, even Missus Linklater from the shop. We were all under suspicion. I nodded, not once but twice. Joined everyone else. Looked downwards. Guilty.

My eyes were shut. Thought about Gail. Yes. It was me up there instead of the Minister.

I was pretendy Minister, with a different haircut to him. Pretendy Minister, delivering the sermon. Different haircut. Gail could not take her eyes off me. She was in a state of wonder. Adoring me. Her hero. Gail. Me.

I got bored with being the pretendy Minister. Why didn't I try imagining someone else?

Moses. I was Moses leading my people to safety. I was leading my Orkney people. Me, on a white horse, a white charger, waiting for low tide to cross over to the Brough of Birsay. Safety. The Promised Land. Bad people on chariots chased us right up to the water's edge. Just in time, the Lord parted the sea. Just in time. A path between the banks of water. Water stacked up. Eggy-yellow. Just in time. The water was eggy-yellow. Me, on a white charger, showing the way. The chariots were in pursuit.

We got there. Me. On a white charger. We're all safe. The Lord collapsed the banks of water. Whoosh. The baddies were trapped in this yellow yuckiness, sucked under and drowned. Dead baddies.

I was a hero. I. Moses. Hero. Everyone was cheering. They were singing my praises.

Alexander – I mean, Moses – is a Jolly Good Fellow.

I was standing at the top of the lighthouse on the Brough of Birsay.

Alexander is a Jolly Good Fellow. Alexander is a Jolly Good Fellow.

Looking down from the lighthouse, hand in hand with Gail. No need to wave or nod. Heroes don't need to do anything. Heroes just *are*.

I wanted to tell you something.

Badness is only someone else's point of view.

Those men on the chariot, were doing the chasing. Maybe they weren't the baddies. Maybe the chariot men were the goodies. The chariot men with their horses. Poor horses. Horses not pure white like mine. Not pure white like my handkerchief (free of snot). Just doing their job. Maybe I was taking away rats like that Pied Piper feller to meet their fate on the Brough. No, that's wrong. It was us Orkney folk that needed rescuing.

All this was in my head. My head fit to bursting. It wasn't a dream. You can never dream when the Big Sky is light.

Everything is clear when my eyes are shut.

Everything is clear when my eyes are shut and there is darkness.

Everything is clear when my eyes are open.

Everything is clear when my eyes are open and there is light.

Eyes open. Eyes shut.

Darkness. Light.

Badness. Only in a dream.

I opened my eyes. Looked up. Where was Gail sitting? I looked away across the pews. Left and right. Right and left. Forward. Sideways. No Gail. No choice. I had to look behind. I didn't want to but had no choice. Well not exactly looking but glancing over my shoulder, once in a while. There she was, sitting two rows behind me. She was far nicer to look at than the Minister.

Beautiful long blonde hair. I was in love. Gail was only fourteen. I was older than her. She was beautiful and she will be mine.

She will fall for me, if she hasn't already. You see, I knew everything that there was to know about eggs. And I will rescue her one day. I will be her hero. I will be like that *Dan Dare* in my comic. I will be her Viking. She will fall for me. Who or what will I be rescuing her from? Not sure. Not sure... as of yet.

"...and brethren, I wish you all a good Sabbath."

The Sabbath service was over. People were having a good chat to each other on their way out. I had to take a close look. The Minister's haircut – DA? Was Ephraim telling the truth? There was the Minister, outside the kirk. At the top of the steps by the main door. I will find out whether Ephraim was telling me the truth.

Stood round to the side. I could take a good look at the back of his head. Hoped no one knew what I was up to. Ephraim was right. Gold top. DA. Like them Yanks. Greased down. Shit pouring out.

Ephraim was right. The Man of God with his Duck's Arse haircut.

The Man of God…

Stupid…

Stupid…

Stupid.

I wanted to laugh. I will never be scared of the Minister again. DA. Greased down. Shit pouring out.

I went over to Mither and Ephraim.

"Mither, did you see how the Minister pointed to us and stared at us and said we were bad people and living in sin… in front of all the others? There must be a way we can win him round and get him to say we're good."

Adult. Hero. Badness was only someone's point of view.

"It is up to the Power of the Lord," Mither replied, but then her coughing took over.

"Alexander's right, Isabella. We don't want to be the centre of attention, picked out in front of others. We must do something to get back in the Minister's good books."

Ephraim was spot on. I nodded.

"Why don't we invite him round for supper? No, he's bound to be busy. Why don't we just ask his faether instead? The Minister's faether, Mister Flett. Mind, we could invite both of them round and double our chances of getting back in the Lord's good books. There is nothing wrong in killing two birds with one stone. What do you think, Isabella?"

Mither gave Ephraim a look.

"Mither, what does this Mister Flett look like?" I wanted to know. I needed to know.

I may be laughed at. I am taking a risk by asking a question.

Mither took some time to answer. "Mister Flett is like his son but older. He wears an eyepatch."

"Over each eye?"

"No, just over the one. Just the one."

"How does he know what eye to put his patch over?"

Mither did not answer. She shut her eyes and looked up to the Big Sky. I don't know why she did that.

Ephraim laughed. I don't know why.

No. No. No. I must have asked silly questions. Next time, when I'm unsure about something, I'll keep quiet. I'll nod. Safer. Safer. Learnt my lesson.

Mither went to talk to Gail's mither and faether. They owned the very big farm next to ours, and after all, it was the Sabbath. You should always speak to people you don't get on with. The Sabbath brings folk together.

"Ephraim, I saw the back of the Minister's head. Is the Minister a swimmer?" Couldn't help myself. I've asked another question. At least Mither cannot hear. I have said it. It was out in the open. I felt better for it being so, but I didn't want Ephraim laughing at me again.

"Alexander, the Minister thinks he is the Lord…" Ephraim smiled and pointed to the Minister who was standing at the top of the steps, "…but he has a Duck's Arse on his head." We laughed. Together. Did we laugh. We have shared a joke, man to man, adult to adult. Phew.

What Ephraim did to me didn't happen. It didn't happen.

My real faether would not have hurt me so. Maybe Ephraim was not my real faether.

Yoo-hoo! I'm home. Your faether's waiting.

I was so wrapped up in the Minister's DA and in thinking about Faether that I plain forgot to say hello to Gail after the service. I dreamt about her that night. We met in Dreamland. She received my dream. I received hers.

Dreamland. Me and Gail. Happy-ever-after.

That's how it should have been.

CHAPTER 4

GOLDEN BANTAM

1951

It came to pass. I got this dream.

There was rain and then there was no rain. There was wind and then there was no wind. There was Goodness and then there was Evil. It was a strange dream, not the dream that I was hoping for. I wanted a Gail-and-me dream. I wanted a lovey-dovey-kissy-kissy dream.

It started off so well. I shut my eyes and opened a door and stepped into bright golden light. Orkney Bible bright golden light.

Then there was me in my brand-new big motor car. Behind the wheel. Wearing gloves. White gloves. Made me feel important.

Then next to me was the biggest bantam hen you've ever seen. Patch over one eye. A big red flabby bit under its chin. Red comb. My passenger was not sitting down. It was rooting around on the floor in search of food. No joy. It kept on looking up at me, sort of sadly. Sort of pleading. *I am hungry. You are an adult. Help me.*

I wanted to help. I knew I must help. I took off my white

gloves and put them where you keep bits and bobs. Glove compartment. There was a pair of specs there. Specs. There. Not my specs. I didn't wear specs. The specs. Significant.

I pointed to the specs. I pointed like that Lord Kitchener feller on the poster in the war before the last war. No nonsense. I gave a *Your-Country-Needs-You* point with my first finger. I didn't have to say anything. The hen got the idea and followed the line of where my finger was pointing. The hen got the drift. Clever hen.

The bantam let me take off its eyepatch. The bantam let me put these specs over the eye that had the eyepatch. Revelation. No longer was the bantam hen pecking in hope. The big bantam had full sight. *I, an adult, had done good.* The bantam could now see where the food was. On the floor of my brand-new motor car. Went straight at it. Yum-yum. Yum-yum.

This bantam was so pleased with itself. Cluck-cluck-clucked. Not just once. Then with a wiggle of its arse, laid its egg. Not just an ordinary egg. Special. Perfectly shaped. Golden. A big, proud, golden egg. Golden with three eggy yolks inside. Not one. Not two. *Three.* Golden. Cluck-cluck-clucked. Then with head to one side, it gave me, the driver, a look. A *Bet you can't beat that* look. And to rub it in, it wiggled its arse once more. *Bigsy bugger. Didn't say thank you.*

I knew this all meant something.

Wiggling its arse and laying a golden egg. It was the Lord creating the world in six days and then forgetting the most important bit and having to lay the golden egg of Orkney on the Sabbath, the day of rest. I had to share my revelation with Ephraim. Right. Now.

"What's up, beuy?"

Ephraim was there on his tractor. I went about this in a roundabout way. Not head-on.

"That's a fine tractor you have, Ephraim."

"It's a Massey Ferguson. I'm the first in the parish to own a Massey Ferguson. It's my *Massive* Ferguson."

Ephraim's tractor had a neon sign over the cab with the words *Massive Ferguson* lit up and bright against the brightness. Orkney Bible bright golden light. He heard me out. Didn't interrupt.

"Hens' specs will make us all rich, Alexander. You're a genius, beuy. Less time needed to look for corn pellets to peck; more time to lay golden eggs. We'll be able to charge top dollar. You'll be wealthy and Gail will be all over you like a rash. Leave it to Ephraim. Let's see, there's ten hens each needing a spare pair…"

"That's twenty pairs of specs," I said, quick as a flash. I did not want Ephraim to take over my dream. I was the driver. I was in charge.

"We'll be millionaires." Ephraim was really excited. He could see the money rolling in, and so could I. In gold coins. Gold coins rolling from the road down the lane to our bu.

All this in my dream. This dream was exciting. It wasn't the dream I wanted. Where was Gail? Where was the happy-ever-after between us? Where was the lovey-dovey-kissy-kissy dream? It wasn't the dream I wanted, but it was an exciting dream nevertheless.

I was very happy so far with this dream. It didn't jump about all over the place like all my other dreams. After all, what use was a wrong-way-round dream when first you've ended up on your arse and the next minute you're slippery-sliding and about to end up on your arse?

One thing was following the other in this dream. I was having an ABC dream. Gold top.

Ephraim came back from the big town of Stromness with this big box of specs. All we had to do now was to fit the specs on the hens. It was a clear day, no wind, but the hens wouldn't come outside. They knew. Trouble in the air. Gale-force winds round the corner. Not having that. Better to be indoors, clucking around in the byre. Company for Popeye.

"Well, beuy, I might as well help you finish off the job. I'll fit the specs. Let's go indoors."

"Ephraim, this is my idea and they're my hens and I'll do it myself," I snapped back.

Ephraim said nothing. Raised his hands, keeping the peace.

I, not Ephraim, carried the box of special specs indoors and started fitting them. I soon found that even indoors, this was not going to be so easy. I tried sneaking up, catlike, behind the hens. I tried grabbing them by the feet. I tried shouting at them, telling them that what I was doing was for their own good. They didn't listen. They were being difficult. *Awkward buggers.*

Ephraim watched all this, smiling. Not I-told-you-so smiling. "Go on. Your Ephraim has been round the Standing Stones more than once. Let me take over."

"Only until I get the hang of what to do."

Ephraim gave me a funny look and then said, out of the blue, "Sometimes you wake up and feel like you've got a snake wrapped round your neck and it's squeezing the life out of you."

I nodded. Didn't think any more of what he had just said. Odd, though.

Ephraim started to fit the specs on the hens. Not getting the specs out of the box and taking them to the hens. No, the other way round. The hens were picked up one by one and taken to the box of specs for individual fitting. They were not happy. Ephraim was an adult. Adult-clever. All was going to plan. One. Two. Three. ABC. Gold top.

But then something happened. Were my eyes playing tricks

on me? Ephraim sneaked up behind a hen, grabbed it by the scruff of its neck, but instead of taking the hen over to the box of specs, he twisted and pulled the hen's head until I heard a snapping sound and the hen was as dead as driftwood. Dead as driftwood. He did the same to the one after, and the one after, and the one after. Murder.

Exciting, though.

All in my dream. Not the dream I wanted.

Exciting, though. I wanted to join in.

"Stop. Ephraim, stop. These are my hens and I don't want them dead."

My dream. Exciting. An action dream; with driftwood. I wanted to join in. *I wonder how it feels to kill a hen or an... an... adult?*

"What are you doing?" I yelled out again. "Stop!" I was so angry. I picked up the spade and was going to beat Ephraim about the head with it, and make him see sense and stop the killing. I was in charge. The driver. Shouted at him. Outwardly. Angry.

What's it like putting your hands round a hen's neck?

All in my dream. Not the dream I had asked for. This was not the dream I asked for.

What's it like putting your hands round an adult's neck?

Was it because of my shouting? Ephraim released his grip round the bantam hen's neck and dropped it. The hen landed on its feet, clucked once and quickly made its escape. I bet it was saying to itself something like, *Phew. Not going to end up in the pot as tomorrow's soup.*

The hen had been so lucky. Ran away. Didn't hop. Hens don't hop. Phew. Lucky escape.

Ephraim turned round to look at me. Not just smiling. Grinning.

When adults grin, does it mean they're happy?

I looked at all the hens. Something different about their feet. Not scrawny, twig-like toes, but cloven feet like the Devil. Cloven feet just like the Devil. The Devil.

"You'll be seeing a lot more of me from now on." The Devil had wheedled his way in. Grinning.

I looked up at Ephraim. Ephraim was extra-grinning.

The Devil and Ephraim were the one person.

All this in my dream. Scary. Not kissy-kissy. Not happy-ever-after. Not gold top.

I woke up sweating and scared. That was not the dream I wanted.

The dream I had reached out for was to be golden Orkney. A kissy-kissy dream with Gail. It had started off a beautiful dream, but it hadn't ended up beautiful. This dream, the night after the Sabbath. Sweating and scared. Not the dream I wanted. I wasn't given the choice.

This dream had arrived without my say-so.

Whoever had given me this dream was warning me that something very bad was going to happen. I had to understand what it all meant. I had to go over it, again and again…

CHAPTER 5

MISTER FLETT

1951

I got a gift of money from an uncle. It arrived on a strong westerly wind.

"Your uncle has met his Maker in Canada," Mither told me. She also told me this uncle's name, but I have forgotten it. Maybe I didn't swill his name round and round enough times before spitting it out.

I knew nothing about this uncle, his meeting with the Maker, nor anything about this 'Canada'. Being from Orkney, I of course knew about the Hudson Bay Company where many years ago, Orkney folk – Orcadians – worked. But this Hudson Bay was in North America and not this place called Canada, and I am never wrong.

With the uncle-from-Canada gift money I bought in lots of fluffy chicks. Ephraim helped me make wooden houses for them. We painted them yellow, egg-yolky yellow. *We* painted them. Together. Equals. A fortune to be made. Gold coins.

And it all happened so. Clockwork. Not a dream. The van came every Thursday to collect my eggs and the postman popped the cheque through our letterbox the following

Monday. Eggs out the back door; money through the front.

"I'm proud of you, beuy. Gold top." Ephraim said that to me at least once a day. Even more important was the look of pride on Mither's face. I was doing what a man was supposed to do: putting food on the table.

I did not know what to do with these cheques coming through the letterbox, so Ephraim opened up a bank account for me. The bank account was in his name. He told me that he had cleared it with Mither.

"Too young for it to be in your name, beuy. Legal stuff. You're only fifteen years old. We are all proud of you. You are special. Beuy, you are putting food on the table for us all."

I am putting food on the table for Mither and me.

This cluck-cluck-cluck dream stopped bothering me. Must have been the wind that took my worries clean away. My dream was a silly dream. Silly.

This fitting specs on hens. Silly.

No point in worrying over a silly dream. Silly.

Smudgy specs. Silly.

Hens can never wipe their specs clean, rain nor shine. Silly.

Hens have no hands, but they always land on their feet.

Ephraim and me have hands, but we fall over. Ephraim has the dropsy.

Nothing bad is going to happen. Silly. Silly dream.

The winds would soon bring something else in its place for me to think about. My sixteenth birthday. Just after Xmas and before New Year's Eve. Sixteen. Not long to go now.

Next year, I'll be seventeen and have to do my National Service. "My Alexander can't go 'cause he is needed round the farm." Maybe Mither will tell them that.

Wouldn't Gail be proud of me if I was to die doing my bit for king and country. "Only seventeen, *my* Viking hero!" That's what Gail will say.

Them Vikings never fucked about. I hope no one heard me say *that* word. *Fuck.* Swearing. *Fuck. Fuck. Fuck.* Adult.

When things went round and round in my head, back I would go to my favourite place. Just outside our bu. Sat down and took it all in. The grassy bumps and Kitchener's Memorial and the Brough of Birsay, only open at low tide.

The Big Sky. The sea. The wind. The Green Land. Talking to each other, but doing their own thing. Talking to each other but ...

I always came away from there feeling much better.

Whatever I think and do is out of my control. I'm always going to be dangling. Not dangling from the gallows like them baddies in the pictures, but dangling on a string like a puppet. Island. Puppet. Alexander. Me.

The Big Sky, the sea, the wind – yes, and I suppose the Green Land as well – pull the strings. I am given no choice. Orkney tells me what to do.

Badness is only someone else's point of view.

There was then this big change to my routine.

It was the day our grandfaether clock stopped chiming. Used to bong-bong on the hour, every hour. Now, no more bong-bong.

The change in my routine. The grandfaether clock no longer bong-bonged.

Two things happened at the same time but I don't think they were linked.

When was this big-change day? Not the eggs-out-the-back-door day. Not the money-through-the-front-door day. On a Wednesday? No, it was a Tuesday. Yes. Definitely. A Tuesday.

The time of year? Way after the midges had left. Between Harvest Festival and Xmas Day. Funny that, I could remember the day of the week but not the month. Couldn't be more definite than what I've just said. I don't own a watch and the grandfaether clock has stopped bong-bonging.

Our Tilley lamp was flickering that day. Mind, our Tilley lamp was always flickering.

Mither, me and Ephraim sat down for our supper. Mither was getting frailer and frailer and I was very worried about her, what with the doctor coming to our house regular and her coughing all the time and using her handkerchief. White handkerchief, blood snot. Blood. Not exciting blood.

Ephraim was busy telling us what he'd heard at the farmers' mart.

I was only half listening. Wasn't dreaming, but *day*dreaming. During the day was always a better time for me. I felt more in control of what was going through my head. Daytime. I was thinking about Gail. Our day out. How much money I'd need for a good day out with Gail in Stromness. What she would give me in return.

The three of us have sat down for our supper. Me, Mither and Ephraim. Here's the odd thing – not the grandfaether clock being silent, but that Mither has put no food on the table. Me hungry. No food on the table. Supper. No food on the table. Hungry.

Where's supper?

I looked at Mither and Mither smiled back. I looked at Ephraim and Ephraim smiled back. Mither looked at Ephraim and Ephraim at Mither... I didn't know what to make of it all. I... was... hungry. I picked up my knife and fork. Pleading. Letting them know. Ephraim looked at me, tapped his nose. His hand shaky.

Our table was set for four. Mither. Ephraim. Me. One. Two. Three. I was angry but didn't want to show it. Where was my food? Mustn't show it. Anger. Mustn't show it.

Sung a tune to myself to calm down. About a birdie and a

pussycat. In my head. Over and over again. One that I heard on the wireless. A funny tune. A silly tune. A Tweetie Pie tune. A cartoon tune. I heard the song on the wireless. *I Tawt I Taw a Puddy Tat.*

"We have a guest who will be joining us tonight, Alexander." Ephraim said.

Mither nodded. Mither was in on this game. Mither coughing. Mither nodding. Mither showed no surprise. Mither nodding. Adult.

I Tawt I Taw a Puddy Tat.

Whoever this guest was, he or she was late. I was very angry at being kept waiting for my supper and hoped that this guest would turn up soon and that we would never see this guest again after tonight. Never again.

Our guest finally arrived, a full half-hour late. Guest. Late. I'm hungry.

I Tawt I Taw a Puddy Tat.

This stranger walked in and sat down at the table opposite me. Said nothing.

No "Good evening."

Sat down at the table.

No "Hello, I'm…"

He was very old. He was wearing an eyepatch.

No "I'm so sorry I'm late."

The guest must be the Minister's elderly faether, Mister Flett.

No "It's very kind of you to invite me."

Who was he?

I had plain forgotten our chat on the steps of the kirk after that Sabbath service, and the invitation to the Minister's faether. It was sometime back, though. I was not going to let on that I had plain forgotten. Not happy. I nodded. Hungry. I nodded. Not happy.

I Tawt I Taw a Puddy Tat.

Ephraim, so friendly-like, pointed at me, Kitchener-style. "And Mister Flett, you know this fine young man to be Alexander A. Alexander. His full title is Alexander, Egg King of Birsay." Ephraim's sweet breath filled the room.

Me. 'Egg King of Birsay.' I felt proud of myself. Important. I looked full on at Mister Flett, eyepatch and all. I … was … hungry.

I Tawt I Taw a Puddy Tat.

The stranger's throat wobbled and he finally spoke.

"Good evening." He stared at Mither. Must be out of his good eye.

Mister Flett was very, very old. I have only seen this man a few times in the parish but there was something very familiar about the way he looked. Couldn't pin it down. Maybe an uncle, or an even closer relation.

There was something special-looking about Mister Flett. Not just the patch over his right eye.

That shock of hair? Five thousand volts must have passed through Mister Flett with hair standing on end like that Chief Sitting Bull, the Red Indian. I was hungry.

Special-looking. Was it his neck? Certainly an odd shape. A drainpipe with a wobbly flab. The flab. Stuck. The bulge. Halfway down. Stuck. A comb. Hen-like. Odd. Very odd. I was hungry.

Special-looking. No. Something else. I could feel it but couldn't explain it. Mither gave me a look. I tried to stop staring. I was hungry. *He* has kept us waiting.

Mister Flett was staring back at me out of his one good eye. Made me feel fidgety.

Mither herself was very fidgety. Even before we'd said our prayers she kept on excusing herself to leave the table. What was it about Mister Flett that made Mither act so?

I was hungry. He has kept us waiting. I could kill him. Fuck.

I Tawt I Taw a Puddy Tat.

On the wall behind Mister Flett were the words of the Lord. Thread stitching inside a glass frame:

> *Life is short,*
> *Death is sure,*
> *Sin the cause,*
> *Christ the cure.*

Mither closed her eyes. "May the Good Lord bless this special meal for a special guest." She was sitting next to Mister Flett.

"My-son-the-Minister blesses the food that is put before us." Mister Flett put his hands together and closed his good eye.

Ephraim shouted out his thanks to the Almighty. "Amen!" Telling us what we're having with such pride, as if he'd cooked it himself: "You'll like the gravy, made from a special whisky." Winked.

"Amen." It was my turn. I wanted just to get all this prayers-stuff out of the way so that I could get at my food. I was starving.

I Tawt I Taw a Puddy Tat.

We ate. The chicken Bonnie Prince Charlie and clapshot was delicious. The gravy went straight to my head. Ephraim took seconds and thirds without even asking Mister Flett whether he wanted seconds. Ephraim licked his plate clean. Slurp. Slurp. Mither had to stop him licking the serving spoon. Mister Flett didn't say no to seconds. Didn't say no. Delicious. The meal was too grand for any small talk. Yum-yum. Yum-yum. I was the last to finish. I looked at Mister Flett.

You were late.

No "Sorry."
No "I have kept you waiting."
No "I must apologise."
I could kill you.
I Tawt I Taw a Puddy Tat.

Ephraim let out a fearsome belch. He had something to say.

"I saw a Russian submarine off the coast this afternoon, bobbing up and down on the waves. How can the Lord protect us good Orkney folk from the Russians when they land and swarm all over us? What says you, Mister Flett?"

Mister Flett opened his mouth. Not quick enough. Ephraim continued with his something-to-say.

"Them Russkis might be good news after all, because once again there will be many soldiers' mouths to feed and us farmers will get a good price for our milk and meat. Them Cossacks are fine dancers too. They could improve the standard of Orkney country dancing. We should welcome them, shouldn't we, Mister Flett? What do you think, Mister Flett? Eh? Eh?"

Mister Flett stared at Ephraim. Mouth shut this time. He gave Ephraim a look like the look Mither would always give me if I had done something wrong.

I didn't know what to think. Perhaps Ephraim had a point here about the Russians being good and not bad news. I nodded a couple of times.

Mither gave Ephraim a look.

"Of course, the Reds will shut down the kirk but that's a small price to pay. Do you think, Mister Flett, that anyone will miss the kirk?" Some gravy oozed out of the side of his mouth. Ephraim licked his mouth clean. Slurp. Slurp.

I Tawt I Taw a Puddy Tat.

Mither had a further bout of coughing.

Mister Flett said nothing. He was cross though. The flab was moving up and down his neck. Like the 'test your strength' machine at the Farmers' Show. You'd strike this hammer thing at the base and the red ball inside this see-through plastic tube would work its way up, ring the bell at the top of the tower and then come all the way back down.

Ting-a-ling. Ting-a-ling. Ting-a-ling. Ting-a-ling.

I tilted back on the chair. Just a bit. A wee bit. Ephraim and his talk of the Russkis closing down the kirk and wouldn't it be a good thing? Blasphemy. Ephraim was going to be struck down by lightning. My chair was balancing on its hind legs.

I wanted to tilt back a bit further, to keep a bigger gap between myself and Ephraim without Ephraim noticing what I was doing. My chair was about to topple over. I quickly steadied myself.

I counted up to ten. There was no lightning. Ephraim had got away with it. I pretended that I was just being fidgety. I put my weight forward on the chair. It was now back to where it was.

"We are just a small island off the north coast of Scotland, too far away to receive the Lord's undivided attention. Banks of clouds mass together over Orkney to form a shield – rain. It rains a lot in Orkney. For the Lord, Orkney is Sodden and Gomorrah." Was Ephraim still talking about the Russkis?

Mister Flett was looking long and hard at Ephraim. I didn't know how this was going to turn out. I decided to take Ephraim's side in all of this. I didn't speak. I just nodded a lot while staring at Mister Flett.

Badness was only someone's point of view. I Tawt... I Taw.

Mither left the table. Two against one. There was a hush. There was a long hush. No bong-bong from the grandfaether clock to break the silence.

Ephraim let out a gale-force wind of a sneeze. Aaah-

63

choo. He took out... well, it was more of a dirty rag than a handkerchief. Put it back in his pocket. Brought out a penknife. Then produced a roll-your-own from behind his ear, as if by magic.

All the while, I was looking at the poker next to the hearth. It would do the job.

I Tawt... I Taw...

No one spoke. No sound. Even the peat fire had gone hush-a-bye.

Mither returned.

"Thank you for a fine meal," our guest said. "I have something for you to see. Something... Something you may find interesting."

... a Puddy Tat.

Mister Flett took out from his waistcoat a fob watch and chain. No movement at first. Then, holding it between thumb and first finger with a blink-and-you'll-miss-it wrist movement, the watch changed position. Mister Flett's elbow was now fully out to the side. The watch, like a steam train picking up pace, was swinging left to right... right to left. Higher and higher. Faster and faster. It would soon be doing a loop-the-loop.

His watch. Such a fine one. *Gold as well.*

My mouth was so wide open. I could have been swallowing a summerful of midges.

Mister Flett could see that I was being drawn into its beauty. It swung from right to left and then left to right, from right to left and then left to right. I was in a special world. I was in Dreamland.

The guest and this watch. In my bu.

"That's a fine timepiece, Mister Flett," Ephraim said. Friendly now. Manner of speaking completely changed. Respectful. No more let's-make-him-angry talk about the Russians and the invasion. Friendly. Let-me-offer-you-a-dram friendly. Do-you-need-some-more-baccy-for-your-pipe friendly.

"Mister Flett, your glass is empty. Let me fill it. Please."

My mouth still open that wide to gulp down the midges. No dram for me. I was too young. Mither would not allow.

Mister Flett did not answer straight away. He tapped his nose, which adults do when they are about to tell other adults a secret. Adults only share secrets with other adults. He carried on swinging the watch from side to side. Right to left and left to right. The light from the Tilley lamp flickered. As did my eyes. Dreamland.

"This watch belonged to King Farouk of Egypt, and its case is made of what looks like gold, but is in fact titanium brushed with gold. That King Farouk he won it in Monte Carlo. The fob watch is as light as a feather."

With his right hand, Mister Flett yanked the watch up by the chain. He cradled it in his left palm with the coiled-up chain underneath. Maybe it will have a life of its own, like a coiled-up snake. They have snakes in Egypt. *I know. I know.* Maybe a bit of music and the watch will rise from his open palm.

I Tawt I Taw a Puddy Tat.

I moved my chair back again. Just in case. I didn't want the watch to turn into a snake and hiss and spit and bite me.

His right hand now free, Mister Flett lifted the watch. The chain stayed put. The watch didn't turn into anything nasty. Mister Flett was holding the watch between thumb and first finger. Lightly, like holding a feather. Now at mouth-level. Mister Flett blew his cheeks and let out a long puff in the watch's direction.

Would the watch slowly float to the ground or would coo-cooing birds appear, as if by magic? Puff. Puff. Magic. All of it magic. Before my very eyes. The Tilley lamp flickering.

"Look – see how when I hold it up to the light and turn

it so, the face of the watch changes colour from the palest of white to amethyst." Mister Flett spoke so softly, it was difficult to pick out every word he said.

'Amethyst.' I nodded.

I want that watch.

I've never owned a watch.

You are too old to need that watch.

That watch should be mine. By rights.

"That is a watch like no other." Ephraim got in first. "The last time I saw anything as remarkable was on the Sabbath when I saw a horse get down on its knees and pray."

Mither was coughing. Coughing loudly. Could not stop. Handkerchief on her mouth. She got up and left the table once more.

There was a further silence. I wanted to say something. I didn't know what to say. My mouth was shut tight. I went red in the face. Red all over. Red evenly spread. Not drip-drip. Not blood-red. Ephraim-red. No point in nodding. I tried to smile, looking friendly-like.

"Gold top. Pure gold top. You must be well connected, Mister Flett, to own such an object. Gold top. Pure gold top."

"Thank you, Ephraim. If you look very closely at the back of the watch there is a catch which, when sprung, reveals… but enough for now. I will tell you more next time, and if the meal is as good as this, maybe I will tell you about this watch's special powers. If the meal is as good as this, maybe I will even let you hold this Eighth Wonder of the World…"

Mister Flett kissed his magical watch and slipped it back inside his waistcoat pocket. All done delicately. All done with love. Just as if he had finished reading Popeye a bedtime story, kissed the cow on his cheek with the words 'Sweet dreams' and turned out the light.

Mister Flett's glass was empty. He jerked his head forward,

not once but twice. His glass raised. Empty. A look on his face like the bantam in my dream. Sort of sadly. Sort of pleading. *I am hungry. You are an adult. Help me.*

Ephraim downed his own dram. Said nothing. He filled his own glass. Looking after number one. Ignored Mister Flett.

Mither rejoined us.

Tonight's show was over, but Mister Flett had one final thing to say.

"Compared to the sheer beauty of this watch, what I am about to say is by the by. I will say it anyway. *The... watch... is... indeed... worth... a... pretty... penny.*"

We sat bolt upright. We were all lost in the holiness of this watch. Mister Flett certainly had our attention now.

"I could buy all of Birsay with it, if I was so minded. There is only one watch of its kind in the whole world. It is the crown jewels of all watches. Engraved on the back are the initials *K* and *F*. That proves it was owned by King Farouk. King Farouk of Egypt." Mister Flett jerks his head forward twice for emphasis. "*K* and *F*."

The Tilley lamp flickered.

He has said that the watch was worth more than all of Birsay. First passed down to this King Farouk, whoever he was, and now to Mister Flett. This dear old man. The king's watch. From ancient times. King Farouk. From the ancient kingdom of Egypt. Farouk – that's not an Orkney name.

What a fine man Mister Flett is. Perhaps I can be his favourite nephew, and when it's time for him to go and meet his Maker... a gift... just like from my uncle in Canada. But that could mean me waiting until I'm very old. I might be thirty by the time...

He has promised to show us more next week. *A catch, when sprung, reveals... special powers. He will let us hold it.* Adults keep their promises – *Sixpence for you if you find the hour before I do.*

"Thank you, Isabella. That was a very tasty meal," said

Mister Flett. He again was looking at Mither in a strange way. "Isabella, I will be only too pleased to let my-son-the-Minister know of your kindness in inviting me round for such a wholesome evening. It's late. I must be heading home."

Mister Flett kissed Mither twice on each cheek, followed up by one full on the lips, shook my hand, completely ignored Ephraim's, put on his coat and left for home, a short walk along a path across the fields. The full moon provided a tucked-up blanket of light on the fast-asleep Green Land. The Big Sky with its full moon had thrown out a challenge to the sea, and the sea rose to it. It made the highest of high tides, that night.

Mither tried to still her coughing. It was difficult to know what she had made of the evening. Fidgety. We did the clearing up. Mither had gone to bed, leaving myself and Ephraim, sitting round the peat fire. He with pipe in hand, roll-your-own behind the ear. Me yawning, sleepy.

"Ephraim, that Mister Flett, what a dear old man."

"Dear and kind. Dear and kind."

"I hope we get to see him again. That watch must be worth a pretty fortune. Such a valuable watch. Gold. Ameth… For him to be given King Farouk's watch!"

"All hocus-pocus. More likely Mister Flett's dog found the watch just along the road beneath a bump in the ground, one of them bumps from ancient Skara Brae times. That Mister Flett, just like his son the Minister… talking out of his arse. Did you see his haircut, beuy? Like faether, like son. Meeting a king from Egypt? You know, beuy, that's as likely as you going down to the shop to buy chocolate and Marilyn Monroe herself serving you. Chiffchaff. Just chiffchaff.

"Mind, I agree that watch was remarkable. Your Ephraim has never before seen anything that looks older than an antique but younger than a newborn, bawling baby beuy. I bet his dog got a large, juicy bone for finding such a watch."

"Maybe we should get a dog, Ephraim."

"That watch must be worth many hundreds and hundreds of thousands of pounds. Imagine what we could do with that sort of money, beuy. We'll invite him round next week for dinner. That'll put us even more in his son's good books. In Orkney, it's always better to pluck the eyebrows off a cow than to skin a cat. We'll find out more about the watch next week. Mister Flett said we could even handle it and get the feel of it."

"It's always better to pluck the eyebrows off a cow than to skin a cat." I repeated what Ephraim has just said. Word-for-word perfect. "Ephraim, I wonder what's it like to kill someone?"

There was a silence as long as a ball of baler twine.

"Beuy, he's taken a shine to you. No mistake."

We both gazed at the mystery of the flames licking the peat in our hearth.

"He promised next week to open the catch of his watch to reveal something more."

"That's some watch, beuy." Ephraim poured himself another dram of whisky. His hand was shaking.

"I come from a good family, Ephraim, even though just now Faether is away looking after his own garden. That Mister Flett, I bet you he comes from one of Orkney's top families too."

"You're right there, beuy. His faether Keith Flett was one of the Birsay Fletts... well connected but not la-di-da with it."

I nodded, not once but twice. I nodded for the third time. The peat fire was now damping down for the night, gently hissing away and puffing those smoky shapes like Chief Sitting Bull does out of his peace pipe.

"Maybe we should get a dog, Ephraim," I said again.

Ephraim started to sing.

"This old man, he played one,
He played knick-knack on my thumb,
With a knick-knack paddywhack
Give the dog a bone,
This old man came rolling home."

The following morning, I woke up stiff and cold in that comfy chair in the in-by. But not told off. Happy. Accepted as a full equal. Mither. Ephraim. Alexander. Three adults.

That Mister Flett and his watch.

I went over to the hearth. I picked up the poker and gripped it as tight as tight could be. I swished it about a bit. Just to get used to the weight of it.

Badness is only someone else's point of view.

CHAPTER 6

THE LATE MISTER FLETT

1951

Mister Flett turned up for supper the following Monday. He was expected.

The Big Sky had dropped a lot of rain on us during the day. Black clouds. Mister Wind blowing hard from the west, but did nothing to puff-puff away the rain.

Drip...

Drip...

Down...

Our lum.

Useless lum.

It was more splish-splash than drip-drip.

Splish...

Splash...

Down...

Our lum.

Useless lum.

Black clouds in the night sky. I could see them. Yes, I could. Black clouds in night-time Big Sky. The night-time Big Sky.

The table was set for four. Like last week, I was sitting

71

next to Ephraim. Mither looking at Ephraim. Ephraim looking at Mither. Me looking at them. Them looking at me. No one sitting next to Mither. We were waiting for our guest.

I wasn't coiled up and angry this time, though. None of this *What will happen next?* Mister Flett will soon be here. He may be late but he will be here. Like waiting for the bus. The bus late, but here soon. Not the school bus, though. Ages since I used the school bus. Too long ago.

I said, I don't know about the school bus.

Waiting for Mister Flett. I was bored. Silence. No bong-bong from the grandfaether clock. I was hungry. I wasn't that angry.

I Tawt... I Taw...

"He is late again." That's what Ephraim said. "We have been waiting for half an hour. He likes turning up late. Beuy, we should call him the late Mister Flett." Ephraim found his words to be right funny.

Mither gave Ephraim a look.

The late Mister Flett.

Mister Flett arrived. The light from the Tilley lamp flickered. Greasy oil. Greasy wick. Tilley. Tallow. Greasy. A smell from it. A smell from him. Not sweet Ephraim-breath smell. Mister Flett. Very-old-man smell. Smell of piss.

It was as if he was here for the first time. It was as if we were strangers. Not dear friends. Not pretendy family. Not uncle and nephew. Not even from the same parish. Coat off. Head down. Took his place. Sat down. Didn't look up. Said nothing. Head down.

Wary. Like we've offered a place to a man of the road, a traveller down on his luck. Hungry. Awkward. Him. Us. The Christian thing to do. *Life is short. Death is sure. Sin the cause. Christ the cure.* Head down.

No "I'm sorry to have kept you waiting."

No "How are you doing, beuy?"
No "I have brought the watch with me."
There was something I'm-so-sorry about him. He was
hiding something. It must have been to do with the watch.
I bet you he has given it away. *My* watch. I bet you he sold
it and has hundreds of gold coins hidden in his bu. Those
gold coins... rightfully mine. He was hiding something. Head
down. I bet you he hasn't even brought my watch with him.

"Guilt is bad. Guilt is after doing something bad. Guilt is
doing something bad and hiding it."

Those were the Minister's words at Sabbath time. Directed
at me, Mither and Ephraim. We were not guilty. We never did
bad things. Those Minister's words should have been aimed
at his own faether. For Mister Flett. No. Let's call him by that
right clever name that Ephraim has given him. For the late
Mister Flett. That late Mister Flett was hiding something.

You could always hear the weather from our bu. The what
was going on outside, from inside. I heard the rain. Heavy
rain. Sodden and Gomorrah. Splish-splash down our lum.

Useless lum.

The flames were licking the peat on the hearth. Smoky puffs
formed shapes and dissolved into thin air. I looked at the poker.
I left the table. I went over. I picked the poker up. I waited 'til
Mither was next door. I took up a position behind Mister Flett.

*All this inside my head... I have left the table... Poker in my
hand... I will finish him off under the lum; not-so-useless lum
because the rain coming down it will wash his blood away. All this
inside my head.*

All this inside my head.

He is to be the late Mister Flett.

The late.

I hummed a tune to myself. It was that silly tune.

I Tawt I Taw a Puddy Tat.

73

Our meal was much plainer this time. Mince, neeps and tatties. Nothing in the gravy to make Ephraim want to lick his plate clean. Right tasty nonetheless. No seconds. No thirds. No slurp-slurp. *The late Mister Flett has promised. Yes, he has.* But all the time he was looking down at the plate. Looking down. Not up at us. He was keeping something from us.

I Tawt I Taw a Puddy Tat.

We were still eating. It cannot wait. I felt the pressure. *All this in my head. Must whoosh out some of this pressure.* I had to ask the question.

"Did you bring the watch with you?" Me with pointy finger, just like that Kitchener feller.

"I did."

I jerked my head back. I hadn't expected his answer.

So he does have the watch with him.

"Where did you get my... *the* watch?" Direct. To the point. I'll be as rude to him as he had been to me. The late. I looked over again at the poker by the hearth. The late Mister Flett. The late.

Mither glared at me.

The late Mister Flett. Smiling. Softly spoken. Had to listen closely. Must show that I was listening closely. I had asked the question after all. I felt better for doing so. I nodded as he spoke.

He has the watch. He says he has the watch. I never had a watch. I never had a faether. Watch. Faether. Unfair.

For the first time since he sat down at the table, Mister Flett has raised his head. No longer head down, he was looking at me. One eye good. Eyepatch over the other.

"Orkney attracts many important people because Orkney is the Centre of the World. Us Orcadians in turn are a travelling people. Travelling brings a maturity to the way we look at things. There are no airs and graces on us Orcadians. There are no flies on us."

74

I was aware my mouth was open. Wide open. Clamped it shut. Crocodile-like.

"We fully understand in Orkney the power that nature holds over us, that the important things in life are outside our control. People are important, but only as important as important people can ever be."

I nodded.

"There is nowhere as uncomplicated and crystal clear and as pure as Orkney. There is nowhere as mysterious, as dark and as filled with menace as Orkney." Speaking quickly now. A lot for me to take in. The late Mister Flett jerked his head forward, not once but twice.

I nodded.

The late Mister Flett. He was straight out of my dream. You know the dream I'm talking about. Him. On the floor of my car, rooting around for food. Speaking. All at the same time.

"Answer the beuy's question, Mister Flett." Ephraim was not impressed by all this flimflammery, all this chiffchaff. Each word shouted out, separate: "How. Did. You. Get. This. Watch?"

Ephraim would never dare speak like that to me.

"The great potentate himself. Yes, King Farouk. The very one. It was his to give. Didn't I tell you that his initials, *K.F.*, were on the watch? King Farouk was…"

"But where did you meet the king?" *Give me an answer. I am an adult like you.*

"Here in Orkney, beuy. King Farouk was following in the footsteps of the great-great-grandfaethers of his great-great-grandfaethers. The Ancient Egyptians came from the best ancient land in the East."

I Tawt I Taw a Puddy Tat.

"What brought them Ancients here?" *An answer. Keep it short. Don't want a Sabbath sermon.*

"Now Alexander, a lot of people got themselves in a right

pickle over where the East actually started, and got their Middle East muddled up with their Far East and Near East. Them Ancient Egyptians not knowing what part of the East they came from were right confused as well."

The late Mister Flett gave me a look. A don't-interrupt look.

The late Mister Flett's head jerked forward again. Not once but twice. A pair of specs would be more useful on him than an eyepatch.

"The Ancient Egyptians had of course heard about Orkney, and that Orkney was the Centre of the World. No ifs. No buts. The Centre of the World. Fact. They'd also heard that Orkney men were strong, and good rowers to boot."

Not staring, but smiling. A fond look. Brought out the watch. *At last.* Patted it like I pat Popeye the cow; fondly. Returned it. Too quickly for me. Like the sun peekabooing. Disappointing.

"This watch is worth a pretty penny."

We nodded. Both Ephraim and me. We nodded.

"Now, where was I?"

Ephraim and me. Me and Ephraim. Looked at each other. Not a peep. We were waiting for the late Mister Flett to continue.

"Them pharaohs loved tall ships. With the wind billowing through the big sails they could travel all round the world. Mind, they didn't want to sail too far in case they fell off. They believed in them days that the earth was flat." The late Mister Flett pretended he was Mister Wind, took in a deep breath and then let out this long puff. *Phew...ew...ew.* Ended up with a cough and a splutter.

The late Mister Flett is a very old man who will die soon. Smells of piss.

He raised his empty glass to Ephraim. Not a toast. Sort of sadly. Sort of pleading.

Ephraim ignored the plea.

I nodded. I was in a muddle in my head. *Pharaohs. Don't know them. What have they got to do with Egypt? The earth is flat. Obvious. Anyone can fall off the cliffs next to Kitchener's Memorial. The late Mister Flett has the watch. It will soon be my watch.*

Mither was staring so at the late Mister Flett.

I heard the rain. Inside. Splish-splash.

Lum.

Useless lum.

"Mister Wind sometimes didn't blow. The pharaoh's tall ships had run out of wind. Them Ancients in their tall ships then needed the slaves to do their bit. Them Ancients were always on the lookout for slaves to do a bit of rowing in the galley, down below. Always vacancies for that position.

"Everyone knew about our strong winds. All the time. Them Ancients. Clever buggers. 'Why don't we visit this place which is the Centre of the World, and whilst we're at it, bring back some of their strong winds? No difference to storing their Orkney winds like we do our grain in the pyramids back home?'"

He was talking less hesitantly now.

The late Mister Flett picked up the salt container from the middle of the table. Jiggled about with it. Gave it a right good shaking. Bits of white flew around like snow. Then settled. Showed us how the winds can be easily stored inside something. White salt. Passed it over to me to do likewise. Smiled fondly, I gave it a good shaking. Good fun. Some even came out through the holes at the top.

He was still waiting for his glass to be filled up. Just a wee dram. Not much to ask for.

"So them pharaohs sailed many days and nights and nights and days and finally got here. They loved it in Orkney. The peace and quiet and birdies and people too. Them pharaohs loved building, and were always at it. Pyramids and the like. Yes, that fine lighthouse of ours on the Brough of Birsay. Who built it? The Ancient Egyptians, that's who. But they could only stay for so long. Time to go home. They threw a big farewell do on the biggest of their tall ships..."

He paused and then lowered his voice. "Us Orkney fellers didn't stand a chance. Didn't stand a chance." The late Mister Flett pulled out a handkerchief. White. Clean. Clean. White. Just the one handkerchief. Free of snot. Dabbed his good eye. He was crying.

His fist crashed down on the table. "They seized the strongest of our Orkney men. Took them away as galley slaves. My great-great-great-great-grandfaether was one of those men. My own blood. Orkney's finest. Born free, now a slave. Us Orcadians, we didn't stand a chance. You get my drift." He shouted it out, loud enough for everyone in Birsay to hear. A disgrace that must never be forgotten.

"How could they get away with that?" Ephraim and myself, as one. Appalled. Not understanding. "Surely the Orkney men had an inkling as to what might happen, with the drink and all?"

"Them Ancients tricked us. They didn't spike the drink. They just offered us drink. Lots of it. As much as we wanted. Being hospitable. Our men were soon legless."

"Why didn't our men just refuse?" Both of us yelling.

"The drink was free."

"*Free? It was all offered for free?*" Ephraim first, in amazement.

"That's right. Free."

"*Free?*" My turn.

"Yes, Alexander. Free."

Why didn't the Vikings come to their rescue? They don't fuck about. Drink or no drink. Them Vikings would have given them

78

pharaohs a good going-over. Them Vikings, our brothers, could have saved our Orkney folk from becoming slaves. Kith and kin. Same blood. If I'd been the man in charge – me, taken charge, adult, the leader – I would have made sure, with my Viking friends. Them pharaoh fellers, they would have soon known who was gold top. Us Orcadians don't fuck about. Us Vikings don't fuck about. Us. Orcadians and Vikings. As one.

"Them pharaohs. Cunning whores." Ephraim was right angry.

I joined in. "Cunning whores." I was right angry too. I did not know what the word 'whore' meant, and did not understand why Mither looked at me so.

"When them Russkis arrive in the next few months, they'll not dare try that one on us." Ephraim was boiling over. He was raging. "Them pharaoh fellers, all nicey-nicey, then this. The hand of friendship and then…"

"The Egyptians have been feeling guilty ever since." The late Mister Flett pointed to his empty glass. Sort of sad. Sort of pleading. Sort of needing help. Sort of helpless. "That answers your question, feller. King Farouk was back here to make amends. *Amends.*"

'Amends.'

I nodded. I'd listened to the dear old man long enough. His gold fob watch. I wanted to touch it, to hold it and to look at it and lose myself in its mystery, and be told again how much it was worth.

"But you still haven't told me where the king gave you the watch." I was steaming.

"Beuy, be patient. I was just coming to that. Now, where was I?" The late Mister Flett's flab was moving up and down his neck.

"I met King Farouk on the Brough of Birsay, the Brochhhh, and we had this grand chat. He treated me as his equal. Him, the great-great-great-great-grandson of the pharaoh from the East, and me, a humble Orcadian from Birsay, the West Mainland and the Centre of the World. I gave him a Craven "A" cigarette and he gave me this special watch and another gift. We could have been long-lost brothers."

I will kill him for my watch.

"We had a long natter, speaking about the Cold War, the price of eggs in Egypt, the Great Pyramids, Birsay and of course all things Orkney. Just King Farouk and me."

The sound of the rain.

Outside our bu.

Continuous.

The rain.

Inside our bu.

Splish-splash.

Down through the lum.

Useful lum.

Washing his blood away.

Mister Wind quiet tonight.

Ephraim was champing at the bit. He has let the late Mister Flett talk for too long.

"You know, Mister Flett, it's always better when strong winds go out than when they come in. People take them winds for granted, but do so at their peril. Some get in a pickle over whether the westerly wind is a wind that comes from the west or goes to the west. Did you get King Farouk to say anything about those Egyptian winds? Eh? Did you?"

Ephraim winked at the late Mister Flett. I saw him do so. Yes, I did. Mister Flett winked back at Ephraim. Left eye.

I did not like that. I am as much an adult as both of you. I do man's work round the farm. There was something going on here.

"Of course we talked about the winds. King Farouk was apologetic, like. He said that back home in Egypt, winds were

80

contrary creatures and went all over the place, wherever they chose.

"I told him that we have disciplined winds here. All the winds started in Orkney and only went in one direction: outwards." The late Mister Flett jabbed his finger, pointed outwards like that Kitchener feller. "Orkney. Outwards and disciplined."

"That'll teach them Ancient Egyptians. They can't even control their own winds. That's one up for Orkney," Ephraim roared in triumph. He winked again. Again, not at me.

I put in my two pennyworth. "That wind can be a bastard. I was on the boat over to Hoy a few days back and the westerly wind gave us many almighty ups and downs. That westerly is a real *bastard*."

I shouldn't have said *that* word out loud in front of the late Mister Flett and Mither. Not once. Twice. Mind on, many a time I've had the parish kids shouting at me, "Alexander is a bastard… Alexander is a bastard."

The others round the table looked at me, stunned, like. I heard this loud taking-in of breath from Mither and from the late Mister Flett. Ephraim was laughing.

They must have not heard me proper. I started to say once more that the westerly was a bas —

The late Mister Flett didn't let me finish. Spoke ever so softly to me, like Mither did when I needed cheering up, not at all angry, like. "Not westerly, Alexander, but outwardly. These outwardly winds, we pay far too much respect to them."

"Winds are important, but not that important," Ephraim said.

"Winds are important, but not that important," I repeated, word for word.

Mither tried to speak but ended up coughing.

The late Mister Flett brought out the watch from his waistcoat pocket.

"I don't know how many more winds I will be able to see before it is time for me to meet my Maker. My-son-the-Minister does not want the watch. My-son-the-Minister says possessions must not come between us and the Lord. My-son-the-Minister says you should never covet your neighbour's ox. Exodus 20:17." He repeated, head jutted forward, "Exodus 20:17."

Ephraim and me, we both nodded, holy-like. Both of us adults. Together. Me nodded faster.

"I do not know what to do with this, my timepiece, when I receive the final call." The late Mister Flett started to swing the watch from side to side.

He was talking about my watch.

"I want to leave it to someone in this parish who will derive strength from it... someone who will cherish it... someone who will be kind towards me... someone close to me in those days remaining. I know I have not long left."

The late Mister Flett gave me the warmest of smiles. He was coughing but not coughing like Mither did.

I nodded. I looked away from him. Towards the hearth. I picked the poker up. That's how I was going to kill him. It will be raining heavily. Splish-splash. The blood will be washed away. Splish-splash not drip-drip. *All in my head.* Job done. *All in my head.* I have returned the poker to the hearth. *All in my head.*

The winds. Always in charge. Moving. Not moving. Their decision. Always in control. The late Mister Flett will give me his watch. When? When he dies. Who says so? He says so. When will he die? Could be years. Should I wait, do nothing? Wait. If I wait, then I'm not in control. Better to be like the winds. Act now. Not yet. The winds. They know. They'll give me a sign when it's the right time.

"Winds. We pay far too much respect to them," Ephraim said once again.

"Winds are important, but not that important," my turn to follow.

"Winds are important, but not that important." the late Mister Flett completed the round.

We were all soon to be shown that we had got this wrong, badly wrong.

Badness was only someone else's point of view.

CHAPTER 7

THE PLAGUE

January 1952

O n the 15th January 1952, the great gales came to Orkney. Took everyone by surprise, me as well. Didn't let on, though. When I spoke to Ephraim about the great gales, I must have nodded up to ten. Same when I spoke to Mither. Same when I spoke to the late Mister Flett. Had this nodding down to perfection. Adult. Not beginner adult. To-be-taken-serious adult.

The local Birsay parish newspaper. That week. Front-page report.

Like the plague in Ancient Egypt, evil has left its mark on every farmstead in our Holy Land. In just a few hours, winds of a force not previously unleashed in our lifetime have brought wanton destruction in their wake.

Nodded while reading it.

Neighbours' stuff. No bits and pieces. Lots. Slabs and posts. Thatch and roof tiles. Outside doors and gates. Trailers and wheelbarrows. All came our way. We were doing repairs there and then, but had to get out of the way sharpish. No blood. No one killed. A scratch here. A bump on the head there. Dangerous, though. *Wanton destruction.* Dangerous.

"Mither, have you seen Mister Flett? Is he all right?"

"I have neither seen nor heard of him, but we will say a prayer," Mither replied.

"Amen."

Did he still have *my* watch? *Amen.*

The outwardly winds had no right to *my* watch. *Amen.*

That watch was mine. *Amen.*

Only right and fair. *Amen.*

The late Mister Flett gone missing. One thing. *My* watch gone missing...

Me. Alexander A. Alexander. Me. Before, special. Egg King of Birsay.

Me. Alexander A. Alexander. After, used-to-be-special.

Only a few months between the special and the used-to-be-special.

Outwardly winds of over 150 miles an hour wooshed away my hens and the hen houses. All my hens. With the wind behind their arses, they'd have got back to Ancient Egypt quicker than them pharaohs ever did. Never to return. One-way ticket. Alexander A. Alexander. Eggless. Insignificant. Adultless. Eggless. No longer Egg King of Birsay.

Our horse, gone. Unfair. *Thank the Lord.* Popeye survived. *Thank the Lord.* I went through to the byre. Had to see her. Had to pat her. Had to rub my cheek against hers. *Thank the Lord.* Popeye would make me feel cleansed. Sabbath-holy. Better than any Minister.

"No faether. No watch. Those outside the shop laughing at me... *me.* Mither... poorly. Those winds were a *bastard, bastard, bastard.* Popeye, why me? Why me? Why me?" I was crying. Hush-a-bye crybaby. It was unfair... unfair... unfair.

Ephraim joined me in the yard. Hand rested on my shoulder. Nothing to be said. Hand on my shoulder. Not a tight grip. Not threatening. Soft touch. Faetherly.

Destruction everywhere. Where's the thatch gone? Holes in the roof of our bu. You could see the sky. The sky could see us. Holes much bigger than our lum.

Lum.

Useless lum.

The kirk, just up the coast road. Lightning struck our kirk. The winds had got in on the act. The roof – where have the tiles gone? Bell tower – what bell tower? Bell tower with bell. Ding-dong. What bell tower with bell? Now fresh air. Was I at the wrong kirk? No. I only go on the Sabbath but it was definitely my kirk. Sabbath-kirk.

I went inside the kirk. Today was not Sabbath. I went inside. I looked up. You could see the Big Sky. The Big Sky could see me. Where was the lum? The kirk never had a lum.

Lum.

Useless lum.

The Big Sky and the winds had made mischief together. Cowardly. Wouldn't have dared so if it had been on the Sabbath day. The sea as well, got in on the act. All angry. All really angry. The sea as well. Badness. All as one. But not on the Sabbath. *Badness was just a point of view.* Never got badness on the Sabbath.

The kirk. Outside and inside. Inside and outside.

Outside the kirk, them gravestones for the dead still upright, but covered in smelly seaweed. I even saw a piece of driftwood on one of the graves. Should be see-sawing from side to side. Should be balancing, precarious, like; even have fallen off. But fixed, like. Should go this way. Should go that way. But the driftwood was fixed, like.

Outside the kirk.

Inside the kirk.

Muck. All over the pews. Left the Minister's pulpit well alone.

Inside the kirk.

Outside the kirk.

The stone wall round where the graves were – fallen down. Like Humpty Dumpty. Hump-tee Dump-tee. Teeeeeeee.

All the king's horses and all the king's men
Couldn't put Humpty together again.

Destruction. Evil.

Outside the kirk and inside the kirk. Inside the kirk and outside the kirk.

Storms and no storms. Evil and no evil. Big Sky outdoors and Big Sky indoors. The late Mister Flett and the late Mister Flett. It was Sabbath. Still a Sabbath day. Still a holy day. The Sabbath after the storm was a sad Sabbath. Folk still in a state of shock. Sabbath.

It was cold.

Men and womenfolk were wearing thick coats so you couldn't tell whether they had their Sabbath best on underneath.

It was cold.

Wearing hats and gloves.

It was cold.

Everyone could see everyone else's breath.

It was cold.

I could see and smell Ephraim's breath.

It was cold.

Mither didn't look well.

It was cold.

Gail was in her usual place. I looked round. I looked behind me. I caught her eye. Gail with her hat on. Lovely long hair hidden. Hair up in a bun with her hat on. I'll buy her a beautiful new hat. With my hens taken, the hat certainly won't be a yellow one. Yellow was the colour of egg yolk. The evil winds must have been yellow. Egg yolk brought bad luck. Yellow was a bad-luck colour.

From up high, the Minister was staring down at us. Didn't beat about the bush. Up in his pulpit, he nailed down the guilty bastard. Bastard. Nailed down from up high.

Fuck. Fuck. Fucking bastard.

Swearing.

Swearing to myself. Adult.

Swearing to myself on the Sabbath. Adult.

Swearing to myself on the Sabbath in the kirk. Adult.

Swearing out loud. Adult.

"The Book of Job will provide you with the name of the One who is the cause of all our trouble. The One has boasted to God that he can turn all men from worship. He will unleash the flood," the Minister said.

"I know the name of the One who is going to unleash the Flood," the Minister said.

The Minister lowered his voice to a whisper. "The One is the cause of our troubles. Sickness, pain and death are all his work."

The Minister made this sound. His mouth wide open. It was not a human voice. Growling. Dog-growling. "There is evil within." Rasping. Loud. Not human. Possessed.

From the back pew to the front, everyone was paying attention now. Fear, not joy.

That tune popped back into my head.

I Tawt I Taw a Puddy Tat.

"Be in no doubt that the Devil was the One. There are those here who have strayed from the true path of the Lord. The Devil, with his cloven feet and tail, sits amongst you."

I looked down in shame and fear. I looked down in disappointment. Hadn't made a ha'penny of difference. We had invited the Minister's faether, the late Mister Flett, round for dinner not once, but twice. For what? Mither, Ephraim and me were still in the Minister's bad books. I was a sinner... I will always be a...

I Tawt I Taw a Puddy Tat.

"Once the egg is taken over by evil, it will float to the surface. It could never return to the bottom of the pan. How many more warnings, my parishioners, do you need?"

I Tawt... I Taw...

I had somehow helped to let the Devil in. Through the front door of our bu. I had done something bad and had opened the door. The Devil had brought destruction. My egg business was finished. But that won't be the end of it. The Devil, once in, won't go. The tears. The shame.

The Devil. Inside our bu. Inside my head.

Not scrawny twig-like toes, but cloven feet like the Devil.

The Devil's face filled all the space in my head. A Mister Punch laughing-and-grinning face. A serious-looking adult face with a crown on his head, a King Farouk face. A late Mister Flett face... when he was younger. All one and the same person. The Devil. The Devil was one and the same with different faces. Inside me.

So this watch, my watch, didn't just belong to one of them. It belonged to all of them and all of them were swimmers-; Mister Punch, King Farouk, the Minister and the late Mister Flett. Watch. This watch should be mine alone.

My mouth was wide open. Not summerful-of-midges open. Different open. Teeth- showing open. Chattering open. My teeth were making a chattering sound. Cat about to catch that birdie.

I Tawt... I Taw...

"The Devil cannot be removed with kindness. You must act now. The Devil is to be thrown into a fiery furnace like Shadrach, Meshach and Abednego."

Shad... Mesh... Abed... These were strange names. These were *not* Orkney names, but the Minister's words rang true. I had to act. The moment had come.

That Sabbath day, Mither was giving me long, hard looks. After supper, she wanted a word.

"Are you feeling all right, Alexander? Has something strange come over you? I'm used to seeing you with your mouth wide open, but at kirk today and here tonight, you've been just like one of those barn cats, your teeth chattering away on seeing a mouse... ready for the kill."

I didn't reply. I... said... nothing.

The following morning, mucking out the byre, had an attack of the sneezing. Eyes open and eyes shut. Aaah-choo. Then suddenly this vision. Aaah-choo.

The Devil-King Farouk-Mister Flett was standing in front of me. I saw something on fire. Not the fiery furnace that Shad and his friends were about to walk into. A big bush on fire.

A voice spoke to me from this burning bush: *What are you waiting for?*

The shovel that I was using turned into a large, wriggly snake. I was Moses. I was in Ancient Egypt. The Lord was telling me that the time had come.

Morning, afternoon, evening; the late Mister Flett was here in our bu. No longer was he treated as a special guest. No longer did he deserve a special place at our table once a week. Here. Here. All the time. Always here. Should we have still called him the late Mister Flett? Not late now. Here. Always on time. Always here. By the peat fire. In Ephraim's favourite rocking chair. By the peat fire. Eyes more often closed than open. Eye that works. Eye that doesn't. More often closed than open.

The chair moved forwards and backwards, backwards and forwards. Asleep, but the rocking chair still moved of its own will. Of its own will.

The late Mister Flett. The late Mister Flett with his watch. The late Mister Flett with my watch. Always here. When he's dead, it'll be a different matter. Won't be on time, then. Won't be the late, either.

My plan to get that which was rightly mine needed the late Mister Flett to be comfy in our bu. Right comfy. Truly at home, like. Day or night. Night or day. Didn't matter. Comfy. I couldn't wait any longer. Needed to act. I would have to use an Either/Or plan. Either would do. Or would do.

Either he will tell me that he will leave me his watch when his time comes, and I will play the pretendy part of the devoted nephew. Love and affection.

Or I will anyway be playing the part of the pretendy devoted nephew. Love and affection. He won't see it coming. I will kill him there and then.

Either. Let's... try... 'either'... first.

I don't know how many more winds I will be able to see before it is time to meet my Maker.

My plan was clever. It was Big Sky clever.

Either first. I will pull up a chair facing his rocking chair. He will be asleep but his chair will be rocking forwards and backwards. I will sit down on my chair. Not say anything. He will know I am there. I will be inside his head. His eyes closed. Mine open. Watching him. Me, not fidgety. Concentrating. Focused. I will be inside his head. I'll be in his Dreamland.

He will open his eyes. I will speak. Not drip-drop speak. Not splish-splash speak.

Not lum.

Useless lum speak.

I will be speaking Orkney rain speak. Continuous. An up-pour. No, a down-pour. Relentless. No stopping me. Downpour speak.

I will tell him about Mither. *Poor Mither.*

I will tell him about Ephraim. *A good man, but he is not your faether.*

I will tell him about the neighbours. *They have a Massey Ferguson, haven't they?*

I will tell him that they are after our land. *Why?* To grow crops so that their herd can eat. He will then say, *My-son-the-Minister would not approve of neighbours not getting on.*

I will tell him about Gail. *You should marry her.*

I will ask him about King Farouk. *It was me he met.*

I will tell him about the rainbow, and how that day I walked out into the water. *I don't know how many more winds I will be able to see before it is time for me to meet my Maker. You can have my watch, Alexander. Here it is.*

Adult to adult. No. Nephew to adult. No. I will be pretendy son. Son to faether. I will pretend the late Mister Flett is Faether. I will tell him so. I will say the words. "You, Mister Flett, not Ephraim, are like a faether to me."

My other son, the Minister, does not want my watch. Here it is. For you, Alexander.

It was a good plan.

Or was even simpler. Let's… consider… 'or'. Or was not so clever, but more straightforward. Or took less time.

Him, eyes closed. Fast asleep. Chair rocking forwards and backwards. I will stand behind him. Thick baler twine in both my hands. Thick baler twine tight to the late Mister Flett's throat. Baler twine against the flab in his scraggy neck. Tighter and tighter. Doesn't put up a fight. What will be, will be. He knows he is very old. The chair no longer rocking forwards and backwards. Deserves it. Kill him there and then in front of the peat fire. Take the watch from his waistcoat pocket. As natural as natural can be. No blood. Bloodless. Would prefer blood. More exciting. But *that* poker could be too hot to pick up, and the sun could be playing peekaboo, which would wake him up. And Mither could walk through at any time from the ben.

The watch would now be mine for keeps. My entitlement.

Either. Or. Whatever way. I will slip my watch into my pocket. I will then look out the window. There it will be: the sign. The sign from the Big Sky. The You-were-right-to-have done-what-you-just-did sign. The Big Sky will reward me with a rainbow.

Purple-blue-green-yellow-orange-red-bright. Shimmering. Playful. See-through. Different colours. Inviting me to reach out and touch.

Some words filled my head.

I Tawt... I Taw...

No, not those words. These words.

Eeny, meeny, miny, moe,
Catch a piggy by the toe.
If he hollers, let him go,
Eeny, meeny, miny, moe.

I remember the words. All the words. I remember the words. *All in the right order. I know. I know.*

It was all worked out. Clever. Adult. Clear-cut. Straightforward. Orkney.

"There is no time like the present." That is what the Minister liked to say.

All this was going round and round in my head. Round and round. Not forwards and backwards. Not backwards and forwards. Not side to side. Not side to side. Round and round.

I was helping Ephraim in the near field. It was only halfway through the first month of the New Year. 1952. January. Ephraim and me were doing fencing work on the Green Land. The first month of the New Year. Just a few days after the Destruction.

Fencing. We had no livestock to fence in. Good fences will not stop the wind.

Fencing. Those winds. Lashing rain. Sodden and Gomorrah. Good fences will make no difference. No difference whatsoever.

"Ephraim, why are we doing this?"

"Beuy, the farm's boundaries must be marked out." Ephraim patted his pockets. "I must have left my knife in the bu. See how strong this twine is."

He picked up the twine. Pulled it tightly between both hands. The twine. Tight enough for a passing birdie to perch on. Ephraim had that look on him. The one he had in that dream I didn't ask for. It was that killing look.

"Nip back indoors, beuy, and get Ephraim his pocketknife. Might as well bring out another ball of baler twine while you're at it."

"I won't be long." It was mid-morning and I knew *he* would be there. Forwards and backwards. Backwards and forwards. Eyes closed.

I went to the byre first and picked up the twine and pocketknife from the top bale of straw.

Then back to the bu. Felt the chill indoors. There was evil here. What had happened to *Life is short. Death is sure. Sin the cause. Christ the cure*? Those words on the in-by wall. Not there. Not there.

But the late Mister Flett was there. Sitting in the rocking chair by the hearth, in Ephraim's chair. The late Mister Flett was sitting in the rocking chair. It was *not* his by rights.

The peat fire was blowing puffs of smoke into the in-by. The wireless was on, with that yellow glow. That voice coming out of the wireless. *I know. I know.* It was... it was... it was George Formby. He was here. He was on my island of Orkney during the war.

Voices in my head, telling me I'm bad. Voices from visitors, there in my in-by. It was the voice from the wireless I liked the best. With the wireless voice, you have to make the picture up in your own head. Your picture is as good as anyone else's. You can't be wrong.

George Formby was in the in-by, singing. George Formby out of the wireless. George Formby was Mither's favourite. He was here in Orkney during the War. Yes. George Formby. Chirpy. Did he have cloven feet? No, not in my picture of him.

The late Mister Flett looked fast asleep. There was a smile on his face. His right foot was tapping away to the tune. Tap-tap. It was a fine tune. Patch over his right eye. His foot tapping away must have put the smile on his face.

I started to tap my right foot. Tap-tap. It was infectious. Dropsy-infectious. The late Mister Flett looked fast asleep, but foot tapping. Me awake. It was not a how's-it-going chat between us. It was not a my-turn-your-turn chat. It was not a let's-tap-together-as-one chat.

But...

His left foot. My right foot.

Both tapping away. Not to the same tune. He was tapping much the faster. You see, we must have had different tunes going round and round in our heads.

Him, *The Left-Hand Side of Egypt.* I could only reckon.

Me, *I Tawt I Saw a Puddy Tat.*

The wireless song had finished.

The late Mister Flett opened his left eye.

"That's a fine watch of yours, Mister Flett," I said, casual-like. Standing in front of him. Pretendy friendly. A smile on my face. Pretendy smile. All worked out beforehand.

No reply. I tried again.

"It's only right. That watch. From the Ancient pharaohs, passed down to you, Mister Flett. Only right."

The late Mister Flett took some time to reply. Did he know what was going through my head?

"That's right, beuy. That was a foot-tapper of a tune! George Formby was here at the Garrison Theatre during the war. George Formby, entertaining the troops. The sea always protects us, but we needed a bit of help then. Us Orcadians – island race. Island race. That George Formby, he was here, in concert, giving us all a bit of help. Him onstage. Him singing the very song. Him saying out loud, 'I would like to dedicate my next tune to Mister Flett.' Him dedicating the song to me."

I nodded, impressed. First King Farouk, then George Formby. He knew important people. The late Mister Flett moved in high places. He was wheezing with laughter. Maybe he had said something funny.

"You know what, beuy? Our memories are as important now as they ever were."

I nodded.

"Without the winds and wireless, Orkney would never be hearing such fine tunes. I've already told you, young Alexander, about there being pharaohs in Birsay before you were even a glimmer in your mither's eye. She was a fine woman. God rest your soul and God rest hers…"

He had just spoken as if Mither and me were both dead. Must have misheard. Must have got it wrong. It's his death that was on the cards. Not ours.

Let's keep the old fool talking. Keep him off guard.

My teeth were chattering.

I Tawt I Taw a Puddy Tat.

"Yes, Mister Flett, who'd have thought that you'd be meeting that Ancient pharaoh in Birsay of all places? Ephraim told me them Ancient pharaohs came all the way from Egypt, from the continent of Asia."

The late Mister Flett snorted. "Stop talking drivel, beuy. Them pharaohs didn't come from Asia." He shook his left fist. "Them Ancient Egyptians came from the continent of... well, never you mind."

This was not going to plan.

"The pharaohs were so pleased to be in Orkney they wanted to dedicate something on the Brough of Birsay to their gods."

I nodded. Once. Twice. I needed him to calm down. I needed him to treat me like his son. I wanted to be gifted the watch. Every time I spoke though, I seemed to make him angrier.

"Beuy, look over to the Brough of Birsay. That white blob, that marshmallow-looking thing with a budgie cage on top, yes, the lighthouse..."

I knew everything that needed to be known about the lighthouse. I would help the late Mister Flett out; tell him this and that. *I know. I know.*

"Mister Flett, Ephraim said the Ancient Egyptians built many lighthouses all over the world, but the one they built here in Orkney was their best.

"*The bit at the top is only thirty-six feet high, but it packs a punch. Its light can be seen eighteen miles away. It does its work without any fuss. Just gets on with the job. Orkney through and through.* That's what Ephraim told me.

"*Pure Orkney. It looks straightforward, but everything is smarter than it seems. Look at the square bit underneath – its castellated tower comes straight out of the deserts where them Ancient Egyptians go riding on their camels.* That's what Ephraim told me.

"And when you step through the front door, you enter the past. Ancient pharaohs. Mummies. You say something once, you hear it over and over again, until silence. Like them smoky shapes in our bu, forming then dissolving. No Big Sky. No sea. No wind. Sounds rarely from inside. A drip-drip. Breathing coming from somewhere. That's what Ephraim told me."

"Beuy, if I hear once more, *that's what Ephraim told me...* I bet Ephraim didn't tell you that our great-great-great Orcadian grandfaethers weren't at all happy, having this Ancient Egyptian lighthouse foisted upon them." The late Mister Flett jutted his head forward. Once. Twice.

"Them ships that used to break against our rocks always had valuable stuff on board. Shipwrecks would help put food on many a table and baccy in many a pipe. This lighthouse was bad news. Still is."

I nodded.

The late Mister Flett is inside my head. He knows what I'm thinking. The late Mister Flett has to be killed now. I wanted to get inside his head but... It must be now. I have baler twine and a pocketknife that will do the job.

Didn't mean to, but automatic-like, my tongue went under the top part of my mouth and my teeth started off. Chatter-chatter. Chatter-chatter. The prey was in sight.

"Beuy. Ephraim this; Ephraim that. Just take care. Don't let Ephraim lead you on. He's given many a person the runaround. I don't want to see you come to any harm. Better you know. Ephraim has a past. The army signed him up, no questions asked..."

At no time has he spoken about the watch. At no time has he looked fondly at me. At no time.

Rocking chair now on the move. Backwards and forwards. Forwards and backwards. He has fallen asleep. Fast asleep, I was sure.

I moved and now stood behind him. The back of his chair. With the pocketknife, I have cut baler twine long enough to do the job. The late Mister Flett was about to take his final breath. The baler twine tight around his neck. The rocking movement would do the rest.

I could have made a last minute change to my plan. A slit in his neck. Drip-drip. That expression on his face. It would have been as confused as a cow in a dentist's chair. But I would have needed to use my Swiss knife to have done so. It's so much sharper. My secret knife. I couldn't remember where I'd hidden it. There was always the poker but it would have been too messy and I wouldn't have wanted Mither's in-by defiled.

No. I would keep to my plan. I stood behind the rocking chair, baler twine in hand.

The late Mister Flett was inside my head. Either him or me.

I heard footsteps.

Mither's? No, not hers. Mither to be seeing her son commit such an ungodly act would be shameful. *Life is short. Death is sure. Sin the cause. Christ the cure.*

Ephraim's? How would he react? As likely to get the police as join in on the murder. Never could be sure about him.

"You there, Alexander?"

It was a man's voice. Ephraim's loud voice from the oot-by, the back room. I could not think straight.

The late Mister Flett woke with a start. Me behind the rocking chair. Me standing right behind him. I tried to behave normal-like, but I was aware of this chill, this dampness, this evil in our bu and inside me.

I rushed out of the in-by. Didn't mean to, but ran straight into Ephraim. Red in the face. Me and him. Different reasons for our redness. Looked down at the ground. A caught-in-the-act look. Had to get out of the bu. Out of the front door. Had to escape.

99

How I got through the rest of the day, I don't know. Ephraim never let on.

That evening, supper and prayers long past, Ephraim said we should all go outside and bear witness to the night sky. The full moon. I took up his offer. No one else did.

"Look at that moon, beuy. Have you ever seen anything so round and bright, full and egg-yolky proud? It's a birthday cake of a moon. Something special is up. We deserve a treat after what we've been through the last seven days. You can have a bigger slice of the birthday cake than me. It's a special cake because something special is up."

Ephraim was grinning. I was grinning... but only pretendy. My heart was still pounding away.

A *birthday cake of a moon.* That's what Ephraim said.

We went back inside.

Ephraim was proved right. Something special *was* up.

Not a nice special, as it turned out.

We had a visitor during the wee small hours.

The Angel of Death had left her calling card.

CHAPTER 8

DEARLY DEPARTED

January 1952

Gail's mither was in the bu, saying how sorry she was. First in our parish to do so. Gail was with her mither. Gail's mither did all the talking. Gail was wearing a dark blue dress. Tight-fitting. Couldn't help it. My eyes followed the shape of her body. Her hair. Lips. Breasts. Hips. Legs. All the way down to her shiny black shoes. Sabbath best. Tip to toe. Toe to tip. My mouth wide open. Couldn't help it. Gail's mither did all the talking. Gail just looked at me.

Her mither went on and on. Moved towards me. Pressed against me. Hugged me. Not enjoyable. Iron grip. Couldn't breathe. Sour breath. Went on and on.

Gail was here. Just for me. I've waited for this moment. In my dreams I've waited for this moment. Not for Mither to die. Gail was here for me. To comfort me. Me. Here just for me. I was in Dreamland. Gail came closer and held me tight. Heavenly.

Mustn't show my pleasure. Mustn't. If only Gail knew the effect she was having on me. No, this was not right. Mither, dear Mither, had just passed away. I was no sinner. Mustn't show my pleasure. Not in front of Gail's mither. Mustn't.

Must look the Minister full in the eye. He'll be round soon. Hope he won't see my true self. Lust and my Gail. Murder and his soon-to-be-dead faether. *Badness in me.* Gail's mither was still here. Will look the Minister full in the eye. Upright. Confident. The Minister. He'll be round soon. Just for me. Dear Mither.

"The Good Lord has your mither in His arms and will ensure that her eternal sleep is of the good." Gail's mither was still going on and on. "Isabella has passed into the light and is now in a state of grace." Gail's mither in tears now. "You poor, poor young man. Your dear mither lies in grace on this day of the Lord, 23rd January 1952. You poor, poor young man."

Gail's mither and Gail. Gail looked at her watch; Gail's mither at hers. I looked at her mither's watch. It was not a special watch. It was ordinary. I did not covet it.

"May your dearly departed mither rest in peace. I will leave a soup plate with some salt on her chest. She will be laid out in her ben. You, Gail, are to spend the night with Alexander."

I will dream about her tonight and she will receive my dream in her dreams, and everything will be happy-ever-after between us.

"Both of you must make sure that the light from the candle does not go out, and that there is enough salt for the mourners. You poor, poor young man. You poor, poor young man."

"Thank you," I said. I did not mean it. Furious. *Poor young man this. Poor young man that.* Not my fault. The winds have carried off my egg fortune. Not my fault. I do not belong in the poorhouse; pauper. I do not want Gail to think me a pauper.

Gail. Me. Dearly departed Mither. All in the same room. Gail. Me. Next to each other. Hard chairs. Candle burning. Soup plate of salt on Mither's chest. Sprinkle on arrival. Sprinkle on departure. Stillness and silence. Gail. Me. I looked at Gail. Smiled. Gail looked at me. Smiled back. I could hear Popeye sobbing, not moo-mooing.

No Faether. Now no Mither.

The rainbow. I can see it.

"Yoo-hoo! I'm home. Come and see me, Alexander. My son. My dear son."

Now joined by a second voice, both together now.

"Yoo-hoo! We're home. Come and see us, Alexander. Our son. Our dear son."

Fidgety. No. More than that. Unsettled. I got up to go to the byre. There was the late Mister Flett. On his own. In the oot-by, the back room. Peace and quiet. Out of the way. Mister Flett sitting on a hard chair. Not his usual rocking chair. No forwards and backwards, backwards and forwards. Something important to say to me. Wiggled his first finger. Finger slightly crooked. *Come here* sign.

"They say in the shop that the Devil held back the first low tide of the day. No one can reach the Brough on foot. Beuy, the Devil is sending us a warning. The taking of your mither's life was only the start of it."

I nodded to the late Mister Flett. I quickly moved on. I needed to go to the byre for a piss. Job done. Not long splish-splash. Straight back to the ben and Mither and Gail.

The Minister arrived. Only right and proper for him to pay his respects. Mourners' laughter and singing were now coming out of the in-by. The Minister was having to shout to make himself heard. The Minister was very upset. Crying and sobbing. Kept my distance. Didn't want to be hugged. I didn't want him staying too long. It wasn't just that I wanted to be left on my own with Gail and Mither. I didn't want the Minister to get a whiff of my evil intentions towards his faether.

The Minister did not linger and when he had finished crying left to join the main gathering in the in-by. I made sure to keep to the old ways. Dipped my fingers from time to time in the salt. Made the sign of the cross on Mither's chest, on mine as well. The cross. Salt. Paid respect to the Lord. Kept the Devil at bay. Salt.

Waited for the right moment to put my arm round Gail. *I was the bereaved. It was for her to make the first move.* Her oaf of a cousin came in. He was older than me and could barely fit into his best suit. Maybe he had borrowed it. Gail was more interested in her cousin than me. There was a ripping sound. The cloth under the arm of his jacket and the seat of his trousers gave way. Gail was laughing. The laid-out body of Mither. Gail was laughing. Not proper. Not right. I was angry. Angry. *The Devil take her. The Devil take this cousin of hers.* Left the room once more, looking for peace.

Our in-by was like the drinks tent at the West Mainland Farmers' Show. Had to watch out for the empty whisky bottles. There were many well-wishers on the floor too. The Devil must have put Slipperene on their chairs. Slipperene. Slippy-slidey stuff. Many had given up the struggle. Well-wishers. Chairs empty. On the hard floor, bodies, fast asleep. Bodies laid out. Arms pointing here, there and everywhere. PC Plods, motionless, on traffic duty, drunk.

Roaring and shouting came from the byre. A voice I knew only too well. Rushed through to find out what was up.

Ephraim had asked me for help, man to man. He was asking me for my help. Ephraim needed my help. I was there for him as I would always be there for Mither.

"Come on, yer fucker, fight. You're no match for me. I could kill you any time of my choosing. I've done it before. If ever you say those words again, they'll be your last." Ephraim, roaring loud with fists raised. Bright red in the face. Steaming with the drink.

There was no one else in the byre. Well, no one besides Popeye. Ephraim threw a punch at who or what. A fresh-air punch. Ephraim lost his balance. Hit the ground. Thud.

All this was at Mither's passing. It was not right. It was not right.

Had to get back to Mither in her ben. The oaf would be gone by now. The late Mister Flett was still there on the hard chair in the corner of the oot-by. Had to stop my teeth from chattering. The late Mister Flett was as calm as calm could be, no change there. Wiggled his first finger. Crooked. *Come here.* I did so. Not the time for dark thoughts. Must stop my teeth from chattering.

The late Mister Flett hadn't moved from his hard chair. Again wiggled his first finger to get me to go over. He leant forward. He had his nose in this large book. Looked up. My teeth were chattering away. Must stop my teeth chattering.

I coughed to get attention. Not like dear Mither's coughing, God rest her soul. Waited for him to put the book down. The book was an Old Testament of a book. Big. Many pages. Dusty. Old. Old Testament.

The late Mister Flett. Not crying like his son-the-Minister. Calm. Spoke in a matter-of-fact manner. Mouth, only open murmur-wide. But so softly. It was difficult to pick out what he's saying.

"I met King Farouk, and being hospitable, offered him one of my Craven "A" cigarettes. Straight from the packet of ten. There was none of this fancy-pants gold cigarette case nonsense. The king took one. The Orkney way. Simple. Plain. Unfussed. Just get on with it."

"What was King Farouk doing in Birsay, Mister Flett?"

"Not now, beuy. No questions on this saddest of all nights. Just listen to me, Alexander. Now, where was I? I gave King Farouk a Craven "A" cigarette. Just the one. The king gave me two things in return. Doesn't that only go to show how generous royalty can be!"

The late Mister Flett paused. Brought out the watch. *The*

watch. *My* watch. From one of his pockets. Showed it to me. Returned it to his waistcoat, safe. My teeth were making that chattering sound.

"That was the king's first gift. His second gift, I now pass on to you to keep. See – a book. Treat this book like your best friend. You will learn a lot from it."

The late Mister Flett then handed over the book; this Old Testament of a book that he'd just been reading. Its front cover had strange symbols on it – Egyptian squiggles; hie-ro... something or other. Like those squiggles on the Dwarfie Stane in Hoy.

"This book will be your Holy Book. If there is anything you do not understand, I will be there to guide you."

I nodded. I must keep paying attention.

I opened this big book. First page, blank. As was the second. As was the third. The first page held closer to the tilly light. Not too close. Still no writing. I was being made to look stupid.

"Alexander, turn the book upside down and start at the back. You will find the pages written in English. Everything will become clear."

I did so. He was right. The letters, words, sentences – all were in English.

"This book is called *The Powers That Cannot Be, Volume I*. It is a copy. The original, so legend tells us, is kept safe on our Brough of Birsay. A parting gift to Orkney from the pharaohs.

"The original is said to be in the pyramid below the lighthouse on the Brough. This copy is rare. Treat it with the utmost respect.

"It is perfectly understandable for you to question why your mither has been taken by the Lord. Within this book lie all the answers you will ever need." He was almost whispering.

I accepted this book with gratitude.

I understood that the book was very important.

I held it with care.

Look, see how when I hold it up to the light and turn it so, the face of the watch changes colour from the palest of white to amethyst. The book.

"I better get back to Mither. I must do my duty."

"Alexander, I knew your mither. Alexander, there are too many grown-up men here tonight who are no better than children..." The late Mister Flett's head jutted forward not once, but twice. Emphatic.

Clutched my gift for dear life. Dear life. I said goodnight to Mister Flett. Returned to the byre; goodnight to Popeye. Then I had to head back straight away to Mither, to sit with her. No, I decided there and then I needed some fresh air. A lot to take in. First Mither. Now the late Mister Flett to think about. That should be my watch but this book that I've just been given... I wasn't going to let it out of my sight. The book was very old and mysterious and must be very valuable too. If only I'd had my Swiss knife with me. Drip-drip. Blood red.

Left the farmhouse. Found my favourite spot. Needed to clear my head.

Night-time. All the colours were asleep. Blackness. Purple-blue-green-yellow-orange-red-bright colours. Asleep. Rainbow. Asleep. All my favourite colours in the Big Sky fast asleep. Night-time. But the air was fresh. Fresh air. So fresh.

No Faether. Now no Mither.

No mist now. Night Big Sky. Black. Suddenly there was light. The Big Sky was paying its respects, just for me now. The Merry Dancers put on such a fine display in the night sky now. A bit of green on black. A lot of green on black. All now swirly green. Swirly green Big Sky. Swirly green Big Sky. Big Sky ever-changing. A bit of black on green. A lot of black on green.

Thank you, Big Sky. All black. Night Big Sky. As it was. The Big Sky has paid its respects. Thank you, Big Sky.

No Faether. Now no Mither.

Realised too late. I forgotten to do something before leaving the bu. Stupid of me. Should have dipped my fingers in salt and touched Mither's toes. Should've before leaving the bu. Laid Mither to rest. Salt when you arrive. Salt when you leave. Salt. You should always do this. The Orkney way. Stupid of me. Forgot. Deserved to be punished. Realised too late.

I have given the wrong message to the Devil. *Yoo-hoo! I'm here.*

I have to hope that the Devil was busy; not noticed my forgetfulness. Forgot. Deserved to be punished. Hands up in front of me. Apology.

Yoo-hoo! I'm here.

Like the Lord, the Devil couldn't be everywhere at the same time. That's what Ephraim said.

Orkney was Sodden and Gomorrah. That's what Ephraim said.

Omnipotent. Lord and the Devil. That's what Ephraim said.

Yoo-hoo! I'm here.

Yoo-hoo! We're here.

I might yet get away with it.

Might do so.

CHAPTER 9

ANTIMACASSAR

January 1952

The week of the burial and mourning. A low-hanging mist over the parish. All week. Last week of January. No downpour. No peekaboo sun. No clouds racing. Stillness. Mist. Dim light. The Big Sky paid its respects. In Mither's memory. Our king wasn't well either.

The sea was doing its own thing, though. *Serves Big Sky and the wind right. Should've told me what they are up to.* The birdies didn't know any better. Us mourners, silent as silent can be. We were there, graveside. Crashing waves. The Big Sky and the wind did the one thing. The sea did its own thing. Birdies made a racket as always. As always.

The Minister. I stood next to him. Could lose his footing. Careful now. I could also. Careful now. The hole in the ground, freshly dug. Adult hole. Whoops-a-daisy. Careful now. Not proper for the Minister to fall in. Freshly dug. Hole. No longer empty. Graveside hole. Fit for one adult.

Earth in a small pile all round the hole. Right round the edges. The hole was rectangular. Earth not clumpy. Earth, baby-on-all-fours-high. Earth, small pile. There for the shovelful. Adult mourners to pay respects. Hole. Dug deep. Hoped there was enough earth to do the job. Mustn't fall in.

The wooden box. The coffin. Coffin. Made of teak, not driftwood. Not driftwood. Mither's coffin already lowered in. The Minister stood next to the hole. Had to be careful now. Both of us. The Minister and me. Mustn't fall in. The crashing waves. Birdies. Felt as if Mither had passed to the Garden of Eden. Careful now. The Minister said his words. I did my bit with the shovel. Just a sprinkling.

Wore my Sabbath best. It wasn't Sabbath. Sabbath best on a day that wasn't Sabbath.

Felt unwell. Mustn't faint. Took a long, deep breath. The strong whiff of seaweed did the trick. Better than smelling salts. Thank you, sea. Thank you, sea. The birdies fell silent. Thank you, birdies. Thank you, birdies. Ephraim was silent. Thank you, Ephraim. Thank you, Ephraim. That seaweed, it did the trick. Not about to faint.

Stood next to the Minister. Ephraim knew his place was not out front, where I was standing. I was next to the Minister. We were the important ones here. Out front. Don't get me wrong, it was right for Ephraim to be there, but not right out front. Took a quick look. Behind, over my shoulder. There was Ephraim and all the mourners. The late Mister Flett. Where was he? All those faces. It was all a blur. Oh, there he was. The late Mister Flett. Over there.

The Minister spoke loudly and clearly.

I stood as still as a statue. In my own world.

"And let me finish by saying that Isabella Seater was a wonderful, kind woman, always there for those in need. Isabella has earned her reward in Heaven. She has proudly taken her place among the righteous."

The Minister could not finish his words. He started to cry. I did not. Manly. Adult. Held in my feelings. Didn't cry. Did not.

The grave was filled in. Me first. Earth. A topped up shovelful. A scattering would not have been enough for dear Mither. The service was over. We had done the right thing by Mither. We had laid Mither to rest.

I wanted to be left to my own thoughts.

I needed to be left to my own thoughts.

No Faether. Now no Mither.

The Minister stood next to me. He held my hand. Did not let go. Not crushed-tight. Not Ephraim's-sharp-nails-digging-into-my-flesh pain. Was holding my hand. Firm. I-am-the-Minister firm. Stared at me. Said nothing. Piercing. Said nothing. His eyes, deep into my soul. Could feel them. Has he seen the evil?

Could hear his breathing. Could hear his breathing. Eyes gentle. Held my hand. Hand light. Spoke. "My son. My son." Released my hand.

Saw Ephraim walk over to the late Mister Flett.

Saw Ephraim hold out his hand.

Saw Mister Flett turn his back on him.

The following week, we had things to do. Gail's mither was there to help. Sorted out Mither's clothes. "That frock will go to Missus Linklater. That shawl to Maggie Sinclair." Tidied up. Water got from the well. Mop. Bucket. Bu was made spick and span. Spick and span. Did the dusting and cleaning. Yes. I did. That rocking chair, very greasy at the head. "You need an antimacassar. Antimacassar. I've a spare one." Gail's mither did the organising. No sign of Gail. "You poor, poor beuy."

I sat by the peat fire in the rocking chair. No forwards and backwards for me. No forwards and backwards. No. The late Mister Flett. My nose was in *The Powers That Cannot Be, Volume I*. I... was... reading...it... slowly. Had to take it all in.

III

A big step up from Dan Dare and the *Eagle* comic.

A big step up from *The Lord is my shepherd*.

A big step up from *Never covet your neighbour's house, wife, ox or anything you fancy*; Exodus 20:17.

But I could follow it all, without help. An astonishing book. I felt a changed Alexander A. Alexander. *No Faether. Now no Mither*. My path. My new path. Wide enough, just for me. A change. A big change. *No Faether. Now no Mither*.

No one was there to see me. I was in my bu and I raised my hand high, palm open. Moved it very quickly from side to side. I was waving goodbye, to no one person. No toodle-oo. No see you later. I was bidding farewell and Godspeed. The Tilley lamp flickered. I and my inner voice were at one. We were in harmony.

Ephraim walked into the in-by. He was holding a piece of paper.

"At least it's you in my rocking chair. Haven't seen that old fucker for a few days now. He's probably upped sticks and found another home where he'll be kept warm and fed. Good riddance.

"I can see you're wrapped up in that book of yours. You don't need to concern yourself with this legal stuff. Chiffchaff."

Smelt his sweet breath. Didn't know whether to trust him. Ephraim, my pretendy faether. I did like him. For five years he has been my 'pretendy'. Five years. Taught me manly things. Looking after goldfish. Then panning for gold and spoots over on the Brough. Then using a Swiss companion knife. Air pistol to air rifle. That Swiss knife. Blade in. Blade out. My secret knife. Taught me a lot.

Have moved on. I needed to be guided not by him but by *The Powers That Cannot Be, Volume I*.

Felt the chill in the bu. Odd that we haven't seen the late Mister Flett for some time.

"Them legal fellers have given me this Power of Attorney, you a minor and that, and in your mither's honour *we* will together make a good stab of making *our* farm tickety-boo. Who knows, maybe in a year or two's time, you will have enough spare cash for a car. That will certainly make Gail look at you. Just sign here... and here... and finally here. No, don't worry about the date. I'll see to that. Oh, this bit of paper as well."

I put pen to paper. Didn't completely trust him. Wanted to get back to my book. My signature there... and there... and there... and on the other bit of paper as well. My days of being the Egg King of Birsay were well and truly over. Ephraim was not my real faether. *No Faether. No Mither.* My signature there... and there... and there... and... I have much more important things to do. Should've read what I was signing before signing but you'd have done the same. Ephraim, my pretendy faether.

Must leave that Alexander behind. The Powers That Cannot Be, Volume I is my chosen path.

Not daft.

Not lum.

Useless lum.

This wiser me, Ephraim's breath smell, Ephraim's shaky hands, Ephraim wobbly on his feet, Ephraim's red face, all came from one thing and one thing only. Not the dropsy. It's the drink. As plain as plain could see. The... drink. The... drink. This wiser me.

I have put pen to paper. There... and... there... and... there. Everything as clear as mustard.

Ephraim would not leave me alone with his plans for Mither's farm. *My* mither's farm. Not *his* mither's farm. *My* farm. Ephraim, with his plans.

"Listen up, Alexander. With the two of us working flat out on our farm..."

Leave me in peace. I am reading.

"…we will keep the tax inspector at bay and be able to save up for a tractor and still have a bit left over to buy up a few spare acres for growing bere barley and…"

Leave me in peace. I am reading. Leave me be.

"…from time to time, I will need to be away. You will be left solely in charge while I source supplies and suppliers, find markets and business opportunities, do deals with fixers and middlemen."

I was often accused of telling lies by my teachers and the soothsayers when in fact the fault lay with them.

"…I'll be doing all this in your mither's memory. All this for our farm."

I was deeply hurt because I knew I was telling the truth about having a sixth sense and special friends who were invisible to the outside world. You go through life and find true companions who are invisible to others.

"Beuy, you were put on this world to do something special. You are not an ordinary Orcadian – if such a person can indeed exist. Both you and I will leave our mark on this world."

From an early age, I knew that I could judge true people and friends by the quality of their light and colour.

(The Powers That Cannot Be, Volume I, chapter 1, page 1, para 3)

Ephraim will never be purple-blue-green-yellow-orange-red-bright but he was not seaweed-slimy green. He has never been invisible to me. He was special to me. I can see Ephraim's light and colour.

I *know* he could be difficult. But I know he could be the best pretendy faether a sixteen-year old could have. He knows the true worth of *The Powers That Cannot Be, Volume I*.

Got up from the rocking chair and looked Ephraim full in the eye. Everything was clear. I was enlightened. It gave me strength. *The Powers That Cannot Be, Volume I*. Astonishing book. Needed to be published. I will pay for it to be published. Don't need the late Mister Flett's say-so. Say-so. Do need the late Mister Flett's money. Do need his watch. Do need *my* watch. That gift of the book doesn't save the late Mister Flett's life. Must make Faether and Mither proud of me.

Yoo-hoo! We're home.

The week of mourning was over. A big storm. Thunder and lightning and lashings of rain. Lashings of rain. Like a dam no longer holding back water. Smoke from the peaty fire up through the lum. Whoosh down through the lum. No splish-splash. Lum.

Useless lum.

Back to normal. Orkney back to normal.

The wind. The Big Sky. The sea. The Green Land. The Green Land. The sea. The Big Sky. The wind. The sea. The Green Land. The Big Sky. Birdies as well.

The wireless was on with that yellow glow. Special.

Not music. Not *I Tawt I Taw*. Not *Ring-a-Ring o' Roses*. Not *Knick-knack paddywhack, give the dog a bone.*

Words. Serious words. Solemn words.

"We mourn the passing of His Majesty King George VI, who died in his sleep last night. Under his reign, Great Britain and the Commonwealth survived its greatest challenge. The young Queen Elizabeth has a heavy and arduous responsibility ahead of her. Great Britain and the Commonwealth. Your loyal people will serve. God Save the Queen."

Mither died first. Then it was the king. That way round.

Yoo-hoo! We're home. Come and see us, Alexander. Our son. Our dear son. King George has joined us here.

The Sabbath service. Me wearing Sabbath best. Empty seat now the other side of Ephraim. Kept empty out of respect. I must be adult. I must not be fidgety. I wanted to hear his sermon. Gail would have to wait. Sermon. Minister made no mention of Mither's passing. Made no mention of the king's passing either.

Didn't understand. Didn't let on that I didn't understand. Mither passing. The king passing. No mention made. As if these important events had never happened. No mention. As if he forgot. Mither passing. King passing. As if there were more important things to talk about in his sermon.

Day after, went to the shop. Waited to be served.

Missus Linklater went on and on. "She was so young to be taken. So young. So young."

I bought a packet of ten Craven "A". Said it was for Ephraim.

"Such a young age to be… "

Waited 'til I was clear of the shop. Waited 'til no one could see me. Opened packet. Took out one cigarette. Didn't light up. Put it behind my ear. Adult.

There was no longer four in my life. Have to come to terms with there being just the three in my life. The late Mister Flett, Popeye and Ephraim. In no particular order. Could have been Ephraim, the late Mister Flett and Popeye. Haven't seen the late Mister Flett for some time now.

I feel this chill, this dampness, this evil in our bu and inside me.

There's four in my life. Mither, though passed, is always in my head.

CHAPTER 10

THE FARMER NEXT DOOR

JUNe 1952

Front door. Men would come to the front door. Strangers. Always asking for him. "Where's Ephraim?" Always asking. Not friendly. Not "Sorry to hear of your loss." Not "She was a fine woman." Some were carrying a briefcase. Others just raised their fists.

Ephraim was never around. Off seeing the middlemen. Off to make deals. When Ephraim was here, he was pretendy faether and real faether, all rolled into one. Ephraim could have charmed the water out of the sea. However, he's rarely at home. These men. At the front door. Always asking after Ephraim.

Me wrapped up in *The Powers That Cannot Be, Volume I.* This arrangement could not go on. My farm like that piece of driftwood, going under. Farm. Mither's and mine. *This cannot go on.* The late Mister Flett not giving up his watch. The late Mister Flett not here when I needed guidance. *This cannot go on.* Must do something. Will ask an expert, but pretend I know the answer anyway. *This cannot go on.*

Ephraim.

Late Mister Flett.

Never here.

Ephraim was back. I asked him for advice.

The world-famous hypnotist Mister Edwin Heath is appearing at the Garrison Theatre, Stromness. Do not go.

Mister Edwin Heath wouldn't be calling himself world-famous if he wasn't. World-famous people have wisdom. Them hypnotists are wise fellers, holy men with insight.

The world-famous hypnotist will take out first one handkerchief, then the other. He will magic cooing birds. I will ask him. He will give me the answer. 'Coo-coo'.

Money for the farm. Money needed for the book. *We cannot go on like this.* Teeth chattering.

I go to see the world-famous. I am disappointed.

I will never let on that I ever did something that did not turn out for the best.

Think of Gail. She only visits me in my dreams now.

Think of Gail's mither, going on and on. Sour breath. *Poor beuy. Poor beuy.*

Think of Gail's faether. Owns the farm next to ours. Big farm. He has twenty cows; we have Popeye. He has four Massey Fergusons; we had one horse, taken by the winds. He has many four-furrow ploughs; we had one, two-furrow, taken. He needs land for silage; we're a piss-poor smallholding.

Ephraim never has a kind word to say about Gail's faether.

"That fucker has got the manners of a whore. We're surrounded on three sides by Mister Splash-the-Cash. Our backs to the sea just like Moses and them Israelites in Egypt. Camel going through the eye of a needle? He can stick his Massive Fergusons up his arse."

Ephraim back now. Don't know for how long. Smile on his face, big smile. Champing at the bit. Good news to tell. Good news.

I have my own news for Ephraim. *Men here at the door. Some carrying a briefcase. Others showing their fists.* Bad news to tell. Bad news.

"Beuy, I am so excited. Gold top. Gold top. I've always had your best interests at heart. From Monday, you will be mastering the whys and wherefores of the Massive Ferguson. Gold top." Pretendy faether. As he tells me this, pretendy drives a car. Pretendy steering wheel. Both hands round the wheel. *Vrrrrrrrrrroooooooooooom. Beep-beep.*

"We are going to be doing a bit of renting out to the farmer next door – yes, to Gail's faether. That spit of land next to the sea is of little use to us. It's bumpy and sandy and no use for growing anything. Renting out; gold-top news for you, beuy."

Ephraim's words. Out of the blue. *The Powers That Cannot Be, Volume I* will have to wait. This is important. Out of the blue. A bolt from the blue. Need to think. Need to question.

"Ephraim, that spit of land – very important. Must be left alone so Devil has something to work on. Otherwise idle Devil will be up to mischief. Without that spit, the Devil will pick and choose. Pick and choose. Round the farm. Round the bu. In our heads."

"Old wives' tale, beuy. Old wives' tale. Gail's faether is not the Devil. Listen to me. His black Aberdeen Angus cows can graze there to their hearts' content. In return, he will make you the best farmer in the West Mainland. You'll still have plenty of time to read that book of yours."

"What? Ephraim, you telling me you've shaken hands with the farmer next door? The one you call a whore and worse?"

"My tongue sometimes runs away with me, young feller. You should know your Ephraim by now."

I am furious.

"What you call 'that spit of land' is a third of our farm. How much did he pay you? While we're at it, how much is there left in the bank? I want answers. This very minute." Am shouting at him. Am taller than him. I am. He doesn't scare me now. Now.

Ephraim plays the injured party.

"Good God, sixteen years old and so suspicious of your Ephraim. I could have taken the pounds, shillings and pence on offer but I swore on the Bible to your dear mither that I would always put your interests first. No money has changed hands. May I be struck down if I am telling you a word of a lie." Ephraim is sobbing. Sobbing.

I have never seen Ephraim sob before. Maybe I have misjudged him.

"Gail's faether will fill your boots with knowledge. Alexander, knowledge is better than pounds in your pocket. Trust me."

I stare at him, but cannot hold my stare.

"Look at the knowledge you've already picked up from *The Powers That Cannot Be, Volume I.* Knowledge is the be-all and end-all. Without knowledge, we are like a fish supper without the fish. How do you think them boats keep upright on the sea? *Knowledge.* How do you think we won the last two World Wars? *Knowledge.* How do you think them birdies get up in the air? *Knowledge.* How do you think you'll get your way with Gail? *Knowledge.*

"You'll be starting next Monday."

I do not nod.

Ephraim has rented out the land for nothing. Me part of the deal as well. Me working for someone else on my own farm. Not happy. Not happy. Not happy. Ephraim and his sweet breath. Ephraim *is* seaweed-slimy green. Not happy.

Leave me in peace. I am reading. Leave me be.

But it all works out so different. Me, not angry. Me, pleased. High up in the Massey Ferguson cab. Me, Minister-important, looking down from my pulpit. Me. Daytime. Have time to reflect on what I've read the night before. *The Powers That Cannot Be, Volume I.* Such learning. Such wisdom and I'm not even at page 7 yet. Me at peace with myself and with Ephraim. It has worked out different than expected. High up. Best position. The dog's bollocks. The bollocks on every animal that went into Noah's Ark. Gold top.

"Beuy, we'll find a way to get it published. We don't need world-famous people to tell us where the money is to come from. The answer lies close to home. It's your duty." Ephraim is spot on. He understands.

He winks. Adult to adult.

"Ephraim, there are old layers here, in our parish. Past their prime. Ready for the soup pot. Too old. Won't be missed. Their money can be put to better use." My teeth chatter. I have the late Mister Flett in my sights. Can't do this on my own. Need another adult's help. He knows I'm not talking about hens. Need Ephraim.

Ephraim just grins. Walks away, whistling. *With a knick-knack paddywhack, give the dog a bone, this old man came rolling home.* Whistling. Roll-your-own behind his ear. Adult.

I now keep a roll-your-own behind my ear when I'm in my Massey Ferguson. Adult. High up like the Lord. High up like the Big Sky. High up in my Massey Ferguson. I have these thoughts.

Profound thoughts.

Thoughts from on high.

Thoughts about living where I do in Birsay.

Ephraim. Gail. Gail's faether. Gail's mither. Minister. The late Mister Flett. Even Missus Linklater, at the shop. All from the same parish. Pulling together, firm, cohesive, all as one, looking after each other.

Friends and family. Caring. Something happens. An event, a trigger, Mither dies. Next-door neighbour sees an opportunity: his cattle to go on someone else's land. His Massey Ferguson. Let's have a bit of Mither's farm. Not a slow drip-drip grab. A quick whoosh grab. A pretend-nothing-has-happened grab. Opportunity – not to be missed. Others benefit. Nearest and dearest.

Folk tut-tut. Folk no longer tut-tut. Folk steer away from tut-tutting. Folk change the subject. Folk do not raise the subject. Nothing untoward has happened. All from the same parish, pulling together. Vroom-vroom.

Things settle down. Dust settles. It never happened. Like yesterday's monsoon. It never happened. What are you talking about? Me and the late Mister Flett and his watch. Will be the same turn of events. It's the way it is. What watch? Oh, that Mister Flett. Wasn't it 'natural causes'? Like the Big Sky, the wind, the sea and the Green Land, it's the way it always will be. Like life and death. That's my parish. Birsay. Bet it's no different to any other.

The late Mister Flett. I'll have his watch. Kill him. It's the order of things. Haven't seen him for some time.

The days that follow are not fidgety. Not sunshine-winds-winds-blue skies-misty skies-black clouds-rain-rain-sunshine-again days. Days of rain. Rain days. Rain. Just rain. Lashings of rain from above. Rain. Rain.

Like the Big Sky. Like the Minister from his pulpit. Me in my Massey Ferguson. I look down. The sandy loam with green bumps, between the bu and the sea. Not exactly green. Belongs to the Green Land nonetheless. No longer sandy. Churned-up mud. All the fault of rain, rain, rain.

The rain from the Big Sky usually disappears into the Green Land. You can see the rain as it falls, but as soon as it hits the Green Land, it is supposed to disappear. The Green Land where I give the cows their feed though is no longer green. The sandy loam no longer sandy. Churned up.

Waterlogged.
Pissed upon.
Defiled.
Days of rain no better than:
Fencing damaged by the wind.
Birdies trying to nest in your lum.
Useless lum.
Taking someone's life for the greater good.
Badness.
Badness is only someone else's point of view.
My spit of land between bu and sea. No longer my land.
"Yes, it is," says Ephraim. "It's rented. It's our land."
Must still be mine. Ephraim says it's our land. It is rented out, but still mine. Must still be mine. The next-door neighbours' cows are there. Does this make any difference? It's raining non stop. The Green Land is churned-up mud. Water lying in the small holes.

From above in the Massey Ferguson, the Green Land looks full of craters. Looks just like honeycomb. Wet honeycomb. That's what Ephraim says. Buzz-buzz. Buzz-buzz. Bees. Arms pumping out like hens', but much faster. Laying honey, not eggs. Honeycomb. That's what Ephraim says. Buzz-buzz.

From above in the Massey Ferguson, I know what needs to be done with *The Powers That Cannot Be, Volume I*. Certainty. Gold-top certainty. Moses certainty. Certainty.

From above, plan the late Mister Flett's ending. He is not *invisible* to me, but where is he? I will have his watch.

I was often accused of telling lies by my teachers and the soothsayers when in fact the fault lay with them. I was deeply hurt because I knew I was telling the truth about having a sixth sense and special friends who were invisible to the outside world. You go through life and find true

companions who are invisible to others. From an early age,
I knew that I could judge true people and friends by the
quality of their light and colour.
(The Powers That Cannot Be, Volume 1, chapter 1, page 4, para 1)

There is so much contained within. Must take it all in.

Too important to let anything pass by. Like panning for gold on the Brough of Birsay.

Nuggets; not smoky shapes forming in my head, disappearing too quickly.

It's the natural order of things. *The Powers That Cannot Be, Volume I.* Gold top.

My life takes a turn for the worse.

Another rainy day. Thunderstorms this time. After the lightning. Yes. Yes. A sticky day. Eyes itchy. Itchy. It's that time of year. Hay-fever time of year. Never-gets-dark time of the year. Middle-June time of the year. Not a run-of-the-mill rainy day for this time of the year.

Something goes badly wrong on that spit of land, on that day. Thunderstorms. Apart from thunderstorms, no change. Squelchy mud. Piss-pools of water spilling over the honeycomb craters. Cows in a huddle. Water dripping off their backs. Water dripping off their noses. Bullied. Beaten by the lashing rain. Popeye there as well, to one side of this black mass of misery. Only one thing to look forward to: their midday feed.

Have this off pat, the feeding. Tractor's gears locked into first. Massey Ferguson moves at snail's pace. From the steps of the cab to the ground. Small jump. Then jump up to the trailer. Trailer always with sides down. Grab pitchfork. Dish out all that lovely silage grass. Cows, yum-yum. Job done. Got it off pat. Even whistle while doing so, adult-like. Even have roll-your-own behind my ear while doing so. Adult.

That morning, eyes itchy. Aaah-choo. Aaah-choo. Lock the gears into first. Whistle a tune, stroke the back of my ear, roll-your-own there... then it all goes wrong. Jump down to... miss my footing... can't jump up. *Isn't my fault. Can happen to anyone.* Fall awkwardly. Shut my eyes in pain. In agony. Not just fingernails-biting-into-my-cheeks pain. Far worse. *Isn't my fault.*

"Bad luck, beuy." Ephraim said afterwards. My ankle. Badly hurt. Twisted. With all this rain, easily done. *Isn't my fault.*

"You poor beuy," Gail's mither said afterwards.

Cows not happy. Make that perfectly clear. Loud mooing. Wouldn't want to pluck their eyebrows, Ephraim-style. Hungry. Wet. Munch, munch. Food. This very moment. Now.

Popeye out at the front. My Popeye must be their leader. My Popeye is not the type. Manage to support myself; lean against her, my dearest friend, my comfort, my Popeye. But then. Then.

Turns her head. Stares at me out of her good eye. Manic. Moos as loud as ever. Headbutts me. Glasgow kiss. Popeye, possessed by the Devil. My broken nose. No longer bothered about eyes itching. The blood. The blood. The blood. Not splish-splash. Flowing. Hand on my face. Red. Watery red. Don't remember it stopping. Support myself against the trailer.

Cows. *We're hungry.* Mad with hunger. Push against the trailer. *We want our feed. We want our feed.* One more heave. *Give us our feed.*

Trailer is turned over. Right leg crushed. Pain too strong. I remember nothing more. Nothing more.

Am in hospital. Many parish folk visit. Next-door neighbours visit; Gail as well. She looks like she would rather be elsewhere. Obligation, that's what brings her here, not kissy-kissy love. Told to be here by her mither. I want to cry, but men aren't allowed.

The doctor is confident. "We'll get you up and running in no time." Leave hospital soon after. Right leg still in plaster. Itchy. Scratch the plaster. Makes it worse. Itchy. Itchy.

Can put more and more weight on my right leg, but better just to sit in the rocking chair with my right foot up, resting it. Know what, though? The right leg's got a mind of its own. Twitches away. Cannot stop this powerful surge of electricity. Every now and then it dances to its own tune. My good leg is as still as the loch at full moon. Good leg plays the straight man.

Back to hospital, a week later. Plaster removed.

"Away you go," the doctor says. He can see my right leg dancing away. Says nothing. My left leg keeps a straight face. It's a good leg.

Ephraim tries cheering me up. "Beuy, look on the bright side. If you were to enter them tap-dancing competitions on the West Mainland, you'd clean up." He thinks it's such a good joke. He won't leave it be. "Beuy, you ever thought of doing that dancing that those Irish lads and lassies do?"

My Massive Ferguson days are over. What happened was not my fault. I must have aaah-chooed at the wrong moment.

Ring-a-ring o' roses,
A pocket full o' posies,
A-tishoo! A-tishoo!
We all fall down.

Plenty of free time to reflect on *The Powers That Cannot Be, Volume I*. So much to take in. Still on Chapter 1. Can't get further than page 6 of Chapter 1.

Have this picture in my head. It's a moving picture. Not a still, one-off picture. It's sort of an all-action picture. It's a waving-toodle-oo-Godspeed-Massive-Ferguson-tractor-with-the-*Blue Peter*-flag-on-top-about-to-sail-out-to-sea picture. It's an up-there-in-the-Big-Sky-moving-slowly picture. Going-in-one-direction-only-no-reverse-gear picture. A chug-a-chug-not-vroom-vroom picture. All in my head. A tractor-sailing-out-to-sea picture. There's-the-*Blue-Peter*-flag-on-the-horizon. Bye-bye tractor. Bye-bye Massive Ferguson. Toodle-oo. A toodle-oo picture.

All in my head.

The Powers That Cannot Be, Volume I. Nothing else matters to me now.

The Powers That Cannot Be, Volume I. Nothing will get in its way.

CHAPTER 11

THE FEAST

29th–30th June 1952

Something special for me. In my honour. A week since I left hospital. Ephraim is in the in-by, putting his boots on. No longer squelchy. Peat fire has dried them out.

"A grand dinner for you, beuy. Tomorrow night."

A grand dinner. Can only be chicken Bonnie Prince Charlie and clapshot. Plenty of gravy, please. Ephraim enjoyed it so much the first time round. Slurp, slurp. So did I.

Tomorrow night comes round soon. The table is set for four.

One. Two. Three. Four.

Me. *One.*

Ephraim. *Two.*

The late Mister Flett is nowhere to be seen. More than a few months since I last saw him. I will kill him. Need him back in the bu. Need him where I can see him. Need to see him to kill him. *Three.*

Four?

One. Two. Three. Four.

Yoo-hoo! I'm home. Yoo-hoo! We're home.

The late Mister Flett, after such a long time, walks in and takes his place opposite me. Head down, just like before. Says nothing. Fiddles about with his waistcoat pocket. No explanation felt necessary. Patch over one eye. That wobbly flab in his neck. The late Mister Flett.

Not good enough. If he thinks all he has to do is to walk in and sit down…

No "Hello."

No "Good evening."

No "I'm so sorry I'm late."

No "It's very kind of you to ask me."

No "Has it been that long? I've been needed down south."

No "How have you been keeping, beuy?"

Takes out his watch.

I'm very pleased to see the late Mister Flett.

Still a spare place, facing Ephraim. Laid out. Can't work out for who. We don't wait. Get stuck in. Right tasty. Nothing said. Wireless turned off. All quiet from the byre. Popeye must be sleeping. Right tasty. Not chicken. The meat not white. Can't be Bonnie Prince Charlie then. Can't have beef Bonnie Prince Charlie. Doesn't exist. Beef. Right tasty.

Wolf it down. Beef of a beefiness never eaten before. Chewy but tender. Succulent, not drowning in slurp-slurp gravy. Meaty, not bloody. Lean but not shrivelled. The three of us tucking in.

Ephraim mops up the gravy on his chin. Slurp-slurp. "Are you enjoying the meal, Alexander?" He lets out a loud belch.

"Thank you, Ephraim, it is very tasty." I belch back. Adult.

"After Popeye's badness towards you, it's only right that she should be making amends in this way."

Popeye is the main course, and right tasty with it. Right tasty.

Belch again. No disrespect meant to Popeye's memory.

More a celebration of her life. Better than hymn-singing. Popeye. A special friend. Comfort. A bit of her is stuck between my molars. Annoying. The fact I've eaten her. I didn't know I was going to eat Popeye. Unexpected. Can't be held responsible.

Not my fault. You'd have done the same.

"Can I have seconds?" The late Mister Flett breaks the silence.

Ephraim leaves the table to turn on the wireless. Ephraim likes his music. He returns. The wireless takes a bit of time to warm up. Confident yellow glow. A song. We all – yes, even the late Mister Flett – sing along to it. Much banging of fists on the table, the three of us swaying from side to side.

A Roy Rogers song from Cowboy Land. On the wireless a lot. A tune borne all the way on the westerly winds from America to us in Orkney. A good song. Just the song for the moment. A hymn. Sacred.

A Four-Legged Friend. It's just right for Popeye. What a right good friend she was.

The song finished, we toast our new queen. Queen Elizabeth the Second.

"God save the queen." We clink glasses. Me too. A dram of the finest Orkney whisky. Me too. We are loyal to our sovereign lady and we are the best of friends; Me, Ephraim and the dear late Mister Flett. All adults.

Ephraim eyes up the spare place round the table. He can see someone.

You go through life and find true companions who are invisible to others.
(The Powers That Cannot Be, Volume 1, chapter 1, page 1, para 3)

Ephraim, calmness itself. Telling-it-as-it-is talk. Speaks to this guest I can't see.

"My account is settled with you. The decision to attend is yours. Yours alone. This is *my* household. I owe loyalty to no one. I have broken many of the Ten Commandments in my time. Make it worth my while and I will be your loyal servant. Otherwise, be off with you."

We suddenly feel a cold draught. The light from the Tilley lamp flickers. The fire dragon puffs out two large, peaty balls of smoke into the in-by.

Ephraim leaves the table. The late Mister Flett goes to his place in his rocking chair.

It is only right. I am left at the table.

Go to my room straight away. Cannot wait. Need the support of *The Powers That Cannot Be, Volume I*. Find my place. I never seem to get beyond page 6. What I read is deep and profound. Profound and deep.

An idea is a being incorporeal, which has no substance but gives figure and form to shapeless matter and becomes the cause of the manifestation.
(The Powers That Cannot Be, Volume 1, chapter 1, page 5, para 2)

Take a deep breath. Popeye ever present in my thoughts, but in body no more. Whirly bits of Popeye are in my gut. This evening's meal. Must remember to brush my teeth. There's a bit of Popeye trapped between my molars. Popeye is making the journey from this world to the next. Popeye is on her way to becoming an idea, a being incorporeal. Popeye a being incorporeal. Holy. Holy Popeye.

The Powers That Cannot Be, Volume I has, in a few simple words, explained the meaning of life to me.

I must make this book known to the good folk of Orkney and good folk everywhere.

I sleep soundly the night.

CHAPTER 12

ACTUS REUS

1St JuLy 1952

Morning tea at our hidey-hole from the north-westerly. Ephraim and me.

"Ephraim, Popeye is gone but still with us. She's now an idea."

"Popeye was right tasty. Don't you think so, beuy? Right tasty."

"Ephraim, Popeye is now a being incorporeal."

"A being incorporeal?"

"A being incorporeal."

"How do you know that, beuy?"

"The Powers That Cannot Be, Volume I."

A pause. He is fiddling about with the roll-your-own behind his ear.

No whistling.

No singing a tune.

No Roy Rogers.

No *A Four-Legged Friend.*

A pause. My pretendy faether is going to say something significant. Significant.

I know. I know.

"*The Powers That Cannot Be, Volume I* must be brought to general notice. Them farmers at the mart are gagging for a copy. It gives answers to problems that even the veterinary man can't fix. This book is the Massive Ferguson of philosophy."

I know. I know.

"Ephraim, Popeye is now a being incorporeal."

"Beuy, a being incorporeal and right tasty with it."

Another pause.

Ephraim's finger, sideways, inside his molars. Upper set, to the back. Fingernail toing and froing in the gap, sawing away. Something meaty to be removed. Gets the bugger. Flicks it to the ground like fag ash. Nail-to-nail flick. Seeks a reward. Has another go at lighting up. Hand shaking. Out comes the pipe. Fills it with baccy. Match after match unsuccessful. Northwesterly comes between what he wants to do and what can be done. Hand shaking. Sweet breath. Oh, that sweet breath.

"Well, beuy. This book has to be published. Your Ephraim hasn't the spare cash. Not like him next door. That fucker won't be helping us. Let's just you and me take a step forward on this."

A step forward. Together. Adult. Man to man. Equals. I like the sound of that.

"Yesterday I was with a middleman. This book of learning of yours – he'll get it published. But the sting is in the cost. One thousand copies at one guinea each."

"That's one thousand guineas." Quick as a flash.

"The late Mister Flett is past his prime. He is past his prime, beuy. All that's left for him is the soup pot. He will be of greater service to humanity if his money is put to the general good. General good."

My teeth start chattering. Smiling.

Him, smiling, genuine. Not peekaboo smiling.

As one, smiling, we see eye to eye.

Ephraim's pipe is full of baccy. No point having another go. Pipe still in his mouth. Morning tea at our hidey-hole from the north-westerly. Hidey-hole, but the wind's a bugger. Doesn't worry about puff-puff now. The pipe, there 'cause he likes it there. The pipe. Can talk with the pipe in his mouth. Talks out of the side. Adult. Adult.

"Alexander, my beuy, in life, before you start off, you need to know where you're going."

"That's right, Ephraim. That's what it says in *The Powers That Cannot Be, Volume I*."

A lot of mankind's time is taken up travelling along the long road. What is particularly infuriating for good folk is that the destination point is always in the distance. The eyes that the Great Creator gave you and me are easily distracted. Many an hour travelling along the road can be valuable time lost.

The conundrum is to bring the destination point as close as possible to the starting point, and this can be done by 'recalibration'. The human eye can be contrary, but when focused, releases its full potential.'
(*The Powers That Cannot Be, Volume 1, chapter 1, page 6, paras 2-3*)

"Beuy, Orkney folk have been waiting for a book like this. *Old Moore's Almanack* and *The Racing Post* have their uses, but *The Powers That Cannot Be, Volume I* takes our thinking to the next level. I have only the one word: holy."

"Let's not forget the Bible."

"We must never forget the Bible, beuy. How far have you got with this *The Powers That Cannot Be, Volume I*?"

"Ephraim, there's so much to take in. It's almost as if the first few pages don't want to let me go. I get to the end of one page but then have to start again. Everything seems new to me."

"This middleman I know, down south; he'll want a copy for himself. He's got a greyhound. The greyhound is fidgety. If this greyhound was less distracted, it would be a world-beater. As fast out of the traps as a three-toed lizard." Ephraim takes his pipe out, then puts it back in his mouth. "Every Massive Ferguson tractor cab should have a copy of The Powers That Cannot Be, Volume I."

What with Ephraim's enthusiasm, I plain forget to ask him about last night. Him laying down the law to that empty place at the table.

"Listen close to what I am about to say. Things have come to a head."

Ephraim clicks his fingers, no longer laughing, no longer easy-come-easy-go; serious now as the hanging judge, him with the black cap. Seen him in the pictures, always saying the same words, "You will hang. Take him down." The hanging judge and his black cap. Adult like us, but extra important.

"The farm has fallen on hard times, beuy. You can walk all right, but your leg will never again be strong enough for Massive Ferguson work. You're no use for the harvesting. Him next door no longer wants you. Him next door is threatening to build a house on that spit of land. There's even worse to follow unless certain debts are met."

"What debts are these, Ephraim?"

"Then there's your book to bring to the world's attention."

My right leg sparks into life. I look over towards Kitchener's Memorial. The black Aberdeen Angus cows on the squelchy loam, heading towards where I used to give them their feed, in a line, a chain, one by one, slowly. Like that caravan I saw in the *Beau Geste* film, making its way across the desert. Camels then. Cows now. Across my squelchy loam. Walking slowly. In a line. One behind the other. None breaking rank.

"Do you really want to go through with this, beuy? I reckon the late Mister Flett's watch will cover all our costs."

My teeth chattering. Noisy. It's inside me. Can't help it. Instinctive.

"The late Mister Flett gave you this book, after all. He didn't have to," says he.

Yoo-hoo! We're home.

"What would your mither say if she was still with us?" says he.

He's playing with my head. Teasing. Surely.

"The middleman knows a buyer at the mart who knows the big beuys down south and they can offload the watch without question. No one will be any the wiser." Ephraim catches breath.

Musical in his telling. Round and round. *Ring-a-ring-o' roses, a pocket full of posies, a-tishoo! A-tishoo! We all fall down.* I need my handkerchief. (Free of snot). *A-tishoo! A-tishoo! We all fall down.* I want my coo-coo birds. Now.

"Beuy, listen closely." Ephraim looks every which way. Conspiratorial. Starts to speak, but then stops. A bird flies overhead. Ephraim waits until it is far in the distance.

"This is how we will kill the late..."

The north-westerly is strong, but not too strong. I hear every word.

"It'll take place on a rainy day. Sodden and Gomorrah. On the Brough of Birsay. The sea will cover our tracks. At night-time. The Big Sky to keep our secret. Must be windy. The wind to blow away all the evidence."

I nod. I can't help but grin.

"Beuy, you look as happy as a cow eating an Easter egg."

I know deep down that to murder someone is a different thing to do.

An unfamiliar thing to do.

But not a wrong thing to do.

Badness is just a point of view.

I live on Orkney, on the Mainland on an island surrounded by the sea, with the wind and the Big Sky and the rain and the special light and the sun playing peekaboo and the birdies.

The reign of King George VI is over. Died in his sleep. Natural causes. Now Queen Elizabeth II is on the throne. Things change.

The late Mister Flett is with us. Soon to be killed. Unnatural causes. Events here are dictated by island rules. Island rules never change. It is only right. This is Orkney.

Ephraim, pipe in mouth, fidgets with his ear. Removes his roll-your-own. He can't be trying to smoke them both at the same time. Gives the roll-your-own to me. Gives... it... to... me. At that one moment in time, that means more to me than any talk of *The Powers That Cannot Be, Volume I.* Much more.

He has given his roll-your-own to me.

We are partners.

We are to be partners in crime.

CHAPTER 13

THE HOW AND THE WHEN

Early October 1952

Tide times are all-important. Low tide going over. Low tide coming back. Four hours in between. The Brough of Birsay. The late Mister Flett to join us. Ephraim needs to be very persuasive. Night visit, after all. *Unusual time for a visit.* That's what the late Mister Flett will be thinking.

Welcome-home-from-hospital meal, a memory. A distant memory. Told just now in the oot-by. Told to make myself scarce this lunchtime. Ephraim to have a one-to-one chat with the late Mister Flett. Ephraim. Sweet breath. Has helped himself to a dram or two. This early in the day.

Keep out of their way, as asked. Walk to the shop at lunchtime. Don't rush back. Buy myself a pack of ten Craven "A"s. Puff-puff. Adult. Go to favourite spot. Must stay there for a couple of hours.

Ephraim tells me how he got on, word for word. I say; he says. Ephraim says; the late Mister Flett says. Ephraim is smiling like the sun in the Big Sky. Not peekaboo. Full-on sun. Must have gone well.

— Meeting the king... the watch... *The Powers That Cannot Be, Volume I*... remarkable... King Farouk coming all the way to see you... When they say important people attract important people, they are talking about you.

— Very kind, Ephraim. I have much to say. Us Fletts aren't hoity-toity but we have a standing, an importance. Us Fletts have no need to put on the ritz. We are what we are: important. Why else would King Farouk seek me out? Me?

—Will you do something? Not for me, for Isabella. Something she so wanted, but sadly her health...

— Isabella was a fine woman. God rest her soul.

—Isabella loved going to the Brough... the Ancient Egyptians thought the Brough of Birsay special, too. The lighthouse and all.

— Before the lighthouse was there, ships would hit the rocks and go under. Strangers' lives would be lost. But us Orcadians would always find something useful, something valuable floating to the top. The lighthouse put an end to all that.

— Totally agree. Totally agree. One man's misfortune should be another man's...

—My-son-the-Minister spoke about this very thing in the kirk, last Sabbath.

— About the lighthouse?

— No... misfortune and salvation.

— This King Farouk. A gold-top feller with a sense of duty. Not so easy to find, these days. One who puts others before...

— Never a truer word spoken, Ephraim.

— Why don't you and me and the young feller go over to the Brough? For Isabella. While there, we'll pay our respects to that fine King Farouk and them fine Ancient pharaoh spirits.

— King Farouk came all that way to see me. Remarkable,

don't you think? Just thinking about it - it gives you a thirst, a real thirst.

— I bet them Ancients left interesting things in that pyramid under the lighthouse. The original copy of *The Powers That Cannot Be, Volume I* and watches and gold and the like. I just so happen to have the key to the lighthouse over on the Brough of Birsay. A wee dram, Mister Flett?

— Thanks. Here's my glass. Isabella and me, as you know, we were... I want to pay her my full respects. That's a grand idea. You never know what you might find. Afternoon would better.

— If only we could, Mister Flett. If only we could. But the natural light and daytime air will spoil everything inside. *The Powers That Cannot Be, Volume I* will fade. Afternoon, morning is no good. Our visit has to be during the hours of darkness.

— Night and day - it's all the same for me. Look what daylight did to that Count Dracula.

— Yes, and to other English folk just like him. That Count Balfour too. Them shutters are always shut in his castle on our fine Orkney island of Shapinsay. Wasn't that Count Dracula the first cousin of that Count Kitchener?

— You're right, Ephraim. There are a lot of English counts in Orkney, and they are still coming to live here. Good people. Some of them are a bit strange, though.

— They may be right English counts but we respect them here in Orkney. Look at that fine memorial at Marwick we put up for that Count Kitchener.

— That Count Kitchener, he was just passing through Orkney.

— Why would anyone in their right mind ever want to leave Orkney? When folk come back they can never get it into their head that things don't stand still. My son-the-Minister says...

— You've made a good point there, Mister Flett. You can

tell a city to fuck off, but not an island. It's there all the time. Never leaves you, though you may leave it. For some it's like chewing gum stuck to the soles of their shoes: when they leave, they can't move on. They've no identity. They're lost.

— Them Yanks here with their DAs and their money and their nylons and their chewing gum. Have you ever left Orkney, Ephraim?

— Why would I? If you don't leave, you don't have to worry about the welcome when you come back. Isn't that so, Mister Flett? Isn't... that... so?

— Never a truer word spoken. I haven't had such a good chat in ages. It is thirsty work having a good chat... thirsty work indeed.

— We speak from the same page, Mister Flett. Another dram? So, it's agreed. Night-time, Thursday week, the 9th. At low tide, of course.

— Did you say Thursday? That's a coincidence. It was on a Thursday that I met that Frenchie Emperor Napoleon Bonaparte in Stromness. He'd travelled all the way over from... from... from somewhere secret. What time?

— Midnight, Mister Flett. Midnight and we'll meet on the Headland Point. Point of Buckquoy. Midnight. Thursday week. Eight days' time. The 9th.

— Midnight, Thursday week. The 9th it is.

"The carrot has been dangled, young feller, accepted and duly crunched. What do you think of that, beuy?" Ephraim is waiting for my reaction. Ephraim wants me to tell him how clever he is.

I nod. Smiling.

Still a detail or two to fill in. Ephraim will have it all worked out. My make-do faether. Ephraim is shrewd. As for the late Mister Flett – past his prime. My teeth chatter. Has to be well

planned. Disrespectful if we were to make a pig's ear of it...
disrespectful.

Ephraim and me. Just Ephraim and me. In the bu.

I start to sing a line or two from *I Tawt I Taw a Puddy Tat*.
Ephraim follows. Me first. Me leading the way. Me in charge.
Make-do faether following son.

The following day Ephraim goes through the final plan,
A to Z. Nothing left to chance. Everything clear-cut. Orkney
clear-cut.

"The front door is on the side. The lighthouse is kept
padlocked but..." Ephraim winks, tapping the side of his nose
with his index finger and brings out a key from his pocket.
"The main room is much bigger than it looks from outside,"
he continues. "On the far wall, there's a concealed door. We
go through into another much smaller room and ignore the
ladder which leads up to the lighthouse.

"On the wall, right in front of us, are large framed photos
of that famous music hall act. One of Wilson. Then of Keppel.
Then of Betty. A gap between each. They were big before the
war."

I nod.

"Between Keppel and Betty there's a second concealed
door. Through that, and we're at a staircase which leads all the
way down to the burial chamber. Ancient books and gold and
diamonds await. Fill our boots. We will kill the late Mister Flett
before we reach the bottom."

"Ephraim, if the late Mister Flett is not wearing King
Farouk's watch what's the...?"

A pause.

"Don't worry, beuy, I've thought it through." Ephraim,
smiling, taps the side of his nose again. His sign. A pause. Says
no more on the matter. No more on the matter.

I look at Ephraim. Ephraim looks at me.

"Why don't I just use the knife on him?"

I look at Ephraim. Ephraim says nothing.

"Why don't I just give him knockout drops here? I saw it done in the pictures, a 'Mickey Finn', the Yanks call it. Just a few drops in the drink."

Ephraim suddenly shakes uncontrollably, makes to say something but stops. Looks possessed. Not smiling now. Looks evil. "No. No. No," he shouts. "We must kill him properly. You're never sure with poison. Believe me."

The following Monday evening, the 6th. Just a few days to go now. Am told to have my supper early. On my own. Ephraim needs to have a further one-to-one chat. *I say; he says.*

"Beuy oh beuy, the late Mister Flett is champing at the bit. Nearly bites my hand off when I say our visit to the Brough has to be brought forward."

— Midnight we were to meet, but there is to be a change of plan, Mister Flett. It is now going to be Wednesday night, the 8th. The runes say so. Headland Point. The Mainland end of the causeway. A day earlier won't make any difference, will it? Make sure you don't turn up an hour late.

— I'll be there. We'll go tonight if you want... it's very important. I remember in the war when Winston Churchill came round for my help with one of his speeches... Top secret it was. Top secret it still is. That line, 'We will fight them on the beaches' – who do you think gave him that line? Top secret. You're looking at the feller now. Keep it to yourself.

"He's agreed to wear the watch?"

"This is how our chat went, beuy."

I say; he says. Again.

— You'll be bringing King Farouk's watch with you?

— My watch never leaves my side.

— We're bound to find other watches in this burial chamber and they'll all be yours, Mister Flett. Could be fakes. Counterfeit. If the initials *K.F.* are inscribed different, they'll be worthless. Bruck.

— Just there for a look. Not interested in filling my boots, Ephraim. With my watch on, them Ancients will know I come as a close friend of King Farouk. It's like that ring folk wear on their finger when they're married. Shows they're trustworthy.

— Trust is in short supply these days. Don't you agree, Mister Flett?

— It was different in the war, Ephraim.

— What? Trust?

— No. It was different in the Great War for those Germans. Couldn't help themselves then. That Germany, a fine country but them folk never get to see the sea. Landlocked, Ephraim. Got doolally. Would do anything to get to the sea. That's why they started the First World War. Needed that smell of seaweed. Lost the plot.

— Are you sure about that, Mister Flett? They did have a navy. Still have… and a port or two.

— But them German sailors don't know what to do on the water. Not like us. It's part of our being.

— Our being?

— Our being.

— The 8th it is?

— The 8th it is.

— Do you want us to pick you up at home?

— No thanks. I'll meet you at the Point.

— The Point it is?

— The Point it is.

"Alexander, we have the late Mister Flett in our pocket and

this is how we'll kill him." Ephraim taps the side of his nose and smiles.

Night and day. Low tide and high tide. Winds blowing in and out. Green Land, sodden. Green Land, dry. As sure as A to Z. The late Mister Flett's fate is sealed.

CHAPTER 14

WEDNESDAY NIGHT

8TH October 1952

The waves make their presence felt during the daytime hours. By nightfall their anger has gone. The waters asleep, lapping against the shoreline. Like moths. That's us. Moths. Drawn to the on-off-on-off beam of light on the Brough. That'll be us. Moths.

Me and Ephraim. Moths. Adult moths.

"I've borrowed the Massive Ferguson and trailer. Easier all round. I know the Point isn't far. The tarpaulin will come in handy to stop those prying eyes." Ephraim winks.

I nod. My right leg dances to a tune of its own. My left leg plays the straight man.

"Thinking about it, I'll take the Massive all the way over to the Brough. A shorter distance for any carrying. The causeway's slippery with the seaweed. Beuy, we don't want you doing the splits again. The late Mister Flett is to be collected at Headland Point."

"I've got the torches. Is there anything else we need, Ephraim?"

"No, that's fine. I've brought the rope." Ephraim winks

again. "There's enough liquid paraffin in the flasks to cover the body and get the blowlamp going. We'll have us a fine blaze. Whoosh." He throws his arms open. "If he wants to know what's in the flasks, we'll tell him it's tea."

We are there in good time. Ephraim in the cab; me at the back. We are there in good time. For midnight. My teeth chattering. We wait. We wait. We are waiting.

Ephraim jumps down from his cab and joins me at the back of the trailer. We sit down on a large bale of hay. A large, damp bale of hay. He is angry with the late Mister Flett.

"Must have been an hour since we got here. Where is that fucker?"

It is raining steadily now. We feel sorry for ourselves, like those cows on that fateful day waiting for their feed. Ephraim takes one of the torches out of my bag. He shines it at his watch.

"They say in Birsay the fucker's done time before."

"The late Mister Flett's always been a good half-hour late for the evening meal. You know that. He's never on time."

"Alexander, you don't understand what I'm saying. Forget it. That's it; we've waited long enough. Home for us, beuy... If before tonight you ever had doubts about taking the late Mister Flett's life..." His words tailed off.

"Ephraim, why don't we kill him at our bu? Leaves less to chance. Won't then have to worry about a tractor and trailer, or tide times. We can go over to the Brough any time to get the treasure. You've got the key."

Ephraim has that look on him. I do not feel at ease. I do not feel at ease.

"No, Mister Flett has to be murdered on the Brough in the lighthouse. It's the plan. We agreed. It's the plan. I'm getting back in the cab."

He jumps down from the trailer onto the track. Looks up at me as he speaks. "The late Mister Flett has made no friends by not turning up, the fucker. He has made no friends..."

Ephraim climbs back into the cab. Starts the engine. The Massive Ferguson chugs away, back to the bu.

No further reflecting over the non-appearance of the late Mister Flett. No sitting by the peaty fire over a dram. Straight to bed.

I sleep in late.

The Big Sky is clear, a bright morning.

Last night – perhaps it was not meant to be. Perhaps the Big Sky has had a word with the wind and the sea and the Green Land, or the sea got its word in first.

Big Sky.

The wind.

The sea.

The Green Land.

In any order you want, one of them isn't happy. Put a stop to his turning up. Worked the strings. Downed tools. Put a spoke in the works.

Perhaps I am wrong in wanting to murder the person who brought *The Powers That Cannot Be, Volume I* into my life. Such a book. Such a book. There is so much there to take in. I am still on Chapter 1. But the late Mister Flett is of no use to anyone. He is past his prime. Good for soup and nothing more. My teeth are chattering. Bonxie-ready, that's me. Ready to swoop down on my prey.

I look up to the Big Sky and see the faces of the late Mister Flett, King Farouk and the Devil joined together, forming *the One*.

I want to. I want to kill.

Then in my head I see Mither's face. Then in my head I hear Mither's voice.

How dare you bring shame on me, Alexander?

I put down my copy of *The Powers That Cannot Be, Volume I* and go outdoors.

I close my eyes and am in my favourite place.

Neck flexible. Coo-cooing birds above. I can hear the 'coo-coo, coo-coo'. Look up but see nothing. There's the hypnotist's watch. My eyes moving oh so slow from left to right, taking it all in. Starting far to the left – the Old Man of Hoy, on to the Kitchener Memorial – and then over to the right, the Brough of Birsay. Left to right. Then right to left. I do this a few times but then just keep with the Brough of Birsay and that lighthouse. Neck. Fixed. Eyes straight ahead.

The Brough doesn't look that special, just a green, flattish pancake. But there is, as we know, a lighthouse there.

The lighthouse is not in the middle of the Brough. It is off-centre. The winds must have lost their puff before the land ran out. The next bit of land, America, thousands of miles to the west. Too heavy a load. Let's get rid of it. Drop it. Here.

Over at the Brough I can make out a slope leading up to the lighthouse. Gentle. Saint Magnus first buried at the start of the slope, so they say. The lighthouse. It's at the highest point. Tad bit farther, I'm at cliff edge. The sea. Rocks and shallow water. Maybe a sandbank or two.

The lighthouse has two parts to it. A birdcage out of which the guiding light sings. It stands on a flat roof. Right in front of all this, a small fort with a dumpy base. This fort is bright white, holy, bright white with yellow edgings for the battlement.

I see it all, helped by this picture just in my head. That was a mighty film at the pictures: French Foreign Legion film with this Beau Geste feller and white fort and sand and camels. We have beautiful sand here in Orkney, but these camels always elsewhere. On holiday. Never see camels here. Never see 'em.

I've been over many times to the Brough, but always stay clear of the lighthouse. The Minister, when he goes on and on about swimmers and the Devil, always finishes off talking about the lighthouse. Swimmers and lighthouse. As if the two go together. Spiritual guide. Welcoming hand. Inner light inside all of us. That's what the Minister says.

I don't like the lighthouse. Gives me the creeps. But can't keep my eyes off it. The lighthouse. I always stay clear of the lighthouse. Makes me uneasy. Haven't told Ephraim that. Keep it to myself.

I hear Mither's voice in my head: *Grace before meals.*

No, surely not right to kill the late Mister Flett. He is very old, but…

I stare out to sea. Too far out for me to spot any driftwood. Just this wave getting bigger and bigger. First a spit of whiteness, then this big, white, fat grin; getting huge, more evil by the second. White chariot. I can see it. Dead centre. Show-offy. Menacing. Wave's job done. Disappears. The next wave waiting its turn like a plane on the runway. Sitting on its shoulder. *My turn now.*

I hear the voice of the Lord. *Alexander, it is your turn now.*

My turn now.

Take a deep breath. I have been given my sign.

It is right to murder the late Mister Flett. Wave follows wave.

If I don't kill the late Mister Flett, someone else will.

Family. I'll pretend that the late Mister Flett is just family. Kept within the… Ephraim, my pretendy faether, is already close family to me. The late Mister Flett's death; a family matter. Badness is just a point of view. Everything is to be kept within the family. It'll all blow over. I know. I know.

Orkney is my family.

Orkney.

Family.

Island life.

I walk back to the bu. A short walk. Mind made up. Decision taken. Clear. Island-clear. Orkney-clear.

How gentle and green our parish of Birsay is. The farm

beyond the farm beyond the farm. On the Green Land, sheep and cows, still as anything. Heads down. Grass. Sheep and cows. Ornaments on a mantelpiece. Pretty. Wee statues. Statuettes. The birds overhead, tweet-tweeting away. Maybe some of them coo-cooing. Just a month or so back, fields full of bales of hay, paired up, leaning on each other's shoulders. Like lovers. Me and Gail. Fields now resting. I take a deep breath. That's my Green Land.

How lucky I am to be born and bred in Birsay.

The late Mister Flett turns up at the farmhouse, early evening. Makes a beeline for the rocking chair as if… as if he owns it… as if it's for his use only. A shiner over his left eye. Supper. Doesn't join us at the table. In silence. Waiting for an apology. An apology. We are. Awkward silence.

The flabby part of his neck moving rapidly up and down like the 'test your strength' fairground attraction.

"I was having a quiet drink yesterday. Minding my own business at the bar. This who-did-he-think-he-was feller started to get up my nose. Gets up my nose. Talking about the past. Exaggerating what I did. Making me out to be…"

Ephraim raises his eyebrows, as do I. Him first.

"Yes, the West Mainland branch of Eggs for the Wounded in the Great War. I was in charge. Yes, I made a few mistakes in looking after the cash. I have paid the price and have squared my conscience with the Lord. Look, my son being the Minister is proof of my redemption. I am no embezzler. I… have… never… murdered… anyone." He stares full on at Ephraim. With that shiner, he looks as stupid as the Minister with his Duck's Arse.

I try to catch Ephraim's eye.

Ephraim says nothing. Just glares.

The late Mister Flett continues. Feels as if he should be saying more.

"I wasn't having that. I wasn't having this who-did-he-think-he-was feller acting all bigsy-bugger towards me. I made sure he came off the worse."

Both Ephraim and myself raise our eyebrows. That is indeed quite a shiner. Who'd have thought? Over the eye with the patch. That's the one with the shiner. Who'd have thought? Lucky, really.

"I was shaken… in no fit state last night." He points to the shiner. No need to. "I'm sure you understand. I still want to go over to the Brough." The late Mister Flett's flab is on the move. Up and down his neck. Up and down.

That shiner-dreichy purple and yellow. Inside; an egg yolk of a big spot. The yellow first, on squeezing. Then the blood-red greyhound wooshing out of the traps. I'm going to rip his eyepatch off. Yes… I… am.

"Mister Flett, we'll give you one more chance. Just the one. Any more malarkey and the beuy and me will go to the Brough of Birsay on our own. I'm the one with the key. Do not forget that fact." Ephraim lays down the law.

"On Friday the 10th, there's a low tide at eleven o'clock at night," I add. "That's tomorrow night."

Me and Ephraim, showing a united front here. We are not taking any more nonsense. United front. Pretendy faether and son. Son and pretendy faether. Equals. Standing firm. Taking a position.

Ephraim dictates the terms. "I'll collect you at eleven o'clock Friday night, Mister Flett. If you're not there, we'll go without you. Wrap up warm. Tomorrow night."

He shows the late Mister Flett the key to the lighthouse. Holds it up between first finger and thumb.

The late Mister Flett nods. In the wrong. Eyes downward; like sheep and cattle looking for that particularly tasty blade of grass – that one, *that one*? The late Mister Flett. He is in the wrong.

I stare at Ephraim. Both of us adults. I'm taller than him, but he's built like a bull. Ephraim has the look on him of a real faether.

Special. Blessed. I have two faethers. A real faether in his Garden of Eden and here, standing before me, a pretendy faether.

I will earn Ephraim's respect. I will. I will.

Ephraim and the late Mister Flett leave the table to sit by the hearth.

I go through to my bed in the in-by. Miss the friendly sound from the byre. Hear laughter between them. Must be the warmth of the whisky and the peat fire that has healed the ill will. Ephraim, the executioner. Mister Flett, the condemned.

Don't want them getting too cosy. After all... After all...

I have a lot to think about. So, the late Mister Flett has been in prison. Him being an adult, he should have known better. You know what? I want to be the adult who does the killing. My faether in his Garden of Eden would be proud of me. So would Ephraim. But ssshhhhh. It's a surprise. It's our secret.

Yoo-hoo! I'm home. My dear son.

CHAPTER 15

FRIDAY NIGHT

10th October 1952

Three seconds of bright white light. Twenty-two of darkness. The light full on. Dazzled. The darkness too brief for our eyes to get accustomed. No point in using the torches. The light's there to warn ships and boats. You'd think it would be on all the time. Not three seconds on and twenty-two off.

Tractor left at the foot of the Settlement. On foot now. We are the blind leading the blind.

Each of us is carrying a large bag. The late Mister Flett's is empty. For now. His bag is low-tide-empty going out. Will be low-tide-full coming back. "The treasure's all for you." That's what we tell him. *The old fool.*

Ephraim's got something inside his. For the strangling and for the disposal of the body. "Just in case we find so much treasure, Mister Flett. I'm carrying a backup bag." That's what we tell him. *The old fool.*

"Flasks of tea in mine, Mister Flett. This'll be thirsty work." *The old fool falls for it.*

I have my Swiss knife in my pocket. This is my secret.

Ephraim is wearing gloves – white, thin. The only one doing so. He is not going to change the plan. On our way up, we pass the ancient Settlement where the founder of Orkney, the great Saint Magnus, was first buried. We keep quiet as a mark of respect. Everything is as planned.

Four hours is all we have. Four hours before the Brough of Birsay becomes an island once more. We have to take care. Slippery. Ephraim leads the way. Slippery. No wind. Rain in the air. You can hear the waters, and hear the stillness too. A high-pitched pip-pip-pip-pip-pip makes us all start. Just a curlew. Perhaps lost. Perhaps a warning. We don't speak. Three seconds on, twenty-two seconds off.

We get there without slipping or falling over. A miracle. I am there, at the highest spot on the Brough. A highlight. Ephraim turns on his torch. There it is: the padlock. Key in. Lock opens. Ephraim leads the way in. Shuts the outside door. Really excited. Uneasy as well. Going to be killing someone. I know that killing is not a wrong thing to do. It is a different thing to do. A new thing to do. Here is as good a place as anywhere else. But I have always kept clear of the lighthouse in the past. Touch the knife in my pocket. Feel reassured.

Pitch-black. Background hum. Drip. Drip. Ancient spirits on the move. Echo too. Yoo…oo…hoo…oo. Yoo…oo…hoo…

I cannot hear the weather. I always hear the weather. I am used to hearing the weather, even in the bu. Even in the kirk. Even in the shop. Even when you're inside and the weather's outside. Not now, though. Pitch-black hearing.

Torches switched on. The hidden doorway. White metal ladder going up. Framed photos of Wilson, Keppel and Betty, and yes, between Keppel and Betty, the secret door. The concrete steps leading down, just as Ephraim said. Just as…

"There are 366 steps down to the foot of the chamber, Alexander. A step for every day of the year. A step for each pharaoh who once ruled that fine, ancient land of Egypt. Male or female. One spare for the leap year."

That's what Ephraim told me. All planned, from getting the late Mister Flett to the Brough, all the way to his moment of death. Start to finish. A to Z.

"When we're inside, feller, you're to lead. You'll be the front runner. I'll be the back marker. The late Mister Flett? You can work his position out. Piggy in the middle. The ham in the sandwich. Won't have an inkling. Mustn't leave a gap between us. Like that tightly-packed phalanx of Roman gladiators going into battle. You remember that film at the pictures..."

Prearranged signal from Ephraim. The words, "Watch out." Not to be whispered. No risk of that from Ephraim anyway. I am to turn around, face *him*, look *him* in the eye. Ephraim with the rope tighter and tighter round *his* neck. Tighter and tighter until... I am to block the falling body.

It will be my hands in the killing. Ephraim doesn't know that. Faether will be so proud of his son. I stroke the knife in my handkerchief pocket. I want to press the lever to open my knife. It is my flick knife.

After his final breath, I am to remove the watch. Frisk his pockets for anything more? No. We are not common-or-garden criminals. We are not. His limp body to be carried down the remaining steps. We set fire to the corpse. The Ancient way. Then and only then do we have a look around.

"There is no man in Orkney more expert in the use of matches and a dram of paraffin. That's what they say about me. That Ephraim, he can suck diesel out of a tractor. He can throw a buttered slice of bread up in the air and tell you what side it will land on."

"That is a very well-thought-out plan." I meant it.

"Alexander, it is the Massive Ferguson of all well-thought-out plans."

We are at the top of the steps. Me to be in front. The late Mister Flett to be in the middle. Ephraim to be the back marker. At the start, though, we are side by side. Silence. Deep in thought. The time has come. Off we go. It's all for real. Not pretendy.

The late Mister Flett is the first to speak. "Beuy, a sup now would go down a treat."

I don't know what to say. Caught out. I better say something. Red in the face. Thank goodness he can't see me clearly. The only light comes from our torches, pointing way down to the bottom of the steps. He cannot see the blood colour in my cheeks.

Ephraim comes to my aid. "It's just a short walk to the bottom, Mister Flett. Then will be the time for our sup of tea. Maybe something more, eh? Beuy, you didn't forget the boiled eggs and the bottle of *medicine*... sixty per cent proof? There we are, Mister Flett. Hold on for just a wee bit longer. A feast awaits, in more ways than one."

In more ways than one... ne... ne. The echo catches the last of Ephraim's words.

The three of us start our descent. I lead the way, Ephraim bringing up the rear. The late Mister Flett in the middle. Him and his walking stick; one and a half sounds for one person. No gap between us. Tightly packed from top to bottom. Ephraim and myself carrying torches. Three hundred and sixty-six steps. Leap-year days.

A crackle. Electricity, all around me. Not just coursing up my right leg. I can feel it. Teeth chattering; mouth shut to suppress the sound. Will I get away with it? Never thought twice about wringing an old layer's neck... but I can see the judge and the black cap. Better watch my step now.

For the sound of wind or sea to be shut out is unnatural. In Orkney, it's always there. Even in our dreams. Outdoors and indoors. Indoors and outdoors. All I can hear is our breathing. Mine quiet, fidgety. Immediate in my ear, the late's; raspy, Craven "A"-raspy. Two steps behind, Ephraim; steam train.

I lead the way. Frontman of our party, the leader of them Roman fighting men, the scout as in them Westerns. Anyone watching us would have been impressed by the graceful rhythm of our descent. Step by step. Don't turn round to check. Don't look back. I am the frontman of the party. I lead.

Foot movement of the highest order and deepest beauty and tightest coordination, like them ice skaters I saw on Pathé News. The right foot is placed on the step below... joined by the left foot... breathe in... feet together... heel to toe... on the same concrete step... pause... us three in our new positions... statues... one directly behind the other... then off we go... right foot down a step. Massive Ferguson-precision.

Us in convoy, a silent convoy, working our way down, step by step. Waiting for Ephraim to give the agreed signal. My breathing, too loud. My teeth chattering, too loud. In my ear, Mister Flett's raspy breath.

A calendar of steps. Everything in proper time and place as we descend.

January, February and March, passed.

April, May and June, passed.

July, August and September...

Not long off the start of winter.

Still no signal from Ephraim.

It must be now. It must be now. Then like the crashing of a thunderstorm, Ephraim shouts out the words that I have been waiting for.

"Watch out! Watch out!" Slight pause. "Watch out! Watch out!"

No mistake now. I bring my flick knife out.

This is my moment.

Watch out! Watch out! echoes around and around and around like a peaty shape of smoke that refuses to dissolve into nothingness.

I feel a sharp blow to my head, and before I can say, "October" there is an awareness of a second blow, accompanied by a kick to my backside. My legs give way and I start to fall.

Something completely unexpected has happened to me.

I know my life will never be the same again.

CHaFF

CHAPTER 16

DUCKS IN A ROW

Early 1960s

The Mainland, a unique mainland, a mainland surrounded by water.

My island, but on the Mainland.

Born and bred in Orkney.

Away for far too long.

Back home.

Orkney, always there in my head.

The blue of the Big Sky, South Sea island blue. Aloha. Aloha. No apology of a blue here. *Cloudless.*

The sea. No shaken fist here. Just a soothing lullaby, a gentle rocking movement. Hush-a-bye baby. *Unassuming.*

The greenness of the grass. Grass from the Garden of Eden. Grass of the Green Land. I want to leave the roadside, get down on my knees and join in. Baa. Baa. *Succulent.*

The wind. Just a wisp of a breeze. You can barely hear it. Just a wisp. *Shhhhh.*

What's this I hear? The rasping 'crex-crex' of the corncrake. You thought you heard it. You thought you saw it. The Green Land provides cover for this bird. *Furtive.*

I wind down the car window and take in a deep breath of wholesome fresh air. *Orkney.*

I should feel at peace... but that gnawing away... no certainties as to why I am here, who I am and the way I look. *Why. Who. The way.*

I have to make a start somewhere.

That's one of the many things I have learnt. If something is broken, no one else but you can try to put it back together again.

You can try. You can always try. You must always try.

Humpty Dumpty sat on a wall,
Humpty Dumpty had a great fall.
All the king's horses and all the king's men
Couldn't put Humpty together again.

It's up to me.

Back home again. A long time away. It feels so.

The Big Sky: *cloudless.*

The sea: *unassuming.*

The grass: *succulent.*

The wind: *ssshhh.*

Why I am here. Who I am. The way I look.

I decide to deal with the last of the issues first. The way I look. *The way.* I haven't had a haircut for at least a month, so it is about time I pay a visit to the barbers. I got a shock when I looked in the mirror last week. A grey hair in the middle of my parting. That shouldn't be there. I'm only twenty-seven. Is my life over?

I work the gears down from fourth to second. I then ease my foot off the clutch, apply just the right touch to the brake pedal and bring the car to a smooth stop. The car is a hire car. Have I said that before? I should have done. It's important. If you're trying to heal yourself, it's always better to travel light. Then if it doesn't work out, you can carry on as before. You can leave no trace behind you. No one needs to know that you tried.

No one needs to know. The car. Hired, not owned. Hired, not possessed.

The hire car is stylish. It has tailfins at the back. It has a car radio. I am driving a hire car on an open road.

Orkney.

I need to know what the time of day is because I do not want to arrive at the police station and find that it is shut. As a good and dutiful citizen, I need to report a matter of public concern and a neat-and-tidy look about me will add gravitas to my visit. Yes, it is a matter of public concern. I was born and bred in Orkney. I have come back. I am going to reconnect. Friends and family are waiting for me.

I am behind the wheel of my Ford Anglia hire car.

I look at my right wrist and then my left. Both are bare. This *lack of* describes how I feel. I am lost without the watch. I am without ballast. The watch is rare, but its value to me is above monetary value. I cannot be healed without it. This is a matter of my concern. It is therefore a matter of public concern.

I feel safe and secure inside the hire car, my hire car with its tailfins. This is Orkney. Car doors; no need to lock, no need to unlock. I have the open road to myself. Just me inside the car. I've even wound my car window fully up. It's a trade-off. The air is so fresh and unsullied in Orkney, but it still has the power to bring in the unasked-for, the unwelcome, the unpredictable.

A foot-tapper of a tune on the radio, that'll help still my thoughts. The signal is playing up, though. I fiddle with the dial. I want a cheerful diddle-diddle reel, but all I get is quacking static. Someone is speaking now. The Cuban Missile Crisis. I am only half listening. I turn the radio off. There goes my right leg again. It never stays still. It has never stayed still.

I need to find the police station before it shuts, but I neither know what the time is nor the opening hours of the police station. I do know where the police station is.

165

Always look for a positive. I've learnt that.

I have a time written on a piece of paper which I keep in my back pocket. *Four o'clock.* I have eaten a few hours back and bright light fills the Big Sky, so four o'clock seems as reasonable as any other time.

At the police station, I'll report the missing of my watch as a loss. No, I'll report it as a theft. That'll put it up their pecking order. The police are cunning bastards, so I better make sure I'm consistent in my reporting of this theft. It is always important to have your ducks in a row.

If everything goes to plan, they'll find my watch. If not, at least I'll get a reference number for the insurance claim. The bastards will be trying to catch me out, asking the same question over and over again, but each time from a different angle.

"A family heirloom? When did you notice that it had been stolen? How did such a rare watch first come into your possession? The Swiss make lovely watches, don't you think? Your faether's side or your mither's? Stolen, did you say? The precise day and date on the watch when you became aware it had been mislaid? Was it Swiss, perchance? A family heirloom, did you say? Ancient Egyptian, did you say?"

Cunning bastards, the police. Cunning bastards.

First of all, I need to find the barbers. Always good thinking time to be had there. Just you and your face in the mirror, reflected back to you, downside up and front-to-back and the chattering of the scissors. Snip-snip.

Key turned in the ignition, clutch engaged, gears smoothly up from second to fourth, foot on the accelerator. I arrive in no time. I could have walked, but like being behind the wheel. I am in control, in my own space, and of course I am paying per day for the borrowing of the car, whether it is on the road or standing idle. My hire car. That's the beauty of a hire car: no emotional attachment. Did I tell you that my hire car has got a radio?

A red-and-white pole outside a dumpy-looking building. The barbers. That's where I park the car, on the hard standing next to the *Paraffin – Esso Blue* sign.

I leave the keys in the ignition and walk towards the shop door. The sun is shining. The Big Sky is cloudless blue. There is no wind. It is going to be like this all day. I am T-shirt optimistic. This is Orkney after all.

The card on the barbers' door says, *Open*. I do so.

Everything has its own time and place. Your life cannot make any sense unless it is laid out in front of you. Look. The magnificent hills of Hoy. Panning out, from left to right, to be taken in strict chronological order. Start point. End point. No in between. No surprises.

I know. I know.

Ding-a-ling. Ding-a-ling.

The ding-a-ling. Ding-a-ling. Not just the ringing of a shop doorbell.

CHAPTER 17

THERE IS NO BLACK CAT

Early 1940s

Ding-a-ling. Ding-a-ling.

"Hello, *boychik*. Good to see you again. Where's your faether?"

I look behind me. There is no one else in the barbers, just me and the adult. He has a kindly face and a pencil-like growth of hair on his upper lip between his nose and mouth. The barber puts down the newspaper he is reading. The man is talking to me.

"Eh, *boychik*, where's your faether?" He repeats the question.

I don't understand why he is asking me this. Boychik? I am nearer to thirty than twenty, and am under no obligation whatsoever to tell this stranger my age.

"He's just gone to the shop," I hear myself saying.

I do hope that Faether has gone to buy sweets for me. Did I just think those thoughts?

The stranger places a plank on the large black chair, then lifts me onto it. I sit on my black padded throne, feet dangling. There is chewing gum on the sole of my right shoe.

If I were just a bit taller, I'd be able to slide the shoe forwards and backwards on the seat of the barber's chair and get rid of the gum. To stand up on the barber's chair makes sense. I feel a pressure on my shoulders. An adult pressure. This-is-not-a-good-idea pressure.

"Now be a good *boychik*. Keep still. Your faether will be back in a jiffy."

The barber asks me what style of haircut I am after. I want a DA and tell him so.

"DA." The words come out clearly, but it is a child's voice speaking.

Whatever you ask for at the barbers, you always end up with a short back and sides. That must have been one of the first facts of life that I ever learnt.

Sitting up, Sabbath-rigid, I look at the mirror. It is a child's face that looks back at me. I look down and think I see something move on the floor. I want a DA, but deep down know… I look up. Reflected back to me is the face of a five-year old.

I start to fidget and am told in a kind voice to stay still; no pressure on my shoulders this time round.

"You look just like your faether." Scissors and comb and clippers go about their work. I swear the barber is smoking. I cannot work out how he can use the scissors and comb and clippers and hold a cigarette all at the same time. He must be a magic man.

He removes the towel tucked in round my collar and gives it a good shaking. Has he finished? My hair scatters onto the floor. Pieces in a jigsaw puzzle. Pieces of broken eggshells for a spell to be cast.

I hear the doorbell ding-a-ling but don't need to look round. I can see in the mirror. I can see in the mirror. It's Faether.

"*Boychik, boychik,* look down at the cat, look down at the black cat. It's on the floor in front of you."

The barber is an adult, and I do as I am told.

I feel the clippers at work from the nape of my neck upwards. It isn't the clippers that make me feel uncomfortable. It's this adult.

He told me to look down to see a black cat, but there is no black cat. I keep my head lowered. Perhaps the black cat will come into view. Where is the cat? Where is the cat? I feel as if I have been misled by the adult. I do not like that.

I do not like that.

The barber is smiling. I can see in the mirror. His work now finished, I feel the tape gently being peeled off the back of my neck. The towel round my collar is removed and shaken for the last time; the contents scattered, landing on top of the other clippings already there on the floor, as if by magic. I can see in the mirror. Has all that jet-black hair come from me?

The barber sweeps the floor. He then squeezes this puffer thing and I can feel the powder, like a splish-splash, on the back of my neck. It is sweet-smelling. What this powder is for, I do not know.

The barber then says to me, "There, that wasn't too bad."

My haircut is a short back and sides. I can see so in the mirror. This doesn't surprise me.

Faether gives the barber a shilling and comes over to me. He ruffles my hair. "That's a dandy haircut," he says. I do not need to look round. I can see it all in the mirror. Faether lifts me off the chair.

"Where is the cat? Where is the black cat?"

Faether doesn't answer.

The barber is smiling and leads both of us to the door. Hand in my faether's hand, I walk out the front door. Hand in hand. Together. It's a lovely feeling.

Ding-a-ling. Ding-a-ling.

I am on my own.

Just a minute before I was hand in hand with Faether. Me and Faether. Now, there is no Faether.

There is no black cat.

There never was a black cat.

I cannot say what hurts me more: the absence of Faether or the lie over the black cat. That's right, *the lie* over the black cat. *The adult lie.*

The *Paraffin – Esso Blue* sign.

I sneeze. Aaah-choo. Aaah-choo. A once-clean white handkerchief. No longer free of snot.

Ding-a-ling. Ding-a-ling.

CHAPTER 18

THE GOLDEN SLIPPER CLUB

Early 1960s

D ing-a-ling. Ding-a-ling.

I do not know what to make of it all.

Thank goodness I am still alive.

I am back in the hire car. The same car with the tailfins that I parked on the hard standing, next to the Esso Blue sign. Driver's seat. I pat myself down even before checking whether I can reach the driving wheel and see out of the driver's mirror.

I must do something just to prove that I am in the here and now. Ignition key in the hire car. Vroom-vroom. Off we go. A quick glance at the driver's mirror. My haircut makes me look neat and tidy. Jet-black except for that one grey hair. I'm only twenty-seven, for God's sake. That one grey hair. It's all over for me. I accelerate to fourth gear. As for what I am to tell the police, my ducks are in a row. All of them.

What happened, didn't. I do not feel ill. There is no way of explaining this shift in time. I must have dreamt it all. Time, all over the place.

My car takes the Kirkwall road, the main road out of Stromness. Still some way to go before I leave the Stromness parish boundaries. There will be a crossing of sorts, a frontier post, a brig, a bridge taking me away from safety and security.

All I have to do is just keep on this main road to get to Kirkwall. The big town of Kirkwall is just a half-hour's drive away. The biggest town in Orkney, with all its pleasures and dangers. Kirkwall for us in the West Mainland is a bigsy bugger. Thinks it's better than Stromness. The police station is little more than a ten-minute drive away on the same road. If I see the spire of Kirkwall's Saint Magnus Cathedral before I get to the police station, I know something has gone drastically wrong.

Kirkwall. Bigsy bugger. Beep-beep.

A bend in the road, the crest of the hill, and then to the left, the Loch of Stenness as it unfolds in front of me. Breathtaking.

Surely this Loch of Stenness is a wide-open sea, not a loch.

It is a wide-open sea without skyline.

A wide-open sea with just a hint of movement on the water.

A wide-open sea…

Fine-down-calm…

Not stubble-choppy.

On the horizon, a speck on fire is heading towards Valhalla; a boat on its final journey to its Viking resting place. All your dreams and wishes, life and its passing are to be seen here. The full circle of life in one eyeshot. Magical. Uplifting. Saint Magnus. Loch of Stenness.

Wait. Be patient. Eyes to be kept ahead. No peekaboo. Allowed to turn your head slightly to take in the view to the left. Count down the number of days in a month and add one for the pot and one for luck. Slowly now. I can dilly-dally. Time to home in on the other side. We've arrived at the Brig o' Waithe. Now's the time to look, on the right. The right. Look right.

What a contrast. That stretch of pretend water on the right is called the Bush, and leads to the Bay of Ireland, or so it claims.

Certainly not free-flowing.

Certainly unwelcoming.

Stagnant. *Sssssstagnant.*

Un-Orkney.

The Bay of Ireland broadens out into the open sea, the outside world and freedom. But this particular pocket of water is trapped, imprisoned, tangled up in its own thoughts.

The Bush, more bog than water, is murky, sinister and stagnant. You can tell by its name that something is up. It'll entangle you. It'll take your footstep and not return it. Witches and hobgoblins and finmen and others not on the side of the good weave their dark Orkney spells here. *Sssssspells.*

Not a place to dally.

I shiver and quickly avert my gaze.

I take my right hand off the driving wheel and cross myself. Just in case. Just in case.

I am at the bridge, the Brig o' Waithe, the Bridge of Waithe. The Brig o' Waithe, only one direction you can go, a crossing not a crossroads. The Brig is no man's land. Narrow, waiflike. I am pleased to reach the other side.

In the short time it takes to cross, bright daytime light has given way to pitch-black: no twilight, no sunset. In a blink of the eye, a snap of the fingers, day has become night.

I have been given directions. The police station is at the Orphir turn, first road on your right after the Brig o' Waithe, first cottage on your left. I am going to the police station to report the theft of my watch.

Who'd have thought that a police station can be so popular? There are so many cars parked outside, bright light and laughter spilling out. Outside, a neon sign glows – *The Golden Slipper Club* – not the standard blue police lamp. This is policing in Orkney; pops up in surprising places. My hire car, I leave unlocked. Police station and the Golden Slipper Club, a well-known, after-hours destination. All rolled into one.

There is nothing wrong in shared buildings. Sharing, that is the Orkney in my head, the Orkney I wish to reconnect with. If a police station is also a social club, that's fine by me. Make do. Orkney. Once inside, it will be like any police station. There will be a long counter, behind which will be the man in blue, pencil and pad in hand, ready to take down my details. Friendly, but not to be taken for granted. Open, but has it in him to be a cunning bastard.

I have what I am going to say all worked out. I will be pitch-perfect. All my ducks in a row. Quack-quack. The front door is on a latch. No ding-a-ling bell. In I go.

I walk straight into a large living room with a peat fire burning, a choice of torn seats for your backside's delectation, a kettle on the hearth if it's just a cup of tea you're after. The walls are decorated with pictures, magazine rough-cut, bringing the allure of Hollywood into this dimly- lit Orkney interior. There's a table, next to which are a couple of boxes and large storage trunks.

It all has an old-fashioned feel to it, and is plain filthy. Spiders and moths and creepy-crawlies and fag-end butts and scraps of food and empty glasses and rubbish are strewn over the floor. Filthy. Filthy, but friendly-filthy. That's why it is so popular, and where else can you go when the Stromness pubs throw everyone out at only nine o'clock on a Saturday evening?

People of all ages there. Sociable. Guests after the dance or from early closing, with nowhere else to go. There seems to be no one in charge. I am very excited. I am bound to meet up here with old friends and uncles and aunties and cousins.

This is my return. I have been away for so long. I have got a lot to tell. Fuck the theft of my watch. This is my homecoming.

I take a deep breath, walk right in and head for centre stage, towards the middle of the room where everyone can see me.

I am there. Everyone can see me. In the middle of the room. I am back.

No one has recognised me. No one.

I am not asking for much.

An "Alexander – long time, no see!" would have done.

A "Well, beuy, welcome home."

A "You're a bit porky for a twenty-seven-year-old."

At least a "No. It can't be..."

No one comes over to speak to me. None of the faces familiar. This is not what I expected. I must not show *the hurt*.

I am here to report the theft of my watch. I cannot leave until I have done so.

The clock on the mantelpiece says ten past five. My piece of paper which has *four o'clock* written on it isn't far out. It's less than an hour out. A few minutes later the clock on the mantelpiece is still at ten past five.

"It's always ten past five," someone says to me. It's a female voice.

The ten-past-five clock hurtles towards me. I duck. The man standing next to me ducks. The clock whooshes over both our heads. It lands not far behind me. At least I think it's not far behind me. I don't hear the sound of a clock breaking into pieces. The clock is intact.

"Time flies, my treasure, time flies," the man standing next to me cackles. He must be talking to the wifey who threw the clock. He is older than a middle-aged man.

"That was a close shave, Willie," someone yells out.

The man standing next to me grins broadly. He must be called Willie.

"Willie, you are a useless good-for-nothing, an absolute waster. Mither told me not to marry you. Why didn't I listen to her? God rest her soul." The wifey was the clock-thrower, I'm sure. She is now staring at me.

I'm not Willie, I feel like saying to her. Believe me, if I ever marry it will be to beautiful Gail and not this loud fishwife.

"Well, Mister Willie Farquhar, are you now in deep water," someone shouts out. There is laughter.

So his name *is* Willie. I watch him.

He is the conductor. The ringmaster. The *maître d'*. The *mein host*. He works the room like a politician at election time, pouring whisky straight from the bottle into tea-stained and chipped cups.

I find a spare cup, empty its dregs onto the concrete floor and hold it out in front of me like a supplicant. I need a drink. I badly need a drink.

I still have to find the sergeant in charge to report the theft of my watch. That can wait. I will enjoy a dram or two of Orkney's best in the meantime.

Warm or cold pies are also on offer. Most folk have brought food with them, and are happy enough to be eating cold baked beans straight out of the can. Willie, I was told, would provide the can opener. No extra charge. Plates are available. Like the cups, these plates have telltale smears of previous use.

As befits his age, Willie Farquhar is an elder of the kirk. Godliness is his forte, not cleanliness.

Everyone is singing and laughing and chatting, and in the dark recesses even a bit of courting is going on. *Another dram? Why not? Don't mind if I do.* The ten-past-five clock still lies on the floor. I look behind me. I stretch behind the chair and pick

177

it up, then give it to the lady sitting next to me. I've never seen her before. She's a stunner. I fancy her. This act of giving her the clock will let her know that I fancy her.

She in return gives me her baked-beans can. A clock that does not tell the right time in exchange for a can of baked beans. A fair exchange. I am hungry. That has to be a further sign. She has left her spoon inside the can. That is a further-further sign. I will ask her name.

That's what makes the world go around.

Broken clock in one direction. An empty can of baked beans in the other.

She speaks first. "A stopped clock is always right twice a day." That's what she says. Profound in its simplicity. Profound. For my ears only. I nod. I am in there.

I give the can a good rattle, slurp clean the spoon and tuck in. Meal finished. A dribble of sauce on my chin. The can is discarded on the floor and given a wee kick.

If a problem looks really difficult, kick the can down the road. That's experience. It can only come with age.

I need to go for a piss. I leave the main room and pass through a small back room – the ben – a few men are having a quiet drink. They are sitting round a table. When I lived here, these out of bounds rooms were the preserve of off duty policemen. These men are not in uniform. One of them is watching me intently. He is holding a pack of cards, ready to deal the next hand. He pauses. He is writing something in a notepad. Maybe he is the sergeant in charge. On the way back to the main room I will give it a go and report the theft of my watch to him.

I feel better now, having answered the call of nature. There is such a loud cheer from the main room that I rush straight back to see what is going on. No time to stop in the ben.

A gorgeous girl, standing on the table, is doing a striptease.

She is wearing high heels and likely to totter over at any moment. She is a right beauty. She looks just like my childhood sweetheart Gail. All eyes are on her, not just male.

The whisky has brought a clarity to my thinking. The clock and the striptease are side issues. I am here to notify the authorities of the theft of my valuable watch.

Why should this be so difficult? I know what I want to do. Why doesn't it just happen?

The sharp shrill of a whistle. What has blown in through the open front door? There are many men in blue. One of them has a crown on his epaulettes. Maybe he is in charge.

The epaulette man shouts out for everyone to hear, "I am the superintendent and I am in charge." He sees Willie. The superintendent starts to read from the piece of paper that he's holding. "Mister William Alexander Watt Flett Farquhar of Bridge of Waithe, Stenness. Is that you?"

"Yes, Officer. That's me."

My gaze switches from one man to the other. Ping-pong.

"You have allowed your premises to be used for the consumption and supply of whisky without a licence... You have sold excisable liquor without holding a certificate."

I don't understand all the words, but I get the drift.

The man in blue with the crown on his epaulettes waves a truncheon over his head and hollers something that sounds like, "Ten to five, ten to five." The superintendent looks like a mad whirling dervish. He looks possessed.

I cannot understand why the police would want to raid their own police station. I can see that no good will come of this, but this is the Golden Slipper Club and Willie Farquhar doesn't seem at all put out. Do not forget, it is his home turf as well.

Another dram? Yes, thank you. Don't mind if I do.

"Officer, I don't recognise you. Are you from Kirkwall

or Stromness? I have to keep the numbers even here." Willie pauses. Now softly spoken, conspiratorial. "Officer, tell me something. Out of those having a quiet drink, who brought their own whisky with them and who did not? How can I be breaking the law if someone's having a dram from their own bottle? Where's the crime in that? Are you telling me that if you pop into your neighbour's bu for a dram and a blether, it is illegal to bring a bottle of whisky with you?"

He has more to say. "And can you tell me, Mister Officer of this raiding party, out of this fine body of policemen in my home, how many are on duty and how many off duty? I have to keep the numbers even in here. Fairness is as fairness does. I am an elder of the kirk after all." Willie, calm as calm could be, smiles.

Things are about to go from bad to worse for Mister Officer of the raiding party.

"And can you tell me, Superintendent, who this attractive young lady is?" Willie points to the star turn, more than worse for wear. A bit of drink inside her, I would guess. Just one item of clothing left. Something telling her not to go the whole hog.

Mister Officer turns towards her. Puffed up, I'm-in-charge, no self-doubt. Goes with the rank. All colour is drained from his face.

"Christ, she's the chief constable's daughter. The raid is called off, now. *Now!*" He blows his whistle and turns tail; him leading the raiding party, his subordinates with him in the front room and in the back ben. A position of authority and status to be maintained.

Willie's wife has somehow got hold of the clock and aims it once more at Willie.

"Time flies," cackles Willie. The clock says ten past five. I know it isn't ten past five, but it is time for me to leave.

There is no more dangerous beast than a policeman who's been made a complete and utter fool of, and I know I will be courting trouble if I stay. This reporting of the theft of my watch, a matter of public interest, will have to wait.

I settle my bill for the evening. Five drams of whisky, a Ferguzade – like an orangeade, but sicklier – two cups of tea, and a lukewarm meat pie.

Willie asks me, "Do you need some rubber johnnies?"

My innards swilling around like a rough ferry crossing over the Pentland Firth, that single-minded stretch of water that separates Orkney from Scotland. Bill paid, hand raised, goofy smile, farewell to no one in particular and I rush out of doors.

Reporting the theft can wait until tomorrow. I have this awareness of time and place and insight.

It is Isaac Newton that comes to mind. He must have been born an Orcadian; *that* Isaac Newton with his common sense and profundity. True, Newton is not an Orcadian name, but my next-door neighbour with the big farm did call his favourite sheep Isaac.

Isaac Newton. There's always an Orkney connection.

For every action, there is an equal and opposite reaction. Those are Isaac Newton's very own words.

Isaac Newton.

I heave my guts up.

CHAPTER 19

ONE FOR THE POT

Early 1960s

I t's pitch-black outside. Not a sound. Stillness. Neither people nor cars, not even a hint of a metallic curve or a chassis. No light or sound from where I have just been. A different feel to the darkness. My car keys being of no use to me, I throw them away. I feel good about that. The car was a hire car. I feel no personal attachment to either the car or its keys. Neither will be missed.

Will I be missed?

I am where I am, but I don't know when I am. If that makes sense.

An acceptance of the situation. It can only come with age.

I now have to walk home, first to Stromness and then up the West Mainland coast to Birsay. This will hardly be a stroll, half a day at least, but the night is dry and mild. The sooner I've crossed over the Brig o' Waithe, the happier I will feel.

I must take care. A misplaced step and that would be that. The Bush leading to the Bay of Ireland, ever-stagnant and doom-laden, is now to my left. The Brig seems much narrower than before, more like a tightrope than a generous cut. No light to guide me.

Made it. I breathe a sigh of relief. I have crossed over and am now on the West Mainland side of the Brig o' Waithe, and the darkness is starting to lift with the birds providing the dawn chorus. I can walk at a steady pace, making due allowance for the occasional contrariness of my right leg.

The Stromness road isn't mine alone. I hear footsteps. I am unable to put distance between myself and this person behind me. Footsteps getting louder. He or she is drawing nearer.

I badly want to look behind me.

A pantomime moment, or a Lot's wife moment. Me turning into a pillar of a salt.

I badly want to scratch that itch.

My contrary right leg makes my mind up for me. Because of this intermittent surge of electricity running through it, it tires very quickly. I need to sit down. At least if I'm sitting down by the roadside, I will be looking sideways-on at whoever is coming my way. I will not need to look behind me.

This person who is almost upon me could be three parts bad and one part good, or three parts good and one part bad.

If there is any bad in this person, I will introduce bits of Orkney good. This Orkney goodness can be infectious. It's inbred. It never leaves you.

If I keep my wits about me, I'll come out of this all right. I'll spread the goodness around. Three generous spoonfuls of tea and one for the pot, boiled water and a good stir. Being Orkney-chipper has never let me down before.

I sit down, but before I can even glance sideways an irresistible need to sneeze overwhelms me. There is a clean, white handkerchief (free of snot) in my pocket. It is a matter of hygiene and personal pride to always carry around with me a clean, white handkerchief (free of snot). Self-esteem. That's what they call it.

If you don't like yourself, no one else will. That's experience. It can only come with age.

In the blink of an eye and a splish-splash of an aaah-choo, I am joined by a middle-aged feller. I say 'middle-aged' because that's how he looks to me. It's a safe guess because when all is said and done, you're always more likely to meet a middling sort of man or woman on the road than any other type.

That's experience.

This mystery middle-aged feller sits down on the grass next to me. I immediately pat my front pockets just to make sure my wallet is in its right and proper place and out of view.

That's experience.

I only have small change left, no banknotes, certainly not enough to buy me a good breakfast. No point checking my car keys are still there. It *was* a hire car.

I decide to seize the initiative. Given the worn state of his clothes, here is a man down on his luck, a man on his uppers, a man in need of a sympathetic ear. I don't want to get off on the wrong foot. I back myself five-to-two-on that my Orkney friendliness will win him round, should this feller prove to be an awkward middle-aged feller.

"A very good morning to you."

"What's so good about it?" He stands up.

"It's a fine morning to be up with the larks and doves." I stand up.

I am having to play the long game here. The sun will soon be shining. The Big Sky will become cloudless blue. Aloha. Aloha. The Big Sky has always been cloudless blue on my return. There will be no wind today. No wind at all.

"That's the second time you've used the word 'morning' and—"

"Well, wouldn't you think me a queer fellow if I said, 'Good evening' to you at this time of day and all?"

Be chipper, he's just shy.

"Morning and evening are mere passing places of time. There are always three different times for every time."

"You are clearly a man who is very good with words, and you have just told me something of great importance. I feel honoured that you have chosen me to reveal such a nugget of wisdom."

We're on the verge of a breakthrough here.

"Beuy, what was the key moment for Joe Louis, 'the Brown Bomber', our great heavyweight world champion?" Raises his fists. "Was it that moment he stepped into the ring for his first fight?" Boxer pose. "Was it the moment he took the title and became world champion?" Watch his hands. "Or was it his first successful title defence? Proof, if proof were needed, that Joe Louis didn't just get lucky first time round." Watch his raised hands.

"It is a privilege for me to be receiving such learning at the beginning of such a fine day. Joe Louis, you say?" *I'd never heard of him. Louis. That's not an Orcadian surname.*

The stranger's hands no longer raised. *Good.*

An edge now to his voice. *Not so good.*

"Have you heard of Chopin?"

I nod. *Chopin. That's not an Orcadian surname.*

"I am cut from the same cloth as Mister Chopin, and earn an extra shilling or two by visiting various households. Calling on the dexterity of my fingers and the razor-sharpness of my hearing, I can coax the white and the black piano keys away from wilful grumpiness into shimmering beauty. I am a piano tuner by trade."

I look him full in the face. His upper and lower gums have parted to reveal an array of white and black stumps which pass as teeth. Here could be a musical friend for life.

"The piano is properly tuned," he continues in a bit of a westerly-wind, matter-of-fact manner. "I then tie the piano owner up and search their property for any valuables and the like. If the owner struggles, I kill them there and then and, I don't mind saying so, enjoy the act."

Not at all good. I would even go so far as to say dangerous.

I'm on guard. Here is a deeply unscrupulous man who stops at nothing to get his way, and is even prepared to use the beauty of music as a pretext for murder. He is four parts bad and no parts good. I am clearly in great danger. I need to think fast. I stand up. My right leg recognises the seriousness of the situation I am in and shakes uncontrollably.

Must watch him carefully. Must not let him get a whiff of my fear.

At the same time, something comes to mind. My early years, growing up in my bu; the piano. All of us standing round it. I remember friends and family there, and Faether. We're having a right good old sing-song around our piano. It's an upright, in the oot-by. The piano. It tugs at the memory.

He is looking me up and down. His mouth open, black and white stumps on display.

"Just humour me." He is smiling.

Watch him carefully.

"I have a sixth sense, and am the seventh son of a seventh son. Not only can I read the palms of strangers, but I can tell folk their age even though they may be in a state of denial..." He moves towards me.

I take a step back.

"Through gauging the distance between a person's eyes and feeling their cranium for bumps and the like, I can pin their age down to within a year or two."

He takes a step forward. I can smell his breath.

I stand still, hypnotised. His fingers burrow into my hair,

touching my skull in several places. He displays a lightness of touch you would expect from a man who earns his living as a piano tuner. He has finished, and takes a step back. He rubs his chin thoughtfully. After less than a few seconds, a figure is decided upon.

"You are thirty-two years old," he says.

"I am not. I am twenty-seven." I smirk.

I should not have pointed out his error. I have made him angry.

"Now, I am not going to waste any more of my time or yours. Time is a valuable entity. I am going to rob you of all your valuable possessions and then slit your throat with my knife. It is Swiss Army." He looks at me, full in the face. "They say that we expect lashings of rain mid-morning, so your blood will be washed away."

Here is a person to whom the wisdom of The Powers That Cannot Be, Volume I cannot be applied.

I open my mouth. No words come out. My right leg is shaking with the intensity of a full-force gale. My fate is sealed. I close my eyes and start counting up to ten, fearful that I will get no farther than five. This is not a good situation to be in. *You can say that again.* My right leg will not stay still. *The experience that only comes with age is not presenting me with any options here.*

He looks me up and down and then his voice suddenly softens. "My friend, I observe that you have had a similar misfortune in your life. See, my right leg shakes also without rhyme or reason, of its own accord without a puppet master pulling the strings. My right leg shakes if it's raining or if it's dry, if it's January or October, if I've had an Orkney fry-up with or without brown sauce. See, I kid you not." His right leg is shaking.

He proceeds to roll up his right trouser leg to reveal a criss-crossed lattice of scars that look similar to mine and could only come from the sewing-up by the medical people.

187

"A question for you, my friend. You have an implant in your right leg. Is it of wood identical to the construct that murderers swing from? Could it be of aluminium, or perchance of feather-light titanium?"

He has said, 'my friend'. I am not home and dry yet. Wooden sounds like the safe option. Should I plump for aluminium, or what about titanium, a word that has passed me by so far in my life, but is of a singular beauty in its pronunciation? Of course, I can always state that there is no implant in me whatsoever. It is a pony trap of a question. The wrong answer and that is that for me. I will try and sidestep it.

"Well, my good man, like your good self, I am an Orkney beuy, born and bred. I am completely without any artificiality, as you can see."

I roll up my right trouser leg to reveal a latticework of surgical incisions, identical to his. I then raise the trouser leg of my other leg, my left leg, my unblemished left leg. The contrast is clear. To anyone chancing upon us we must look like a meeting of those secret men, the Freemasons.

He lets out a cry of delight. "We are *family*, and this is a most unexpected way for me to meet a long-lost brother. In return for you telling me how you came to be under the surgeon's knife, I will tell you my story. You are a hail-well-met fellow. My name is Billy Fury – and yours?"

Billy Fury. That is not an easy-come-easy-go sort of name.

I shake his hand vigorously and am about to give Billy Fury my name when I hesitate. After all, this man boasts of using music as a cover for the vilest of murderous acts. However, there is no menace in him now. I decide to give Billy Fury my name.

I cannot remember my own name.

Various names are vying for attention in my head, but I lack the certainty to claim any one of them as my own.

Am I Captain Hurricane, who can straddle an already-fired

torpedo? In a raging fury, I defend king and country single-handed. Job done, I return to the mess in time for roast beef and Yorkshire pudding. *Captain Hurricane.*

Am I Trigger the horse? In between Hollywood film-shoots, I dine out on the finest oats flown in from Latin America, have my dressing stable carpeted with hay and scented red petals, and can speak Esperanto? *Trigger.*

Am I Olga Olkovski? The beautiful Russian ballerina who each day receives a sackful of fan mail. A black-and-white photograph of me in my white sable coat hugging my snow-white Pekinese called Natasha is sent to each fan. The photograph is signed by one of my assistants followed by three kisses, a hammer and sickle and the words, I dedicate my life to the Soviet Union. *Olga Olkovski.*

Captain Hurricane. Trigger. Olga Olkovski. *None of these names feels right. Why are they popping up at this very moment?*

I shake his hand vigorously, a broad smile on my face, but I know that he is looking for more from me than a handshake and a smile. He is waiting for a name.

Odd, that. The issue has become a different one now. Not so much a question of entrusting my name to this stranger, but more one of simply not being able to remember my own name. Having secured my life from this dangerous man, I have to come up with a name or run the risk of putting myself back in harm's way. I close my eyes again, hoping against hope for inspiration.

He wants an answer. Any answer. It doesn't matter what the answer is. That comes with experience.

"That's a coincidence, my friend, you going by the name of Billy Fury. The name on my birth certificate is... Gracie Fields." This strains credulity, but it is the best that I can come up with. *Let's run with it.*

"Gracie is a fine name, a name of distinction," my new brother replies, quick as a flash.

Billy Fury and Gracie Fields, now facing each other. Our right legs are having a mighty chat. Neither wasting our breath. It's Morse code. It's in Morse code, and Billy is tapping out most of the dots and dashes.

"We are cut from the same cloth. I would as readily harm a member of my own family as pluck the eyebrows off a cow. I am elected as the leader of All the Right-Leg-Shakers on the West Mainland, and can muster an army of hundreds at the click of my fingers. Should I hear of anyone disrespecting you, I will track this person down and they will breathe their last breath. I am a person of my word."

"This is a rare honour for me indeed. I have not met a leader of any persuasion for more years than I can remember. Can I have your autograph?"

A few well-chosen words of flattery won't go amiss here. Knowing when to turn on and off the tap of flattery. That can only come with experience.

I know. I know.

"Instead of my autograph, Gracie, let me give you this banknote as a token of my esteem. It will meet all your cooked-breakfast needs, even allowing you seconds of black pudding. Please use it in the first cafe that this road takes you to."

I nod.

"It is considered bad luck for you to see the exact denomination, so I will fold it and put it into my fist like so, and you will look away with your fist open like so, and you will receive it like so and will transfer it to your back pocket like so."

We successfully complete this Freemasonry of a manoeuvre. Eyes not meeting, feet tapping away but each waiting for the other to finish his move, one arm stretched out but fingers never touching. A curious *pas de deux*.

"Thank you for your generosity." I pat my back pocket.

"This is my turning on the left now. Before I bid you

farewell, could you satisfy my curiosity and tell me what such a fine man as yourself, a blood brother, is doing on the road at this dawn-chorus time of day?"

"I am going to Stromness Police Station, Billy. It is a police station, isn't it?"

I don't want to end up in another Cinderella-type, after-hours sort of place.

"Why shouldn't it be?" Billy Fury gives me a look.

"Am I on the right road?"

"Continue along this winding road for a mile or two, and the fair town of Stromness will unfold in front of you. Your breath will be taken away as you see the harbour and the water and the backdrop of the mighty hills of Hoy. The police station will be on your right just as you enter the town.

"Well. Fancy that. You going to the police station of all places. This morning it's bound to be shut because of the Great Event. If you do find someone there, tell them Billy Fury sends his regards." He is smiling again.

I shake his hand and bid him farewell. He in turn wishes me well on my travels, but then says something curious about the good folk of Stromness.

"In Stromness, you stand a better chance of seeing Three Wise Men in the afternoon than in the morning."

Is this a three-spoonfuls-informative-and-one-spoonful-derogatory comment, or is it the other way around? No, it is to be taken as both clockwise and anti-clockwise in its perspicacity.

Yes, a comment can be both clockwise and anti-clockwise in its perspicacity. You'll find out. In time.

The encounter with Billy Fury has been a close call, but I have, using my experience of life, come out on top.

I go on my way, my right leg quietened now that the moment of danger has passed.

Ding-a-ling. Ding-a-ling.

CHAPTER 20

THE GREAT EVENT

Early 1940s

D ing-a ling. Ding-a ling.

The road to Stromness becomes busier and busier, due no doubt to this Great Event.

These vehicles whizzing by, toing and froing, vroom-vrooming, are not police cars. They are Land Rovers with the back flap open and soldiers peering out like kittens from a new-found hiding place. Soft top, yellow and green and brown camouflage, splashes of muted colour merging into the background. Each Land Rover, though, is bathed in a brightness of its own, in celestial and radioactive light. Counterproductive camouflage.

It is odd. Why are there so many military vehicles? There goes another black staff car with its pennant on the bonnet, shoogling in the wind. I swear the driver looked just like Captain Hurricane.

Where am I? I am no older. Though without seeing my face in a mirror, I cannot say for sure that I am still twenty-seven.

The road goes quiet. The birdies' call and reply takes centre stage.

I can hear the clip-clop of a horse, getting louder and louder. I see it in the distance. An outline at first, but becoming more distinctive; a stallion of a horse, fine breeding, majestic, many hands high.

Sitting proudly in the saddle is a lady rider, a beauty from her cheekbones to her toes, possessing a balletic assuredness.

The stallion feels no need to move to a faster step. Clip-clop. It passes me on this now empty, open road. The horse speaks as it does so. "I am Trigger and this is Olga Olkovski. We are both of superior stock."

Where am I? What's happening to me?

The military, with their Land Rovers and staff cars and shoogling pennants and 'top brass', reclaim the silence. They feel they have every right to do so. Entitlement.

I have no understanding of what is taking place. I keep focused on the road ahead, one steady step in front of the next. This, I hope, will still these thoughts going round and round in my head. This, I hope, will shut out the unwelcome and the unreal.

After an hour or so I come to the crest of the hill and Stromness is laid out in all its glory before me. The stunning backdrop of harbour, sea and the Hoy hills, all set in crystal-clear Orkney morning light. Better than the pictures. I am hungry. Time for breakfast. Bacon and eggs and enough money for seconds of black pudding.

I pat my back pocket and take out the folded banknote. One hundred pounds in denomination. Yellow. Half the size of a normal banknote. Monopoly money. What cafe will accept this? On the back of the note is scribbled *Billy Fury* and a telephone number. I do not throw the yellow banknote away.

It may come in handy. You never know. You'll find out. In time.

I reach the police station. The sign outside the front door is handwritten – *Closed Until Afternoon.* No Wise Men here. There is a black-and-white poster in the window, no words attached. It is a photograph, not of Billy Fury but of a fine-looking young lady instead. The photograph is of Gracie Fields. What crime has she committed?

A few minutes later I am at the heart of this fine West Mainland town. Stromness is alive today. It feels like Xmas Day, my birthday, the king's birthday, the-day-the-pictures-first-came-to-Orkney birthday, and Saint Magnus' birthday all rolled into one.

The sun is shining. The Big Sky is cloudless blue. There is no wind.

Flocks of starlings loop the loop. The houses either side of the narrow, cobbled street have had a fresh lick of paint. Hanging baskets full of purple, red and yellow petunias. Shops are doing a roaring trade. There is a party atmosphere. The street is crowded and I am swept along the street by a tidal wave of the good folk.

People are giving me odd looks, and I in turn think that there is something hand-me-downish about their clothes. There aren't many young men about. Those you do see of my age are in uniform. Maybe people take me in my civvies for a spy or a conscientious objector.

Then the penny drops.

I have returned to a previous decade – the 1940s – while holding on to my current age. Best not to tear myself apart seeking the whys and wherefores of this. Let's just enjoy. See what happens.

I stand with my back to the waterfront facing the Stromness Hotel. Some old-style black vehicles are parked up in front. The hotel is the top brass' HQ; the most comfortable in town. Nothing changes. A war to be won for the many; comfort to be enjoyed by the few.

I speak to no one and no one speaks to me.

There are only three policemen on duty. They have little to

do. The good-natured crowd have enough sense about them not to spill over the harbour's edge. Too exciting a day for high jinks. The Pierhead Parliament – Stromness men lounging about putting the world to rights, sharing gossip and roll-your-owns – has adjourned early for the day.

All eyes are on the balcony immediately above the entrance to the Stromness Hotel. Everyone expectant. No reason to be silent with it. A joyous day, not a day of remembrance. Yes, even in wartime, a joyous day. Everyone is in high spirits.

I am not observing. I do not stand to one side, cool, detached. No, I am in the thick of it. I share the excitement. I share the anticipation. I am at one with the crowd. I am standing in the middle of the crowd. I do not recognise anyone. No one recognises me.

"All the way from across the Atlantic, not bad for a Lancashire lass. Will she chew gum and speak like a Yank?"

"They say she's here for a few days to entertain the troops."

"I bet she doesn't need to darn her stockings."

"I wonder what her hairdo's like? Will it be swept up?"

"They've cut back on our chocolate ration. I heard it on the wireless."

"Will Gracie sing for us? I hope it's *The Biggest Aspidistra in the World* or *Sally*, they're my favourites."

And then the balcony doors open and out she comes. She knows what needs to be done. A star here in our Stromness, and not just for the few. We Orkney folk keep our distance. Fans, loyal fans, but respectful with it. No 'Gracie, Gracie' chant from us.

The sun is shining. The Big Sky is cloudless blue. There is no wind.

She smiles, waves to us and then blows us all a big kiss, a gesture of unlimited love. Her hands sweep out in as wide an arc as our empire, British red. Gracie has done this many, many times before, up and down our Sceptred Isle. A star in our midst.

Our Gracie makes us feel privileged.

Our Gracie is shedding tears.

Our Gracie is here not for us all but *individually, for you and for me.*

V is for victory. She is our Rochdale lass. She is our princess. One more wave and kiss and she steps back from the balcony. The curtains are pulled.

Everyone is cheering; even the policemen, even me. I am so happy. If only I had a bouquet of flowers to throw onto the empty balcony. I am crying with joy. All of us are singing *Walter, Walter (Lead Me to the Altar).* Will she reappear? No fairy dust left to scatter over you and me?

My gaze from the Stromness Hotel balcony back to the Pierhead.

The crowd not wanting to leave.

Me part of this crowd.

Me not wanting to leave.

Our Gracie, in our Northern Isles, an outpost of Great Britain fighting for its very survival. She will forever be a tonic to the troops and to us. The might of the British Navy, based here. We are the island of Orkney. Small. Separate. We are the Mainland. The sea protects us. We are also the outpost of Great Britain. An island race. Heroes. Knights of old. Defiant. Orkney. An island within an island within an empire.

She has been here for us. She will come back out for us. I know she will. I know. I know. For one more time. We are waiting.

I look up at the balcony. There is someone there. It isn't Gracie Fields I see. It is *me* up there. Just me. On the balcony. A magic moment. *My* magic moment. From the balcony, I am waving to the crowd. From the balcony, I am waving to myself.

The curtains open once more. *She* walks out once more. She may live in America now, but there are no airs and graces on *my* Rochdale lass. We embrace. We are *one*, Gracie and me. We are holding hands. The balcony is more than our stage. The balcony is our crow's nest, looking beyond this horizon to the next horizon, and to the horizon after that. What a glorious sun-specked future awaits.

We, as one, shield our eyes from the piercing sunlight. I move my right hand slightly away from the top of my brow. Gracie follows. First me, then Gracie.

We let the Orkney sunshine dazzle us.

Gracie moves the angle of her hand. I follow. First Gracie, then me.

Imperceptible at first. No longer flat and shielding. A definite slant now, and defiance with it.

No – first me and then her.

No – first her and then me.

As one. At the same time.

We are saluting. Our nation will get through this. We will win. Victory will be ours.

We hold our salute.

I look outwards, not at anything specific but into the distance, into the great unknown, into the big Blue-Sky future.

A parliament of black rooks surrounds us. They are offering to be our escort to this better future. They are offering to protect us from evil. Their offer is heartfelt and genuine and for the good. Gracie and I thank the birds. The birds say that they are always here for us, should we need them. Caw-caw. Caw-caw. The black rooks fly off, looping the loop as if they were starlings.

I am on the Mainland of Orkney. I am on the group of islands called Orkney.

I am on the Mainland of Orkney. I am on the largest island of Orkney.

I am on Orkney which forms part of our nation, a great island: Great Britain.

And we are at war.

I gaze fondly at Gracie. She parts her lips. We kiss passionately.

She turns to the crowd and leads us all in singing *God Save the King*, and during our patriotic rendition she whispers to me, "Don't I look like Frowsy Fanny in this frock?"

I look out to sea towards the future, our land and sea of dreams. From my crow's nest, I see a tall ship. On its bow, there is something special: a figurehead of Gracie and myself entwined, a Viking tall ship seeking good fortune, proud in its bearing. I watch our figurehead sailing away until it becomes a mere speck on the horizon.

The Great Event now over, the crowd disperses. I am aware of being back on the waterfront, on the Pierhead. There is one more surprise in store for me.

All that has been taking place has not met with the approval of the sea. It craves recognition. It feels it deserves the limelight. Enough is enough. The sea is no longer prepared to hold back its pent-up anger, its resentment.

I am the sea. The British Navy is based here in Orkney because of me. Yet Stromness folk care more for this Gracie Fields. I can pack a punch. You just watch my waves with their white, foamy phlegm, spitting white horses and heads rearing. My threat is not gesture-wispy. If you think I'm just gunsmoke evaporating into nothingness, think again. I am here all the time. The same cannot be said about our visitor.

The waters threaten, are being whipped up into a frenzy and will exact revenge. The message is clear. If the sea has its way, the good folk of Stromness will pay a price for worshipping at the feet of this upstart, this matinee idol, this fattened golden calf of the Great Event.

The Big Sky does not intervene. It plays superior and lets the sea get on with its tantrum because that's all it is, just a childish tantrum. The wind, having let rip in solidarity, reins in its spite. The Green Land has no role to play, so goes about its business.

The sun is shining. The Big Sky is cloudless blue. There is no wind.

I am back in the here and now. I have seen my own future and it is an uplifting one, and I am confident and happy. There is a spring to my step. For the first time since my return to Orkney, I feel that there will be no further twists and turns to deal with. I walk straight ahead and will soon reach the police station. My right hand of its own volition moves towards my forehead and I pretendy salute.

Everything is going to work out fine.

Stromness Police Station will soon be open for business and I can finally report the theft of the missing watch.

It is all played out in my head.

I will report the theft of the rare watch. I will explain my predicament to the man in blue; me being hungry and having money, but it's not real money and it's not my fault. He will then invite me to join him for a hearty fry-up. I hope he has some brown Daddies sauce that I can smother the rashers with. With a full stomach, I will start the second leg of my West Mainland journey. Homeward bound. The sun will be shining. The sky will be cloudless blue. There will be no wind.

I know that this time round the police station will be open for business, what with the Great Event now being over.

Everything will turn out as I want it to. Everything will fit into its time and place. I might even know the man in blue who I will be reporting the theft to.

There is a blue light outside. It is switched on. That means that the police station is open. It is just left for me to push the door and enter. This I do.

Ding-a-ling. Ding-a-ling.

CHAPTER 21

DARLING

Early 1960s

Ding-a-ling. Ding-a-ling.

The anteroom is bathed in sunlight. It is barely furnished.

There is a framed picture of Queen Elizabeth II on the wall above a large radiator, and on a small table in the far corner is an old-fashioned candlestick telephone, its earpiece hanging on a hook with a mouthpiece to speak into. They are still in use here, but I have been away for quite a few years.

It is a no-frills sort of room. I want to sit down, but there is no chair. I can feel the warmth of the sun on my cheek. I press the bell on the counter. *Ping.*

A hatch slides open on the wall behind the counter. I see this face looking at me through the hatch. The face fills the hatch. I hope above hope that this face belongs to the man in charge.

I need this man in blue to be on the ball. A run-of-the-mill policeman is of no use in finding my watch. I have worked out what I am going to say. Pitch-perfect. All my ducks in a row.

"In Orkney, always make sure you know where you are

200

going, otherwise you will never know when you have arrived."
These are the man in blue's opening words.

I have found the right man.

He closes the hatch. The side door opens. He walks round
to take up a position behind the counter. The man in blue is
now facing me.

We eye each other up and down. He does not recognise me.
I do not recognise him.

He has a ruddy complexion. His face is on a body as round
and beefy as a big button. Before me stands a cross between
a St Bernard and a Humpty Dumpty sort of man, a Humpty
Dumpty-before-the-fall sort of man. A man of medium height
with a face out of proportion. No neck on him. He sports an
unusual head of hair. His rug is not a Duck's Arse, a DA. It sits
lopsidedly.

"My name is Sergeant Tulloch and I have kept law and order
in this parish for as long as I can remember. I know everyone in
my patch, but your face, sir, rings no bells. What brings you to
the police station on this fine, sunny day? Your name?"

I don't recognise him. He doesn't recognise me.

"Officer, spring is in the air. Isn't that the chiffchaff birdie
that I hear? I have come to report the theft of an Ancient
Egyptian titanium watch."

The sergeant's head jerks back. I could have been that Joe
Louis feller landing a left uppercut. His hairpiece takes up a
slightly different position.

"You are not here to report the theft of a rocking chair?"

I shake my head.

"The theft of a three-piece suite?"

I shake my head again.

"... of a dining table chair?"

"Not a dining table chair." I nod.

"....... a fold up chair?"

"No chair at all."

"Are you here to report the theft of a garden bench?"

I dismiss such a suggestion with the contempt it deserves.

I am in the right place and time. I have found the right person to report the theft to. But this is proving to be far more challenging than I expected. I have not taken into consideration that the man in blue might be a single-issue man, a man so fixated on furniture.

"I repeat. Are you here, mister, to report the theft of a garden bench?"

"Not a garden bench."

"Are you sure?"

"Positive."

"This is a unique and inexplicable visit. So, you've come to report the loss of something that has nothing whatsoever to do with items of furniture." The sergeant looks at me, wide-eyed in amazement.

"That is why I am here."

I'll tell him the bare minimum for starters. Let's be as skittish as a baby lamb.

"This is grotesque. This is unbelievable. This is bizarre. This is unprecedented. Nothing to do with furniture, you say. Mister... Mister...

"Orkney folk are in great danger and we, the police on the West Mainland, are undermanned. There are only three of us here to protect the whole community. We are the thinnest of blue lines. We are the Three Wise Men, but there are still only three of us.

"I have never known times like these. The good folk of the West Mainland are in a state of heightened danger. Threats from all sides. There is talk of raiders from the north; them Vikings plundering gold bullion from the hold of that ship that Lord Kitchener was travelling on... Vikings."

202

Vikings. That word sends a shiver of fear through me. I know the Vikings don't fuck about. I know. I know.

"There is talk of a Japanese invasion, with their advance party of knotweed doing all sorts of things under the surface... under the surface... to demoralise Orkney gardeners."

They've got a long way to travel.

"But it is the transference of molecular energy that is giving me sleepless nights..."

"Transference of molecular energy?"

First Vikings, then this. It sounds all a bit Isaac Newton to me. I'm unprepared for any of this. I haven't a clue what he is on about. I'll nod.

"There is no escape from it."

I nod.

Sergeant Tulloch stands in the doorway and ushers me into the main office. It too is sparsely furnished. There is only a large table, just big enough for a telephone switchboard and space to write. There are no chairs. I feel this overwhelming feeling of emptiness, but at least there is the warmth of the sun shining through the window.

"Everything, from the snout of a pig to the ferry that brings visitors to Stromness from down south, consists of atoms and molecules. These molecules are invisible to the naked eye and have no loyalty.

"That's Stooshie over there." Sergeant Tulloch points to the police station's mouser. "These molecules and atoms are as loyal as this beautiful lady before you, who purrs when it suits her... Katy Strike-a-light Custard and Johnnycake Union Jack... her mum and dad... she comes from good stock. High tea, then she's off to see what tasty titbits are on offer elsewhere. No self doubt. She knows what she wants. She gets what she wants. Grandad served in the army during the war. You wouldn't know it by looking at her. Stooshie is half cat, half..."

All this has nothing to do with the theft of my watch, but I better humour him, especially since I want to be offered a tasty fry-up smothered in Daddies sauce.

"Does this mean that a farmer can have his molecules muddled up with those of a fox?"

"Not a fox, there have been no sightings yet of predatory Mister Fox in Orkney, but it is not beyond belief for a farmer to have his molecules muddled up with, say, those of a cow. There have been sightings of a cow delivering the morning pinta, and of a farmer being paraded round the auction ring at the farmers' mart by an Aberdeen Angus and – you will not believe this – not even reaching the reserve.

"It's these molecules moving around and upsetting the natural order of things. Our fire crew couldn't cope last Xmas. We had to get reinforcements from down south. It was the pantomime horse. We had to get the man out of the horse and the horse out of the man. I've already got enough on my plate.

"Men and women up and down the West Mainland enjoy the feel of a soft, comfy chair while drinking their cup of tea and reading their horoscope and studying the form for the runners and riders at Newmarket Races. There is no immorality in that. But it has been known for certain men of the parish to be particularly attracted to furniture that ladies favour. Men take pleasure in giving their arses a good wriggle. I think you get the gist. Do not be shocked at what I'm about to say.

"Furniture is not necessarily a force for the good. That's right. Furniture can encourage indecency. Both parties are at risk here. The lady can have her honour compromised by a man showing interest in her at such close and unnatural proximity, and the man runs the risk of melding into the seat itself, powerless to prevent his individuality disappearing into this inanimate object of carnal desire. The chair or sofa in question has to be removed before it goes through the community like a dose of salts."

I don't even nod here. I haven't a clue what he's going on about.

I open my mouth to say something, but the sergeant is in full flow. I look around for somewhere to sit. I look out the window. The sun is shining. The Big Sky is cloudless blue. There is no sign of wind. I've never known such a run of days when the weather has been so perfect.

"We are short-staffed here. We depend on receiving tip-offs from concerned members of the public about certain items of furniture that, in their eyes, have been receiving excessive male attention. Men are not attracted to sideboards and tables. Let's be clear. Not all furniture comes under our close scrutiny. The wardrobe, for example, can go about its business without having to look over its shoulders. From these tip-offs, we cross-check against the register of furniture that we hold for every household. It is a full-time job, keeping the register up to date.

"Do you now see, Mister... why we need more than *three* here? We are understaffed. Criminally so. Constable Mowat is my right-hand man." He lowers his voice. "You will observe in good time that Superintendent Glue walks with a slouch, and I fear that he has been irreparably affected by daily contact with such contaminated furniture." He takes out a handkerchief to blow his nose. I note that it is white and free of snot.

So at least I now have the names of the Three Wise Men of Stromness: Sergeant Tulloch, Constable Mowat and Superintendent Glue. He hasn't finished yet. The sergeant is still spelling things out. I am getting tired. Without anything for me to sit on, I want to lean against something. I quickly jerk back upright. There could be contamination anywhere, even in the construct of the walls.

I am here to report the theft of my watch.

"My hands are full with this furniture problem..." the sergeant extends both hands out wide "...and that's why today's Great Event has been such an unwelcome distraction."

The panel of the switchboard lights up. The sergeant puts his headphones on and scribbles something on his notepad. He says out loud, to no one in particular, "Man... missing. This is all I need. I haven't even the time to run my own business from these premises." The sergeant mops his brow. "And your name, please?"

I feel as I have now reached a tipping point.

There is nothing to stop me walking out of the police station. I am getting nowhere with this Sergeant Tulloch. I am a bit on my back foot, though. I have no name to give.

Captain Hurricane. Trigger. Olga Olkovski. Whoever I am, it doesn't matter. I have to see this through. To attach such importance to the theft of an inanimate object that I have never owned may seem like madness. It is not. We are talking about something that has always been missing in my life. The answer and the cure lies here in Orkney. That's why I have returned. To back out now would be like removing the tablecloth from a fully-laid table. It would remove my whole reason for being.

I suddenly feel very hungry. A fry-up graced with brown Daddies sauce, that's what I want. I will try and bring the conversation round to this, but I must just get a clear picture of the menace of furniture and the like.

Get him in a good mood.

"Just one more question. When you receive such tip-offs about furniture and you confirm that preventative action needs to be undertaken... if you get my drift... what happens then?"

"That is both clockwise and anti-clockwise in its perspicacity. As soon as the paperwork is complete, it falls on Constable Mowat, with the help of Friar Tuck Removals, to remove the item of furniture in question. It is, of course, not released from quarantine until the molecular relationship is restored to its equilibrium.

"Our stores are full to overflowing. If it were not for the usage of kirk hall premises, where would we be? Note that we have no chairs in this police station. We need to set the right example to the general public."

"How do you know when the furniture's 'equilibrium' means it's ready to be released back into the community?"

"That is a profound and perspicacious question, if I might say so, Mister… It is an exact science, Mister…"

I am not going to give him my name.

"Now I've clean forgotten Orkney hospitality. You look hungry. I certainly am. Come and join me in a good fry-up of bacon and eggs. I might be able to find some black pudding and sausages as well. We'll be eating standing up."

I smack my lips. "Have you any Daddies sauce?"

We go through to the back room, which has a large table and no chairs, and the sergeant prepares an excellent late breakfast and there is a bottle of Daddies sauce.

"I'll be Mither," I say.

There is an art to all this; the releasing of the sauce of the gods from a bottle with a narrow neck to it. I know my way round a bottle of brown Daddies sauce. *I know. I know.* Phut-phut. Out come dollops of delight.

Bliss. Plates empty. Sated.

All is washed down with a piping hot mug of strong tea. Poured from a pot. Not one teaspoonful but four. All brimming with Orkney goodness.

We have eaten.

We have belched together.

We have clinked mugs.

Standing up.

Both Sergeant Tulloch and myself are full and silent in our contentedness.

We return to the main room.

"I have come here to report the loss of my Ancient Egyptian titanium watch."

"A watch, you say? The watch must be entered in the police ledger… and your name?"

I do not know my name. I am not being wilful. Captain Hurricane. Trigger. Olga Olkovski. I will give him my date of birth, hopefully that will keep him happy.

"The 27th December 1935."

The sergeant holds my gaze.

"What is the number of your family tree?"

I look away. I do not understand such a question, but want to appear as helpful as possible, especially after such a feast. Many numbers came to mind. A tune does too.

Heigh-Ho. I add Snow White to her seven dwarves and arrive at that fine number, eight. Eight will do.

"Eight is the number of my family tree."

He sucks on the point of his pencil, carefully writes the number *8*.

I peek over his shoulder at the 'lost and found' and see that under the heading *Name* is a '?' symbol, and in the last column has been entered a 'T', presumably for 'theft'.

Sergeant Tulloch makes a loud noise and shuts the ledger. He looks at me thoughtfully.

I smile back. I do not want to be treated as a man who goes around plucking the eyebrows off a cow. To report something that never took place is not madness. I wait for him to break the silence.

"I am expecting a routine visit from an anonymous person who carries out inspections on behalf of the Scottish Police. Because you have no name, you must be that very same man, and it is a pleasure to welcome you. It is my duty to be of the utmost assistance in your visit, sir." He salutes me.

This is a turn of events, most unexpected. Something remarkable in nature has turned up. Things always turn up. Experience. It comes with age.

I nod. I try to suppress a smile. I have been given an unexpected Get Out of Jail Free card.

"Before you start your inspection, you need to be aware of the following. We are holding in our cells those yet to be sentenced but who, as sure as night follows day, are guilty. We give the term, 'being held in custody before trial', a singular island interpretation, here. Rest assured, due process is always followed in Orkney. Those kept in custody are treated with the utmost hospitality before appearing 'in front of the beak' and being found guilty.

"Space is at a premium here. We have six inmates tonight, separate cells. I will get Constable Mowat to accompany you during your rounds. By all means see the inmates – I mean those in custody– in whatever order you wish."

Sergeant Tulloch rings a bell. I am put in the good hands of Constable Mowat. Sergeant Tulloch has some final words for me to chew over.

"Furniture can be a force for bad as well as good."

I carry out my duties with the due authority invested in me, aided and abetted by this Constable Mowat.

Constable Mowat is the exact opposite in appearance to Sergeant Tulloch. Lean and wiry, he is a whippet to the sergeant's St Bernard. He is sparing in his words. When Constable Mowat speaks, white mucus makes a stringy connection between his lower and upper lip.

"You look tired. Here you are. In luck. Empty cell, used more as a guest room. Sergeant and myself charge top dollar, but bill sent direct to Scottish Police HQ. How many rashers for breakfast? The Daddies sauce? On the house. What name on invoice?"

"I can't give my name to you because my visit is of an anonymous, official nature; it is a spot check."

Quick as a flash.

"Of course. Should have thought. Get head down. Nothing better than a good night's shut-eye."

I nod and Constable Mowat takes me to the guest room. There is a bed to lie down on. It looks comfy.

On the wall is a large map of the world, and it correctly shows Orkney right in the centre of things. Orkney is given the due prominence it deserves. The USA, the Soviet Union and China look smaller.

I slip between the crisp white sheets. The mattress, though firm, is not unforgiving. The pillow is just right, of a perfect plumpness. The two hundred-watt light does not bother me. What a full and wondrous day it has been. The sun has been shining. The Big Sky has been cloudless blue. There has been no wind.

The light is switched off. The light switch must be on the outside. It is now dark. I hear a jangle of keys. A mortice lock, not one but two. I cannot get out of the cell, but on the other hand no one can get in. I am safe and secure.

My sleep is rich and deep. I sleep the sleep of the deserving and the untroubled. I know I will be meeting Gail in my dreams, here tonight. We will be together on a white, fluffy cloud.

The gift of Orkney keeps on giving. She is here in my dreams. We kiss passionately and she whispers in my ear, "Darling, I love you."

Darling, that must be me.

The mystery of my name has finally been solved.

Darling. Now, what finer name can there be?

CHAPTER 22

BATTENBERG

Early 1960s

There is a loud knock on the door. I see an eye through the peephole. I hear a jangle of keys. One mortice lock is released and then the other. The door is opened.

"Up you get. Here's towel for wash. Business to sort out before breakfast. Don't need me to tell you what time is. We're in for another sunny day." Constable Mowat, speaking in that Gatling-gun way of his, brings in the day. His manner towards me is friendly but correct.

I am on official Scottish Police HQ business; business which has required me to be incognito. VIP. To be given honoured-guest status.

The constable stands in the doorway. I can't help but notice that his policeman's trousers are too short in the leg. He gives me a sealed polythene washbag that includes a cake of soap, a miniature bottle of shampoo, a fingertip-tube of toothpaste with disposable toothbrush and a razor with a small tube of shaving cream. I wonder whether all this will be added to my bill.

I do my ablutions in the shower room. I have cut myself

on my right hand, but I don't know how or when I did so. I manage to stem the bleeding. There is a skylight in the corridor. The sunlight is streaming in.

"Here, quick slurp of tea, then we're off. No time for real McCoy this morning. Have to meet Superintendent Glue on the Brough of Birsay. We're late. Better make sure the blue light on roof of police car is at full pelt. Cut yourself on your right hand. Bandage, just the man. In you get. Join me at the front. Passing back through Birsay on my return. Can drop you off home…"

Neither policeman let on that they knew me. How then would they know where I used to live? I feel distinctly uncomfortable now. It might only be a short hop, step and jump before they realise that my official authority is an artifice.

"…Mind, no breakfast for you, but authorities still need to be billed. Sorry about the rush. Causeway to be crossed at Brough. Low tide. Must finish business before tides cut us off. Don't want to be marooned for twelve hours with just sheep for company. *Baa, baa, black sheep, have you any wool?* Complete waste of time."

I am delighted after all these years to be back on the Stromness-to-Birsay road. This is *my* road. On the right, the Loch of Stenness; a glimpse of a whole hand petering out to a mere fingertip of water. Then a few miles farther, this same A road plays the snake and on a sharp bend, takes a coily notion to the right. Best to say goodbye here. We turn off to keep straight on.

This B road is minor, but in designation only. Careful now. All this water on the left at the Loch, and then the Bay at Skaill. My road teases, but then plays the straight man and keeps a respectful distance from the coastline. The sea can be throwing a tantrum for all you care; you are out of its spit-and-fury reach.

It is *my* road. I have been up and down it over and over again. In person, in my youth. In my head, while away. I have never been the actual driver along my road. I am jealous of Constable Mowat. He is behind the wheel. It is unfair.

This road consists of one stretch after the other. A consecutive road. One stretch following another. A one-year-after-the-other road. All fitting in, seamless. A road often not wide enough to accommodate two-way traffic, but wider than a vehicle. A road of its time and place. An Orkney road.

Morning, afternoon, evening.

Spring, summer, autumn, winter.

Night, day.

A should-be-one-stretch-after-the-other road.

A should-be-road-that-you-can-join-at-any-point.

A road that sometimes is back to front.

A road that surprises.

The Loch. The Bay. Skaill. Two different types of water. Between the Loch and the Bay, Skara Brae. Home of the Ancients. A settlement of prehistoric wonder.

My road can be single-minded and single-track. We are, after all, only halfway along my road.

Orkney County Highways Department have created, every half-mile or so, hello-stops.

Hello. Passing places. Encouragement to be sociable, as if we needed it. *Hello.* Encouragement. Man-made bends in the road. Encouragement. Passing places. Good manners.

Hello. A Japanese tea ceremony of good manners. One car waits until the car travelling in the opposite direction has passed. A smile and a wave along my road – *After you, dear driver. No, please, it would be an honour, after you* – that is the Orkney way. *Hello. Hello.*

Yoo-hoo! I'm home. Come visit me.

It gives me no pleasure whatsoever to report that we have a stand-off between our police car and this tractor pulling a trailer. There's two of us and eight of them. We are pillars of authority. They are young women engaging in malarkey. All this nonsense next to a kirk of all places, Skaill Kirk.

What a right royal racket; them banging the side of the tractor with blocks of wood, shouting, blowing whistles. Too early in the day for such an Orkney ritual – the Blackening. Alcohol-fuelled and raring to go, the bride-to-be and her friends are wearing old clothes. The bride is covered in treacle, flour and feathers, and on her way to be tied to a statue for an hour or so.

Marriage will be a piece of cake after this.

"What is world coming to?" Constable Mowat curses, but pulls into the passing place, giving way. Not even biting when these young scallywags, female to boot, make disrespectful gestures towards us. No excuse. Our car is a police car. The constable is in uniform. I am carrying out inspections for the Scottish Police HQ. What indeed is the world coming to?

The Blackening goes on its way. Constable Mowat's manner is as before. Short and sharp. Authority in all its shortness and sharpness.

"Farmstead there. Used to be one of the largest egg enterprises on the West Mainland." The constable points out of the window, acting as a tour guide. He is pointing at *my bu*.

I bite my tongue. I know he is keen to show me something. Best to keep in with him.

Experience that only comes with time.

"Ever read *The Powers That Cannot Be*?" he asks casually. Oh, so casually.

To say that I am flabbergasted does no justice to the shock. Maybe he is talking about a different book altogether. Maybe I have misheard.

This is my book. This is my book. *Mine. I am entitled to call it mine.*

"You surely don't mean the Ancient Egyptians' *The Powers That Cannot Be, Volume I?'* My tone, casual and light. A throwaway feather of a tone.

"That very book." Constable Mowat is gruff and smug, as smug as smug can be.

How is it possible that my interest in all things Ancient Egyptian can be shared by this common-or-garden, lower-rank member of the Orkney Constabulary? I must not drop my guard here. I will play along with the man. No, I will take the initiative. I am the expert on this Ancient Egyptian work after all.

"We owe a lot to the Ancient Egyptians," says I.

"Ancient Egyptians, dogs' bollocks," says he.

"The Ancient Egyptians were around before the modern Egyptians," says I.

I know. I know.

"Ancient Egyptians... gentle, kind people, like us Orcadians, whereas Ancient Phoenicians, more like Shetland Islanders... whores," says he.

The constable certainly has a point worth considering here, but I am not prepared to lower the tone and we can't all be lucky enough to be born in Orkney.

"The Ancient Egyptians regarded the Ancient Phoenicians as equals and fellow travellers along life's highway," says I. A loftier tone should always be used when one discusses the Ancient Egyptians.

I know. I know.

He does not reply.

I have finessed him. Game, set and match.

He needs to be taught a lesson. I will put him back in his box.

"Constable, have you read the follow-up book to *The Powers That Cannot Be, Volume I*? It gives sound advice about matters of the heart. Now, what's... what's its name?" I ask, in a casual and friendly and tra-la-la way.

Constable Mowat doesn't reply.

I have him here. He clearly hasn't heard of *The Book With No Name*.

Put that in your pipe and smoke it.

Game, set, match and fucking tournament.

No further word passes between us for the rest of the journey.

Constable, you may be the one behind the wheel, but who is top dog now?

We arrive in Birsay. The tides have parted to reveal a clear and distinct causeway all the way from the Point on Birsay Mainland to the Brough. We can continue to drive all the way up to the lighthouse. We do so. We stop outside the lighthouse. There is a very large white van parked there.

With its dumpy base and yellow battlements, the lighthouse looks as if it's straight out of a *Beau Geste* film. This fort masquerades as a lighthouse. The French Foreign Legion in the Sahara Desert and their fort thousands of miles away from home. The fort belongs to someone else's empire.

So, this must be the 'business to sort out before breakfast' place.

The constable winds down the window and speaks to the driver of the van. "Aye, aye, Superintendent. Calm sort of day, don't you think?"

"It's a sun-is-shining sort of day. It's a Big Sky-is-cloudless-blue sort of day. It's a no-wind sort of day. And is this the man you were telling me about with the bandage on his right hand?" The superintendent looks me up and down. The constable winds up the window.

We get out of the police car and both the constable and I shake hands with the superintendent. I use my left hand to do so. It is the first time I have met him. He is carrying a fair bit of weight on him. The superintendent has clearly been in some altercation or other, as there is an impressive shiner over his right eye. He is grinning, which with his shiner gives him a sinister hit man sort of look.

"The bandage on the man's hand is only certain thing about him. Hasn't even told us his name. Comes to report theft of… Have you heard anything like it?" The constable is filling in the superintendent with details about my good self.

The two of them then go off to discuss something out of earshot. Superintendent Glue is laboured in his step. He isn't going to break any world records. I feel that they are going to be some time. I go to sit in the police car. It has a radio. It is not a hire car. I do not have to wait long. Through the front windscreen I see Superintendent Glue open the back doors of his white van. It's a no-wind sort of day. Constable Mowat makes a circular movement gesture with his right hand. I wind down the window on my side.

"Out."

I do not like his tone. Probably he's still smarting.

"Right, we only have a short amount of time so let's get down to work." Superintendent Glue grins. "Did you bring the white chalk? We need to put a cross against those pieces of furniture that are ready for return. Mister Whoever-You-Are, you will help us with the lifting."

Sergeant Tulloch is right about the superintendent. The molecules have got to him. With drooped head and shoulders, he walks with the freedom and liberality of an overweight crab sitting on an Ottoman chair. Movement in any direction is an agonisingly slow process. He looks to me like the sort of feller who's always walking against the wind.

I get out of the police car.

Close up, this lighthouse looks small. Where can all the furniture be stored? The superintendent locates the key from his bunch and in we go. The first door we come across, the superintendent takes a different key from his bunch.

I see straight away how very wrong I have been. There is a look of wonder on my face. Here is a storage facility to top all other storage facilities.

"A sight to behold! An Aladdin's cave full of things to sit on. Quarantined to protect the moral decency of West Mainland." The constable is back in tourist-guide mode, gushing in pride at the utilisation of, to all intents and purposes, an annex of Stromness Police Station.

This inner door is banged shut.

Will I ever see the sun again? Two against one. I must be on my guard here.

The constable and superintendent set to work. The superintendent holds a Geiger counter of a box in front of him. The dial has the numbers one to ten written on it, in Roman numerals. If the needle points to less than a III, the piece of furniture is given a white chalk mark and therefore deemed safe to return to its owner. Straightforward, not complicated. Orkney.

They could be playing with me, deliberately creating a false sense of security, waiting for the right moment.

"That's a I, that's a II. They're ready. They can go. I'll mark the rocking chair with a cross. Where's my chalk?" The superintendent is grinning. "Right, you, Mister Whoever-You-Are, help me lift this one into the van. This one's still high at a VI. It's not ready yet. Another few weeks and it'll have a lower count.

"Mister With-No-Name. Here. You're still a young man. I bet you wouldn't be seen dead sitting in one of these oldie rocking chairs. This is for you. A bright-coloured chair. Orange. Now that's the modern colour. I bet them lovable moptops from that fine English city of Liverpool, them Beatles, have at least one of these modern chairs in their bu. We'll take it." The superintendent presents it to me, cod-formal.

I do not like his tone towards me.

After less than ten minutes, we have finished. The items of furniture with crosses on them are deposited just outside the lighthouse. Constable Mowat and myself have done almost all of the heavy lifting. The superintendent locks both inner and outer doors with his bunch of keys.

We must have removed ten items of furniture from the store. I could have sworn, though, that only half have chalked crosses against them. It's left to Constable Mowat and myself to carry all the furniture to the very large white van. It is downhill, mind. All ten items are loaded. The Superintendent's van is now chock-a-block-full. I slam the back doors shut.

I am aware we don't want to be stuck on the Brough of Birsay. We are working against the clock. The waters are making their pincer movement. Back to the police car. The constable starts the engine.

The superintendent, with crablike movement, takes much longer to get to the van. We watch him through the windscreen. *Come on. Hurry up.* The superintendent gets in. Then he gets out. He walks in his distinctive way back to the lighthouse. He disappears inside.

What's he up to?

The superintendent emerges a few minutes later. The constable rolls down his car window and shouts out to him; rank and status forgotten. The superintendent shouts for him to come over, just the constable.

Something's up.

The constable leaves the car running. I change seats. If I were to drive off now, that would play into their hands.

I have never been the actual driver along my road.

I sit in the driver's seat, waiting for the constable's return, my fingers drumming on the dashboard.

The superintendent and the constable talk to each other for some time. I am being pointed at.

I am entertainment. I do not like that.

The sea is starting to reclaim the causeway, which is our one and only return route to the Birsay headland.

The constable comes back. Fixed grin on his face. Says nothing. He gets in the car. We wait for the superintendent to do likewise. Takes ages for him to do so. He beep-beeps. We beep-beep. Off we go, a two-vehicle convoy, the superintendent's white van leading the way. First to arrive. First to leave.

We drive back over the causeway to Birsay, the gateway to the glorious West Mainland. The police-car light on top is blue flashing away. We are starring in the films. The constable and I are pretendy-playing at providing security for a gold bullion van. At the Stromness turn-off, we part company and the superintendent's white van continues on the Kirkwall road.

"I was pleased to be of service,"

No answer.

"Two pair of hands are better than one." I try again.

Still no joy.

"An extra pair of hands is without doubt as useful as a loofah for a cow, but I have no clarity as to the *raison d'être* behind my *actus reus*. An explanation, like a fine dram, would go down well." I am hoping that by being more expansive, I can draw him out.

"One question. That's all," the constable barks at me. He pulls into a passing bay, leaves the engine running. He certainly is still licking his wounds over all things Ancient Egyptian.

More than a frisson here. I must have really put his nose out of place with my superior knowledge of all things Ancient Egyptian.

"I think I understand why we put crosses on the three-piece suite and the comfy chair and the rocking chair and the easy chair, and these have all been loaded onto the superintendent's van to be returned to their previous owners. Loading furniture that hasn't got the white chalked crosses, though..." I don't need to spell it out. There is something very fishy going on.

"Us policemen in Orkney earn a wage, a living wage but not a special wage. Cannot afford basics. Have to forego the pleasures of life: second lump of sugar in tea; extra Tunnock's chocolate biscuit for morning break; slice of that pink-and-yellow squared cake, the Battenberg, every day. Not asking for much in life. Policemen's lot, not an easy one."

I nod. *Want to show I'm hanging on his every word. Watch his hands.*

"The Battenberg is a fine, royal cake: full of goodness and no adjectives. The pinkness comes from rare, partially ripened grapes from the vineyards of Egypt, and the yellow comes from... the goodness of the sun." I am keen to show that I too love the Battenberg cake.

He has raised his fists.

"The three of us have an arrangement with Whatever You Want. They sell anything and everything. Crockery, crash helmets, canoes, carpets..." He pauses as if he has lost his train of thought. "And chairs... chairs. We supply the chairs and indeed sofas to Whatever You Want. Do you have a problem with that?"

He strikes a boxer pose.

"So you supply Whatever You Want with confiscated chairs and sofas from your quarantine store on the Brough of Birsay?" This is remarkable. Did I hear right?

"Whatever You Want proud to be helping Police Charity. They store items in old hangar at Hatston, outskirts of Kirkwall. Doing nothing wrong. Furniture we donate has the words *Police Approved* on the sticker. No one's taken in. Public know what they're buying. All above board."

"What happens if the actual owners were to find out where their furniture has ended up?"

"I said one question. You've asked the one question. No more." He jabs his finger at the windscreen. He is certainly not speaking in a friendly manner now. "Whatever You Want also sells handcuffs. You've been warned."

We move off. The return leg of the Stromness-to-Birsay road.

There's my bu, my home, nearer to Marwick Head than the Broch. I am looking at it from the top road.

He does not drop me off, as he said he would. He does not drop me off.

I say nothing, thinking about my late breakfast treat of a fry-up back at the police station. The sun is shining. The Big Sky is cloudless blue. There is no wind.

The police radio is switched off. Even though the atmosphere between us has become decidedly frosty, I am happy with life. I will enjoy that extra rasher smothered in Daddies sauce, thank the police for their hospitality and make my way home on foot. It will only be a few hours' stroll. I need the exercise.

Constable Mowat is whistling Perry Como's *Magic Moments*. I join in. A duet. Reconciliation. We are friends again. As soon as the tune is finished, I will engage the constable in sweet and open-hearted conversation and return to our shared passion.

Experience comes with age.

"Constable Mowat, the Battenberg is the king and queen of

all cakes, but don't you think for Orkney the Madeira is gold top? The Madeira has a yellowy goodness about it, without being showy. It is the most understated of cakes. Sumptuous."

Silence.

A final gambit. "Have you ever tried Black Forest gateau, with its cream and chocolate and cherries? Scrumptious."

Frosty silence. And that is that.

We pull into the police station. We get out of the police car. *It is not a hire car.* I have tried my best. At least a fry-up beckons. With rashers and Daddies sauce and other delights on the plate before me, I will be in no need of conversation.

There have been no more time-shifts. I cannot find the right words to express how they unnerve me. Keeping me on my toes is one thing; experiencing something so inexplicable is another. It strips me to the raw. It makes me question who I am.

I am in the police station car park.

I am about to go in.

Side, not main entrance.

The door will make a 'ding-a-ling, ding-a-ling' ringing sound when I do so.

I know. I know.

CHAPTER 23

ONE-EYED LAWYER

Early 1960s

"Constable, a word please." Sergeant Tulloch whispers something in Constable Mowat's ear.

They then walk over and stand either side of me. Sergeant Tulloch to my left. Constable Mowat to my right.

I can tell by the looks on their faces that something is up. I hope it isn't bad news.

I am distracted. Pleasantly so. Taking in the fresh Orkney air and the aroma of fried bacon and pork sausage; a grand get-together of molecules assailing the nostrils. Bliss. After the cooked breakfast, a little shut-eye. The sheets crisp, the pillow plump, the sleep refreshing. Then, refreshed, a stroll back along my favourite road. Homeward bound. I have it all worked out. The sun is shining. The sky is cloudless blue. There is no wind.

"A body has been found in the lighthouse on the Brough of Birsay. It has been there for some time. Stab-marks on the corpse. Stab-marks, I say. The corpse is charred in places. Burnt. Murder most foul." Sergeant Tulloch comes straight to the point.

I am respectful. I nod in sympathy on hearing of this heinous crime, then shrug my shoulders. Sad to hear of this calumny, but there we are. These things do happen, but fortunately only once in a lifetime. That smell of pork sausage...

"The body has been identified. A Mister Flett from the parish of Birsay."

Mister Flett. I have heard that name before.

Mister Flett. It means something to me.

I close my eyes. *Where is this missing link? I am struggling here.*

Mister Flett. Yes. No. Elusive, like a butterfly.

"Take this man down to the cells." Sergeant Tulloch is referring to me.

This is a most unexpected turn of events. I hear a voice. This voice is a voice I do not recognise. I cannot put a name to this inner voice.

Well, my friend. Wasn't that the plan all along? Both you and Ephraim planned to kill Mister Flett. Mister Flett's dead body has been discovered. Where's the surprise?

I don't know what you're talking about.

I am to be led down to the cells, cells I visited only yesterday in an official capacity. Sergeant Tulloch tells me why I am the prime suspect. He has a strong case.

"All evidence leads to a man who goes by the name of Billy Fury being the guilty party. He is the leader of All the Right-Leg-Shakers on the West Mainland and has a record as long as his arm. He has been at large for many a year. However, the level of proof needed to nail him is higher than a cow can jump over a gate. You being a person without a name, it's much easier for us to... I'm sure you understand."

I nod.

"You have provided us with a ready-made solution. You have had ample opportunity to identify yourself. Because you have no name, we can hurry this one through without the higher authorities raising a cow's eyebrow."

"I was born on 27th December 1935. Work it out for yourself." I am hoping that by giving them a bit about myself I can delay my fate.

"Case closed. It is too late now. Too late to muddy the waters by implicating and naming others. Case closed. No one is going to miss someone who has no name."

I nod. I cannot disagree with Sergeant Tulloch's logic.

"Our high conviction rate is a matter of pride. We are used as best practice. When the storms make Orkney well-nigh impossible to reach, full authority is vested in us to fast-track any case. Keeps things simple."

I nod.

"Orkney has unique powers." Constable Mowat's mouth is slightly open. I am fascinated by the stringy white mucus that links his lower and upper lip.

Sergeant Tulloch continues. "A judge, jury and trial is unnecessary. This is an open-and-shut case. Mister Flett was murdered. We have our man. You are he; whoever you are. Have you anything to say?"

"I demand the right to see a lawyer."

"Granted. The lawyer will be with you after I've suppered the cat. The hanging will take place the day after tomorrow. Wednesday, noon, twelve o'clock, lunchtime. Carpe diem. Constable, I will say this to you for the final time: take this man down to the cells. I do like a juicy steak after a hanging."

"Where does that leave me?"

Go away.

"Down you go. Any nonsense, handcuffs." Constable Mowat is to the point.

No guest room, this. It hasn't been cleaned for some time. The bedding is soiled and the mattress lumpy. I shut my eyes. No

Dreamland for me. It is the wrong time of day for the gift of sleep. My right leg does not keep still. The jangle of keys, the sound of the mortice lock and my cell door is locked. The two-hundred-watt bulb is full on. I am going to swing. With the smell of sausages and bacon and eggs wafting in from God knows where, my misery is complete.

Sometime later, I don't know how much later, the peephole moves. The door is opened.

"Good news. Lawyer. Waiting for you. Interview room. Now. Talk until cows come home. Utmost confidentiality. Will bring mugs of piping hot tea and London macaroon biscuits. Lawyer's name... no, in providing name you've been stubborn as mule. Lawyer. Best in Orkney. All you need to know."

I am led to the interview room.

"This is... accused. Reported theft. Not furniture." Constable Mowat shrugs. "This is the famous one-eyed lawyer. Only one good eye and one tongue. His eye is as good as his tongue. His tongue is so good, sees better than most men with two eyes. He's from Finstown. Will spell it. F-i-n-s-t-o-w-n."

Constable Mowat has made his introductions, but does not leave us to it. He stands in the far corner, out of earshot, a legal fiction.

"I am a busy person. My name is Horace Batchelor and you will swing unless you can come up with an alibi."

He hasn't wasted any time with niceties.

"How can I provide an alibi when the police won't tell me the time of the murder?"

The one-eyed lawyer is having none of that. "Why should they give out such information to someone who will not provide their name? That is their line of thinking. I'm your lawyer. Give *me* your name."

Captain Hurricane, Trigger or Olga Olkovski? Go away.

"How can I help if you refuse to cooperate?" The one-eyed lawyer looks at me long and hard. "Look, I'll try to get a message through to someone who may be of help." He opens his briefcase and takes out a football coupon.

"I am an agent for Vernons, a football pools company from the 'lovable moptops' city of Liverpool. Go on, put a cross against ten teams on this coupon and if you get eight draws and twenty-four points, you will win a small fortune. The entry is for next Saturday. I get a small commission on every pound collected. If you're not in, you can't win!"

These words do not cheer me up in the slightest. Today is Monday. I am to be executed on Wednesday. I have only one full day left to live. Even if I were to win the jackpot... I stroke my neck instinctively.

Mister Horace Batchelor does not give up easily. "Give me the names of your next of kin. I will guarantee that each receives an equal share of your pools winnings."

I say nothing.

"Have you drawn up a will?"

"No, I have not." I spit out these words.

"Given the way things are going for you, you should. I don't charge a flat fee up front, just five per cent of your estate."

I nod.

"And your name...?"

I should be at peace... but that gnawing away... no certainties as to why I am here, who I am and the way I look... *Why. Who. The way.*

"My visit has been a complete and utter... Without a name, Scottish Police HQ will not accept my invoice. I have tatties to sow in the ground and a new Elvis 45 to listen to on my radiogram. Due to your lack of cooperation, I earn no fee. A complete and utter..."

Legal niceties have been carried out. The guilty has seen his lawyer.

I am led back to the cells, now handcuffed.

I am going to swing on the scaffold on Wednesday morning, the day after tomorrow.

It's not looking good for me, is it? Experience can only get you so far in life.

CHAPTER 24

A GHOST OF A MEMORY

Early 1960s

Tuesday morning, a tossing and turning of a night. Constable Mowat escorts me to the shower block. The water is cold. I am led back to my cell. No pleasantries exchanged. The breakfast – well, you can be the judge. Cold toast, just the one slice. Something congealed and off-yellow, for the spreading of. The tea is hot and wet.

Soon after, Constable Mowat comes a-calling. He takes me to a different room than before.

The room is empty in its largeness. One door in, same door out. Jingle-jangle of keys. I am left to it. The room is bare, just two chairs stacked one on top of the other. Concrete floor. A whiff of dampness. The walls recently whitewashed, but black mould is as black mould does. No windows, but a large mirror on one of the walls. You can't look out, but you can look at yourself. You hardly notice that the light is on.

Do not play their game. See what happens.

I remain standing up, hogging the door. I take the opportunity to glance at the mirror. Thank goodness I am still the same age.

"Twenty-seven years old," I shout out.

Sergeant Tulloch enters the room. He then faces the door, bending down. He collects the bits and bobs that he left in the doorway. Both hands needed for the unlocking of.

He does not close the door behind him.

The sergeant sees the stacked chairs. There are just two chairs, in chair wedlock. You cannot separate the yolk from the egg using just the one hand. Both hands needed.

I know everything there is to be known about eggs.

So down go the bits and bobs that the sergeant has just picked up.

The door still open.

He carries both chairs to the centre of the room. They are not placed side by side. The chairs are facing each other. He knows he has to go back to the doorway to collect the just-put-down items. The sergeant hesitates. He is stroking his chin.

There is an order to chairs as there is to a stretch of road. The door remains open.

Bits and bobs collected, the sergeant goes straight for the chair facing the mirror on the wall. I take this as my cue to sit down also. We are both sitting down. I have no preference. His choice of one over the other is fine by me.

I am facing the open door. My back is to the wall mirror.

"Let's have a wee friendly chat, like next-door neighbours over the hedge." The sergeant is sizing me up. I watch him stroke the back of his ear. No roll-your-own there.

"We don't know what your name is, but we know what you've done. You are now being formally charged with the murder of Mister Flett, late of Birsay. Anything to add to what you told us yesterday?"

That would not be difficult. A whiff of sarcasm?

I nod.

"Put your right index finger like so on this inky pad." He points to one of the bits and bobs on the floor. "Then press like so on the sheet of paper next to the pad. Your thumb, if you please."

I do as I am told, bending so far forward that I almost fall out of my chair.

There is a box camera on the floor, next to the ink pad and paper. The sergeant looks intently first at me and then at a point in the distance. I have no idea what he is looking at.

Constable Mowat rushes in through the open door.

"Great danger. Even inside sanctity of the police station. Furniture not safe from radon gas of impropriety." The constable's gaze takes in chairs and occupants over and over again. A fast tick-tock, almost possessed. The constable is in a state of agitation.

The door remains open.

"Sergeant... tip-off from a reliable source... both chairs must be quarantined... for our own and West Mainland's good..." The constable is readying himself.

The sergeant stands up. I follow suit. He is not best pleased. Points to the insignia on his upper sleeve. Glares at the constable. Does not need to say anything to Constable Mowat. Points to the three chevrons on his upper sleeve.

I have a status as well, even though I am about to swing. Sonny Jim, I am an inspector from Scottish Police HQ, incognito. Do not forget that!

The constable is not deterred. He tries to grab both our chairs, in one fell swoop. I wait to see what the sergeant does. I am being hanged for murder. I do not want a secondary charge of assaulting a police constable to appear on my curriculum vitae. This is the second stand-off that I have experienced in twenty-four hours. Three chevrons against one epaulette. There can only be one winner here.

The door is open. Shall I make a run for it?

The constable plays the wounded party. Goes back to where he came from, empty-handed. Leaves the sergeant and myself to continue chewing the fat.

"In Orkney, furniture is the real McCoy of bad bastardy. What passes as criminality is just a run-of-the-mill bawlin' baby of a nuisance." He moves his chair closer to me. "Stacking chairs is like a knife through butter. It's destroying our community. The same chair is in use by different groups every night of week. If it isn't the Women's Institute in Stenness one night, up it pops in a different village hall used by praise-the-Lord Esperanto converts. As for the Orkney-Norway Friendship Society... it can't bear thinking about.

"After these meetings, chairs get stacked. One on top of the other. You don't know who's been on top of whom. Inviting immorality. The kirk is doing its best to alert folk. I tell you, it's a real worry. I see no answer to it all. Where will it all end? Where will it all end?" Sergeant Tulloch is drowning under the enormity of it all, seeking relief in the biting of his knuckle. He is at the end of his tether.

I feel sorry for him. I pat down my trouser pocket. My white handkerchief is there. If it is free of snot, I'll happily pass it over to the sergeant for a good blow.

Sergeant Tulloch pulls himself together. "And now, back to the matter in hand. We have your fingerprints, so there is just the question of a photograph on the charge sheet." He picks up the box camera from the floor – his Kodak Brownie.

If this is going to be the last image of myself, I would like posterity to remember me as a happy-go-lucky chap. Mouth open, I face the sergeant with the broadest of smiles.

"How dare you! Turn around. Face the mirror," he barks at me. "Turn around. Turn the chair around, I say. Face the mirror on the wall behind you. Do not look at me. Do not dare look at me. Keep still. If you disobey me, you will swing today, not tomorrow."

Sergeant Tulloch has, like his colleague, become most contrary.

I do as I am told. I turn around and face the mirror.

Mister Flett? You remember now. The neck. Some baler twine. No time to put up a struggle. No time even to turn around. His body limp. Knife in my pocket.

The sergeant stands up and goes outside. He shuts the door behind him. I am on my own.

There is a loud click and a sudden change of light. Pure white light refracts into a kaleidoscope of colours, pulsating and increasing in intensity. I am at one moment outside the rainbow and the next inside the rainbow; the colours still bleeding into each other.

As the pure white light refracts and disperses, air is being sucked out of the room.

I am in a vacuum.

Cannot breathe.

Fighting for breath.

Suffocating.

Drowning.

The colours became more and more vivid, no hint of whiteness now. A crackle of electricity. The kaleidoscope of colours takes shape and form. Boundaries are established. The rainbow is an archway, pulsating red and orange, indigo and violet and… I am near to breaking point.

A loud crackle. An image of my face seared onto mirrored glass. The ordeal is over, everything now back to how it was. Stillness. I wish it could have taken that extra step. Everything is now back to how it was, but *not* back to how I want it to be.

It crosses my mind that if this is death, it will be a rich experience indeed. It will be the tomorrow coming before the yesterday and the present looking both ways at once.

Calmness. I have nothing to fear when the noose is put round my neck. Reassuring.

I hear footsteps. It must be the sergeant re-entering the room.

"Good, you can turn around now. Out of the chair. Take a step to one side. I can now take your photo from the image that's seared onto the mirror. Like so." The shutter of his Kodak box camera opens and the picture is duly taken.

"It is bad luck for all involved to take a direct photograph of a person before their death. The Ancient Egyptians always believed that if you do so, you are stealing their soul. Have you ever read a book called *The Powers That Cannot Be, Volume I?*"

"*The Powers That Cannot Be* is revelatory, but a mere taster for *The Book With No Name*," I say, quick as a flash. I have retained my composure even though he is challenging me here on home ground. I am pre-eminent in all things Ancient Egyptian, but in truth the fight has gone out of me.

The sergeant looks at me, saying nothing.

I nod.

"I have good news for you."

I nod.

"In keeping with Orcadian hospitality, it is our wish to make sure that the last day of your life is made as comfortable as possible. You will be granted more fitting accommodation... the guest room is yours once again." He emphasises the words 'guest room'.

"We will be at your beck and call. You will have the best of tea, food and drink. We'll share a smoke." The sergeant, all conspiratorial. "A card table with fold-up chairs is provided for a friendly game of cards. You will even have a comfy chair for your exclusive felicitation." This is privilege indeed.

I nod.

No certainties as to why I am here, who I am and the way I look.

"May I be permitted one small favour?"

"You have only to ask."

"Before I enjoy the delights of the guest room, would it be possible to pay a quick visit to the exercise yard, so that I can on my last day on earth go outside and breathe in our freshest of fresh air?"

"Of course, Constable Mowat will accompany you."

"Thank you. I will only need a minute or two."

On my last day, I want to see the sun shining.

On my last day, the cloudless blue sky.

On my last day, the special Orkney air, wind fresh.

"You will have your moment of private contemplation."

Sergeant Tulloch starts to gather together the items that he brought with him.

I help. It is the least I can do.

"Oh, I nearly forgot. Constable Mowat will be taking you on a wee treat. He'll be showing you what only the few ever get to see. Is there anything else?"

"I could murder... a full Scottish breakfast with bacon, rashers, runny eggs and black pudding."

"I will get Constable Mowat to serve you such a feast, and the black pudding will be of a blackness blacker than you have ever put knife and fork to." Sergeant Tulloch is smiling broadly now, hands extended wide, unlimited in friendship. "We have two unopened special reserve bottles of Daddies sauce, kept back for special occasions. One is their vigorous brown-sauce number; the other is their tomato ketchup vintage 1937, should that be your flavour of choice. Both will do justice to the full Orkney fry-up. Daddies never lets you down. Tell you what, we'll throw in a lit candle or two. A take-a-deep-breath-and-blow-out-the-candles full Orkney.

"We like to put a new take on The Day. It will be a chocolate box of a day. A celebration. A new beginning."

236

I nod.

The cooked breakfast is brought to the guest room, eaten sitting down. Right tasty. I belch. I make a wish while blowing out the candles. I do not drop my guard here.

"Right, you've eaten. No time to waste. The sergeant has put me in the picture. We'll head off," the constable says, all smiles.

"A minute or two in the yard is all I need." I am pleased that the sergeant has kept his word.

But we don't go outside. Sergeant Tulloch – so much for his word.

Him an adult.

Down a long flight of stairs. The constable first. I am even more determined to keep him in full view at all times.

There are so many steps in this flight of stairs, there could be one for each day of the year.

Him in front. I have this irresistible urge to push the constable in the back and make a run for it.

I have been here before, and it did not end well for me.

I quickly dismiss that memory as one belonging to someone else.

A memory detached and lost, looking for its home.

A ghost of a memory.

CHAPTER 25

THE WIZARD OF OZ
LIFE-AFFIRMING

Early 1960s

Ground level. The walkway is a car-width wide. At least that fact is clear. As for height, you might as well be looking at the Big Sky. I see a speck in the distance; impossible to judge how far ahead. Impossible to make out what it is. Lined up on both sides of the walkway are neatly-stacked sets of chairs. Each set of chairs is labelled. I have never seen so many chairs in my life.

The walkway is dimly lit. I must be in the main furniture repository for Stromness Police Station. Underground. The Brough of Birsay lighthouse is a mere overspill. Perhaps that speck in the distance is a three-piece suite. You never know what you may find underground in Orkney. It could be something much, much older.

"Sprinkler system overhead for this section. Twice daily. Mainly used on chairs in store. Prevents overfamiliarity. Cold water works wonders. Dampens things down." Constable Mowat, once again the tour guide. Constable Mowat setting a fine pace.

We then enter a part of the walkway that is unlit. Maybe I will be 'disappeared' in this blackness. I can just about see the outline of Constable Mowat. He stops. It is the end for me.

This is it. I am to enter the Pearly Gates a day early. Mind the Pearly Gates are up above, not down below.

We continue our walk. All my senses seem speeded up. On overdrive. Rat-a-tat-tat.

Far in the distance now, I see a pinhole of light. My attention moves from the speck. I look ahead. I am not going to look down at the floor. I do not want a black cat to cross my path.

Darkness scrambles the senses.

Darkness. Opening hours for Dreamland.

Darkness.

We are side by side as we walk into the light. I can see the constable's face again. He grins. I look for that white mucus thread between his lower and upper lip. I can see it. I can see it. Stringy.

Constable Mowat takes a piece of paper out of his back pocket. There are many numbers on this piece of paper. He puts on his spectacles. Torchlight. Easier.

"0809, 0811, 0825, 0852," the constable recites in a clear, Sabbath-pulpit voice.

"0-8-0-9, 0-8-1-1, 0-8-2-5, 0-8-5-2.

"0903, 0905, 0919, 0946.

"1109, 1111, 1125, 1152.

"1209, 1224, 1242, 1252."

Constable Mowat takes a deep breath. He is rattling through these numbers. More to come, I'm sure.

"1926, 1941, 1953, 2007, 2009.

"2020, 2035, 2047, 2101, 2103.

"2226, 2241, 2253, 2307.

"2336, 2351, 2409."

Two-four-zero-nine is the last of the numbers read out.

Constable Mowat returns the piece of paper to his back pocket. No explanation of or context to these figures is provided.

I haven't said anything for a while. I am still trying to make sense of today's events; a day of such richness. My last full twenty-four hours on this earth. Constable Mowat can kill me at any moment. I know there will be another twist and turn to this.

I know. I know.

Magic Moments. Magic Moments. Magic Moments.

I whistle the tune. Constable Mowat joins in. Me first this time. Me whistling. Nervousness. Him joining in. Why?

"The numbers that you have just read out are music to my ears. It has the rhythm of *The Wizard of Oz* about it." I need the reassurance of a human voice. Any will do.

"Glad you think so. Darkest moments. Perry Como. Always there for us. Coming into the light. Uplifting. *The Wizard of Oz*. Life-affirming rhythm. Seed of life in search of an egg. Always."

Constable Mowat fills the silence. It is his turn to start us off. No toe-tapper, more of a Sunday-morning celestial air to it this time. Whistling, I join in. Our whistling could be mistaken for birdie song. *Somewhere Over the Rainbow.*

Rainbow. Yoo-hoo! I'm home.

A whooshing sound overhead, louder and louder. I look up. I can just about make out, in the infinite up there, a there-and-back straight man of a single rail track. All aboard, off to the future. All aboard, time for the return.

'Woo-woo', goes the train whistle. 'Woo-woo.'

'Coo-coo. Coo-coo.'

A model train set of a single rail track. Doesn't have to be one long piece from start to finish. Bitefuls of track will do. All the pieces will fit. In any order. Male/female. Female/male. Female/female. Male/male. A one-four-three-two-five of a track.

'Woo-woo. Woo-woo.'

'Coo-coo. Coo-coo'.

Above the rail lies a power cable, which crackles and shorts and lets off sparks.

Below the rail hangs a large Perspex tube inside which are small, orange-coloured cylinders. These cylinders are upside down and on the move. Rolling stock which are in a state of perpetual motion but look stationary, waiting for permission to move. One part of you waiting for the other part to catch up.

The small orange cylinder carts, to be filled and then emptied, emptied and filled up again, and so on and so on and so on. I am looking upwards at my life. Filled and full. Emptied and empty. Continuous. Infinite.

Never always full.

Never always empty.

Never completely satisfying.

Never completely disappointing.

Never one thing nor the other.

What is inside these carts? I am soon to find out.

I have looked upwards for some time now.

I have always taken my neck for granted.

Isn't the neck a marvellous construct that enables you to turn and flex your head fully to the left and fully to the right but not all the way round!

Fuck off.

"Constable Mowat, what is inside these orange cylinders?"

"Full of files containing confidential information about furniture movements. Duty-bound to open a file for each episode. Even for false or malicious sightings."

I can hear the sound of hammering from outside.

We have come to a large, steel-reinforced vault door. We can go no further. This must be the end of the walkway. On the front of the vault door is a combination lock, as well as a sturdy-looking lever. It is not a door to disrespect. It is an MGM sort of film door, all that gold bullion in a tightly-packed safe room and a bank heist in the offing.

"This is where the numbers come in handy. Important to listen. Click all-important. Must concentrate. Don't interrupt me. Over there... take a seat... I'll let you know when the combination has been cracked."

Ear to the tumbler on the door, Constable Mowat works his way through the numbers.

"0809. 0-8-0-9. Zero clicks clockwise. Eight clicks anti-clockwise. Zero clicks clockwise. Nine clicks anti-clockwise.

"0811. 0-8-1-1. Zero clicks clockwise. Eight clicks anti-clockwise. One click clockwise. One click anti-clockwise."

There is nothing I can do to help.

I have already worked out that the numbers, in their compactness and pattern and solidity, are of the nature of a timetable. I have only got that far.

Conveniently positioned just to the left of the steel safe door is a settee. The settee is all on its own, as I truly am at this stage of my soon-to-be ended life. There is a tacit recognition between the settee and me that we need each other's company. It has various Ancient Egyptian symbols etched upon it. I ease myself into the settee, a melding together.

I am able to shut out all extraneous sounds. There is a steady drip-drip of numbers coming from the constable. A monastic quality in his intoning.

"1125. 1-1-2-5. One click clockwise, one click anti-clockwise, two clicks clockwise, five clicks anti-clockwise."

It is no surprise that my eyes become heavier and heavier. I close them. There in front of me is a chamber full of large, pink, fluffy cushions and pink birthday balloons. I see myself in this chamber and I am asleep on a settee, dreaming that I am in another chamber full of large, pink, fluffy cushions and pink birthday balloons, enjoying the pinkness of it all and in this other chamber I am asleep, and in my dreams...

"2409. 2-4-0-9. Two clicks... We're nearly there. Wake up, Sleeping Beauty. Wake up."

Shaken vigorously by the shoulders. I do not want to wake up. It requires a determined effort to get out of the settee. The settee is reluctant to see me go. We have been very relaxed and comfortable in each other's company.

The steel door is heavy. Constable Mowat cannot open it in one go. He is straining to open it. It opens inwards. I help him.

A light of sorts, from the 'other side'. A murkiness. Brighter than before, but that's not saying much.

A wall of sound, a throbbing, getting louder and louder; all coming from the 'other side'. No one thing recognisable to my ears. A babel of tongues.

There to meet us is Superintendent Glue. I last saw him on the Broch of Birsay.

"Aye, aye. Do you hear me? Aye, aye." The superintendent has to shout to be heard.

"Superintendent Glue, here is our friend again." Constable Mowat points to me. The superintendent, staying put on his side of the vault door, extends his right hand over the divide, truncheon gripped in the other.

I stay where I am. I hesitantly move my head forward and peer into this 'other side'.

Don't do anything unless you have to. That's experience. It'll come.

The contrast between over here and over there cannot be more pronounced. The superintendent's world has a low-hanging layer of mist between sky and earth. There is a mustiness in the air. It is abattoir-noisy. I neither like the look nor the sound of it.

A wall of sound, a throbbing, getting louder and louder; all coming from the 'other side'. A babel of tongues, voices from my past, inside my head, now released. Phrases chopped up. The soup. The main course. The dessert. All in one big tureen. Lid on. Lid off. These voices have served their time. They have never been my friends.

Yoo-hoo! The Battenberg is a fine royal cake. Hello, boychik. Time flies, my treasure, time flies. Good to see you again. I'm an agent for Vernons. I'm home. Before leaving, I tie the piano owner up. All the way from across the Atlantic, not bad for a Lancashire lass. Full of goodness and no adjectives. Otherwise you will never know when you have arrived. In Orkney, always make sure you know where you are going. Yoo-hoo!

I cannot put the lid back on. I cannot.

"I'll wait here for your return. Superintendent Glue will look after you now."

Who says I'm going?

My hand goes to my pocket to find some loose change. I should give him something as a thank-you. The constable has led me from one world to the next. I feared the worst. Maybe he's not such a bad feller after all. My pockets are empty, though. No jingle-jangle of coins to pay this particular ferryman.

I hesitate. A reluctance to take that final step.

Ephraim has taken me by the scruff of the neck and the seat of my trousers and thrown me through the door that the Devil has deliberately left open.

I notice something. My shoelaces are undone. I bend down to tie them up. A tremendous kick to my backside. My mind is made up for me.

The steel door shuts behind me.

Clang.

Clang.

Ding-a-ling.

Ding-a-ling.

CHAPTER 26

THE WINNER OF THE 3.30

Timeless

Ding-a-ling.

"Welcome, my friend. Welcome. It's good to see you again. I must first ask you to step on these scales."

I have no problem with this. After all, I have yet to have my weight taken.

"Twelve stone eight pounds," the superintendent shouts above the hubbub. He is grinning.

There are stalls as far as the eye can see. Some modest as a trestle table; others as elaborate as a Harrods inside a canvas wrap, strong enough to resist even the strongest of a north-westerly.

No distinctive themed areas here. No segregation. No aristocracy in the siting of the stalls. No A to Z. 'Higgledy-piggledy' best describes the randomness of it all. You can find just about anything here. *Whatever you want.*

There is a stall selling gold bullion next to a stall selling bicycle bells; baby clothes on offer next to a stall selling the rarest of spices from Africa; cat carriers, and I swear a little bitty kitten has just popped its head out and popped its head back in. Next to all things kitty is a stall selling lace doilies and antimacassars. Stalls as far as one eye and the other can see.

"Your mouth is so wide open you'll be catching midges," the superintendent says.

Our walk round this open-air market of a place will take a lifetime. The stopping and starting of Superintendent Glue does not help in all of this. Every step is a cog in a slow-turning wheel of foot movement. He walks with the freedom and liberality of an overweight crab. Patience needed.

The mist is still hanging low. What a contrast between this world and the open skies of Orkney. The superintendent has seen someone that he wants to talk to. Over we go.

"I've got someone for you, Madame Mainland." Superintendent Glue, shouting to make himself heard above the hubbub. "Madame Mainland, will you please give this feller a reading? Forewarned is forearmed."

This Madame Mainland is tip-to-toe in expensive-looking trinkets. She is dressed for the part. They must have an arrangement. No money is asked of me. The superintendent remains within earshot.

"Your love line is clear and well chiselled. That is a good sign. Your lifeline, least said, best mended.

"Now this is good news for you. That money line is as straight as the Forth Road Bridge, with steel girders of certainty. You will return to your world the wealthiest man in all of Birsay."

"Now doesn't that bring you unexpected happiness, the best sort of happiness anyone can have? I'll leave you to it. Some business to attend to. I collect a voluntary donation for the Orkney Police Charities fund from every stallholder. A time-consuming business, and I must make a start. Be back here in an hour's time." The superintendent is grinning as he swings his truncheon.

"But I don't have a watch – how will I know when the hour is up?"

An hour is not long enough.

"Don't worry. I won't leave you here. Now, I have wonderful news for you. You can fill a wheelbarrow full of *whatever you want*. Take one of those three-wheeled jobbies. There's a stack of the extra-large ones in the pen next to the kirk. Should anyone ask, just give them my name. Fill it to the brim with whatever you want, all for free. They've all heard of me."

The superintendent then leaves to concentrate on his charity work. He walks with the gainliness of a man wrestling with an octopus on a conveyor belt.

I am soon to have wealth beyond my dreams.

The best gold ring from the jewellery stall; for Gail, in it goes.

An ingot from the gold bullion stall; quite a weight.

Several bundles of the finest silk from Samarkand; so smooth to the touch.

Sable coats of pure white fur; my cheeks, so soft.

Spices with the most pungent and mysterious of Far East aromas; breathe in.

An ornate Ancient Egyptian grandfaether clock from the grandfaether clock stall. Half the size; easily tucks in.

Before I know it, I have room left for one more item only.

I choose a Persian magic carpet with a bird pattern heralding my flight to freedom; a bird inside a cage, like that beam of light trapped inside the lighthouse on the Brough. On the top it goes, balancing precariously.

I feel like a million dollars, and I'm sure that that is the sum value of what I am pushing in my wheelbarrow, full to the brim with untold riches.

I nick my right hand. A kind person at the first-aid stall stems the bleeding. My right leg has not been shaking all the time that I have been here. Odd, that.

With the wheelbarrow full, I sense my hour is up. This hour has sped by as fast as a hare running around a dog track. I return to our prearranged meeting place.

"I see you've made the most of this once-in-a-lifetime opportunity. We mustn't keep the constable waiting." Superintendent Glue is, as always, grinning. It is fortunate he sets a slow pace. Pushing a heavily-laden wheelbarrow is not easy work.

The open steel-reinforced door is ahead. I can make out the constable there. He is waiting for me, on the 'home' side. Maybe he is waiting for the superintendent as well.

The constable is waving. "Cooee, cooee."

I "Cooee, cooee" back.

I am suddenly surrounded by faces. Faces I have known during my life; all the time or at some part. Faces disembodied. Faces fleshed out and lined to reflect life's journey. Faces who seem to know me but I cannot place. Faces desperate for an escape and seeing me as their last hope. Faces upsetting me.

I snap my fingers. The faces disappear.

The problem… fixed.

I sing a little ditty.

"Time to go home,
Time to go home.
Do-be, do-do. Do-do-be, do-do.
Time to go home,
Time to go home.
I am waving bye-bye, bye-bye, bye-bye.
Bye-bye."

Well, that is that. Impatient to return with all my riches, I lead the way back to a world that offers little for me.

My life is to be cut short, but I will die a wealthy man.

"Isn't this the best that you've ever felt?" the superintendent is shouting in my ear.

I nod. No need for reply. I am grinning the broadest of grins. Grinning.

That'll be taxing your neck muscles.

Fuck off.

"This is better than the exploration of a woman's inner sanctum," the superintendent shouts. A pause. He is giving me the space to say something in return. He is looking for my thanks.

I nod. I will play along.

"This is more arousing than holding a betting slip that has that name of the winner of the 3.30 at Newmarket on it."

I nod. A faint smile.

"This is even better than standing at the bar and being offered as much drink as you can down, and it is being bought for you." The superintendent has a pleading look about him.

I nod. A grin.

My wheelbarrow is almost halfway across. Constable Mowat, willing-me-on hand gestures, smiling aplenty, the home side beckons.

"Stop. Stop. The wheelbarrow, beuy. The wheelbarrow," Superintendent Glue barks, piercing voice. Loud. Acting the drill sergeant.

I drop the wheelbarrow.

"You cannot bring the wheelbarrow with you. It must stay on this side. Don't worry. All is not lost. We can unload and empty its contents into this large, reinforced linen sack."

This we do. I am still to be the wealthiest man in Birsay. This will take some time. I'll have to put up with more 'how lucky I am' blether. Price worth paying.

"Isn't this better than enjoying a 99 cone on a warm Saturday afternoon, lounging around at the Pierhead? The *St Ola* soon to be arriving from down south; passengers all wearing the latest fashions, speaking like they do on the wireless. Ever so frightfully."

I lift up my end of the full swag bag. I need both hands to do so. Quite an effort. He is not doing his bit. Most of the goods slide from my end of the sack down to his. I try inching my way backwards to the doorway. There is a bit of pushme-pullyou going on.

"No. Stop. You can't go through with the swag bag." The superintendent, in drill-sergeant mode once again. I drop my end.

The superintendent has a crown on his sleeve. I wonder why someone of his high rank has been posted to Stromness Police Station. He must have blotted his copybook.

I should have thought of that earlier.

"You come back at different weight. Laws of physics and theology. Burnt to cinders."

Shadrach, Meshach and Abednego.

"Einstein and Newton and Marconi. Scientifically proven," Constable Mowat shouts back through the gap. "Must leave bag behind."

"Must leave the bag behind," shouts Superintendent Glue. No echo here. Full force eight.

They are winking at each other, the constable and the superintendent.

I am the entertainment. I do not like that.

I don't mind saying, I'm reduced to tears. The injustice of it all. Nothing positive for me to take out of this, whatsoever. Unimaginable wealth within reach, alluring as a bubble, just for a brief moment. Not so much a gradual fade-and-die; a pop. All over. Gone.

To top it all, my Persian magic carpet, my means of escape, snatched away.

I have been cheated, mocked and laughed at by these two grinning policemen. And let's not forget the role played by the sergeant. All three of these men in blue deserve to be in the Gallery of the Bad.

I am the entertainment.

The superintendent confirms my weight. "Twelve stone eight pounds. Same as before. Off you go. I still have some work to do here."

I am given a firm helping hand – well, it's more like a shove.

The superintendent waves goodbye. "Cooee, cooee." One hand on the swag bag, to be returned to the stallholders or to be treated as a 'donation'.

My hands. Redundant hands.

The constable shuts the steel door firmly behind us.

So much for the 3.30 at Newmarket.

Ding-a ling. Ding-a-ling.

CHAPTER 27

THE HAND OF CHOCOLATE

Early '60s.

Ding-a-ling.

"No time to dilly-dally." Constable Mowat is setting a fast pace. We retrace our steps. The walkway. There is light at first. It's natural light.

Silence. Silence from me. Deliberate. Pointed.

"What do you think of Tunnock's tea cakes? Joy to behold," the constable says, friendly-like, trying to break the ice. "The Battenberg befits its name: cake of royal delight. That Garibaldi, she's a sly biscuit, those sweet raisins. Tried Wright's ginger nuts; quality from South Shields, near Glasgow – well, down south anyway?"

I feel empty inside. I want to be put out of my misery. Maybe my execution can be brought forward to today.

I stroke my chin. It feels stubbly. I shaved less than an hour ago. It should be as smooth as a baby's bottom. Aaah-choo. Aaah-choo. I take out a white handkerchief, free of snot, with my right hand and have a good blow. There is no bandage on my right hand.

The whooshing of capsules overhead is the soundtrack to our return to Stromness Police Station.

Natural light gives way to artificial light. This, at least, is as before.

I am completely disorientated and downcast. Everything is the same but not the same, and will never be the same.

Talk to the constable about anything. That'll steady the pulse. Give you a grounding, something to hold on to. He's open to cakes and biscuits. There is no sweeter subject.

I don't have anything to say.

Well, if that's your attitude, just start an argument. You're good at that. I'm off.

I give it a go.

"The macaroon is Scottish by name and Scottish by nature. A biscuit of the utmost crunchiness and spikiness." My voice is hesitant. "You bite it without knowing whether it will bite back. It offers you the hand of chocolate, but there is a price to be paid." My conversation hat thrown into the ring, but my heart isn't in it.

"Never a truer word spoken," the constable agrees.

This friendliness, after all that he has done to me. I'll show him.

"Can you, Constable, be so kind and explain to me the peculiar timings of the Orkney Railway timetable?"

"Rumbled. Safe combination for steel-safe door. Look up Mainland Orkney Railway timetable. Rumbled."

"But Constable, the numbers come from an out-of-date timetable." My old chippiness is returning.

"Memorises railway timetable but as for own name, hasn't a clue." The constable pauses to let that inescapable nugget of truth sink in.

"My timetable is official and published." That'll show him. "I am talking about the Mainland of Orkney rail timetable, the Burwick to Brough of Birsay route. What has the Orient Express timetable from Wick to Constantinople got to do with all of this?"

I have accused him of saying something he hasn't said; clever tactic.

"You remember your place. You're only twenty-seven. A bit young to be a know-it-all."

"I will not be spoken to like that. I have rights."

"You've already seen your lawyer, him with the one eye. We can always return to this discussion tomorrow…"

Never mind the Brough of Birsay being separated from Birsay and the Mainland; tomorrow my spinal cord will be saying goodbye to my neck. I am not winning here. I do not want to put at risk the tasty fry-up on my return. Given my run of luck, it will probably be my last.

Through the darkness into the light.

"Well, here we are. Back at the top of the stairs. Back from the underworld. Wasn't that a once-in-a-lifetime experience?" The constable smiles.

I cannot ignore the sound of hammering overhead. Work on the scaffold is at an advanced stage by now.

If only there were some vision of beauty to distract me from the sound of hammer against wood.

Easier to catch an elusive butterfly than recapture that lovely pink-fluffy-cushion-world dream served up last night.

My right leg is now shaking.

And here I am. Back in the guest room. Safe and secure and about to snuggle under.

Before I enter Dreamland, I mull over an indisputable fact.

If I hadn't been drawn back to Orkney after these years, I wouldn't now be on death row.

CHAPTER 28

A RICH TEA

EarLy 1960s

I am in the in-by. Ephraim and myself, sitting by the hearth. A bottle of Highland Park, half full and half empty. The smokiness from the whisky is at one with the wispiness from the peat fire. We are enveloped in warmth. We are profound and shapeless and eternal. It is good to be back home.

A pink flamingo joins us in front of the hearth from the byre. Neither Ephraim nor I bat an eyelid. This is Orkney, after all.

"Flamingos are a bit like us people in Orkney: hospitable, but with a weakness in one leg, and this weakness means that them flamingos often stand on one leg with the other leg tucked in behind their body," Ephraim says.

I don't nod.

"Ephraim, what do the flamingos hope to achieve by this tucking-in of one leg?"

"Keeps the heat in, beuy. Keeps the heat in. Flamingos may have less legs and arms, but come from the same family as them octopuses. Octopuses feel the cold but they have a different centre of gravity. It's a well-known fact."

I nod.

"Beuy, pull up a chair for our guest."

I pull up a chair. The three of us in front of the peat fire. Ephraim, honours graduate in whisky, delivers a masterclass on all things flamingo.

He tops up his glass and then continues. "Those Ancient Egyptians thought that the flamingo was the living representation of the god Ra—"

I am being roughly shaken. My sleep has been a long and deep one.

The land of dreams is no more. Peaty balls of smoke dispersing into nothingness. A pink flamingo and an Ephraim inside this bubble. I reach out to touch the bubble. It has burst. I yawn and rub my eyes. Still in bed.

Sergeant Tulloch stands before me. No breakfast tray.

"It's a fine, bright morning. No need to look at your watch. It's seven o'clock. Today is *your* day. Carpe diem. A *special* day.

"Them hens are refusing to go outside this morning even though the sun is shining and Mister Wind is still on holiday. Them hens not going outside means, as sure as eggs are eggs, Mister Wind will be back tomorrow with a vengeance and the heavens will be chucking it down. Hens are an example to us all. How they manage to get the weather right and lay eggs and cluck-cluck-cluck all at the same time is a mystery. Isn't life in Orkney a wonder?

"At least a few midges will be there to watch, paying their respects. Orkney always puts on a good show. We'll be turning *your* special day into everyone's special day. I know you're more than happy to play your part. I'm sure this not giving us your name is just shyness." The sergeant gives me a slap on the back. It is well meant.

"You like an audience. You deserve an audience. You'll get an audience. Let's *carpe diem.*

"Our yard is large, but not large enough to take everyone who'll want to watch. Some West Mainland folk are bound to be disappointed. Everything has to be tickety boo. We'll make sure those wooden bits and bobs are sturdy enough to take your weight. Plenty of time yet to apply the finishing touches. You're not due on until noon.

"*To every thing there is a season*
And a time to every purpose under the heaven:
A time to be born, and a time to die..."
Sergeant Tulloch bursts into song.

I know full well what he means by 'bits and bobs'. He probably even wants me to see whether the noose and hood are to my liking. Wide awake now, getting focused, I look up at the ceiling and am so taken by surprise that I crick my neck.

There are black pencil lines and markings on the ceiling. These trace yesterday's journey. There are the dashes representing my steps downwards. Those long lines, a finger-width apart, the narrow underground chamber and the wide walkway. A dot for the door. Small rectangle for the large open-air market. Dots and dashes higgledy-piggledy for the stalls. An arrow for the return journey through the chamber.

This map makes a far better record of what took place yesterday than any written entry could.

But it doesn't just stop there as diaries do, backward-looking, a record of. If only it did. The map spills into today, into the what-is-in-store-for-me, all etched out on the ceiling.

My route from the guest room, out into the courtyard to the rear of the police station, and here in the middle of the yard is a set of gallows with an X and a matchstick man.

Hangman, that's the game we used to play in school – white chalk, blackboard.

My end is nigh. All mapped out, as I look at the ceiling above.

I did not see this the night before. I did not. It has appeared overnight. The Angel of Death with a unique calling card.

"Throw something on. Let's just go outside, shall we? Let's see whether the scaffold is done and dusted; dry after that final lick of paint. What do you think? Plenty of time later for you to have a shower. Up you get."

I am given no choice in the matter. The sergeant watches me as I throw on yesterday's clothes. Once I am dressed, he secures my right arm behind my back and I am frogmarched out into the fresh morning air.

What'll happen to me when you hang?

You'll soon find out.

It is very noisy outside in the large police yard. Workmen are hammering away, still putting the final touches to this wooden construct.

In my mind's eye, I can see a body swaying to and fro from the scaffold. It is my body. I can see my soul plucked from my body, cupped in disembodied hands and then offered up like a white dove for the final part of the journey.

'Coo-coo. Coo-coo.'

"Come on. Forget about those heebie-jeebies. What a corker of a day. The sun, shining. The sky, cloudless blue. No wind. No wind. Not many have such a fruit-machine-jackpot of Orkney weather on *their* special day."

It's a crapshoot.

Don't come all Yankee with me.

"Tell you what. Choose your fruit. Lemon, orange or banana?"

"What do you mean?"

"Just choose your fruit. Lemon, orange or banana? The lemon was the fruit of choice of the Ancient Egyptians. Not many know that. Between you and me, I always thought the orange a bit too perfect in its roundness. The banana is too bendy a fruit. Think of your neck, man.

"The lemon it is. A lemon for the sun. A lemon for the sky. A lemon for the wind. The lemon does each one of them proud. Three lemons in a row. You've won. A fruit machine of good fortune. Pull the lever and just wait for the jingle-jangle of gold coins. It's going to be that sort of day. A 'lemon' sort of day. Just think on that.

"You're a very lucky man indeed. Here's Constable Mowat. And a very good morning to you, Constable. Please join us. We're having a fine chat."

Constable Mowat stands the other side of me. Sergeant Tulloch to my left; Constable Mowat to my right. Flanked.

"Now, let's just see if this black hood fits. Constable Mowat, if you please."

The rolled-up hood is unfolded over my head, balaclava-style. Sergeant Tulloch probably thinks I will struggle and be awkward. No. This is to be my fate. It is fitting. In more ways than one.

I try to speak. A muffled voice. Sergeant Tulloch continues." We don't want the hood to be so tight that you cannot breathe. Has to be tight enough, though. It's the way these things are done."

"Thank you very much, Constable, a comfortable fit."

Blackness. I can make out what they're saying. I am not gasping for breath.

I wouldn't, of course, know which of them removes the hood. It is carried out with consideration. Not yanked off, short and sharp. My opinion on the hood's comfiness is not sought. At least a fry-up should now be offered. My morning shower can wait.

"Constable, you can leave us now and go back to looking into this problem with the police radio. There's been some airwaves jiggery-pokery this morning. The outside phone line is dead as well. Most unusual. Most unusual."

Sergeant Tulloch then whispers, "You know what? It's such a grand morning, wouldn't it be a shame for me to waste it? I can get some fishing done. The trout are biting like nobody's business. Let's just bring forward proceedings from noon to nine o'clock sharp. Of course, that leaves us with a little under an hour, but still plenty of time for a full run-through. Saves you the waiting."

No. I don't believe it. They are going to hang me before I have had breakfast and my final words with a man of the cloth. The bastards.

My right leg starts to tremble uncontrollably.

My teeth start to chatter uncontrollably.

I am going to be hanged before breakfast, and *no last rites.*

The finishing touches to the scaffold are being applied by some workmen at the far end of the yard. From this group, a workman walks towards us. He takes his time.

"Sergeant, is this prisoner 'The Man with No Name'? Is he the one due to swing at nine o'clock this morning for the murder of a Mister Flett?" This stranger is pointing at me.

"He is that man." Sergeant Tulloch confirms the fact.

The workman stares at me long and hard. "I better get back to my men. They'll be thinking I've gone for an early lunch."

The sergeant holds me in a firm grip. He can see that the news of the bringing forward of my hanging by three hours has not gone down at all well with me. He is still grinning.

"Let's have a cup of wet tea, hot, not scalding, and who knows what delight of biscuit will be available for the dunking of. It's these little things in life. We'll turn *your* day into a nice social occasion, like going to a housey-housey bingo night in the village hall without the numbers being called. There's someone I'd like you to meet."

We enter a small hut in the far corner of the yard. From

the outside, it looks no different to one of those temporary workmen's huts. Inside, no different too. A table, on which there is a wireless; a few chairs; a sink and a kettle. Spartan. A tea-break-and-sandwiches hut. Nothing more. Built for purpose. Dismantled easily. A put-up-and-take-down hut.

There are four corners to this hut.

There is one man sitting in that corner? No.

The man is sitting in the far corner.

A solitary sort of man; a bright orange helmet on his head. A health-and-safety sort of man. A sempiternal sort of man wearing a brown smock of sorts, a large crucifix dangling.

I'm looking at a *priest* sort of man.

He looks vaguely familiar.

I know him.

We are invited to sit down.

This is to be it. No full Orkney breakfast. Man-of-the-cloth time. Dummy run, my arse.

It all isn't meant to finish like this, my intuition tells me. I know. I know. Experience. It'll come…

From the kettle into the pot.

From the spout into the mug.

From the mug…

That hits the spot.

The man before me, in his brown smock with his crucifix dangling round his neck, has a soft voice, a kind voice, a purring, friendly Orkney voice. The man.

I know… I know.

"Here I am. I hope you're impressed. Freshly boiled. One for the pot. Just think of me as Polly." The nice man shakes my hand. His hand is sympathetic to the touch, not clammy.

"I have already put the kettle on. Do you know who made me do so? *Our Lord. He* told me that I am to have a special visitor this morning. And here you are. The Lord has even gifted me this song to sing. And you know what the song is? Well, it's nearer to a nursery rhyme. Ach, come on, have a guess."

I know that man. He's the Minister. What's he doing here?

The Minister starts to sing.

"Polly put the kettle on,
Polly put the kettle on,
Polly put the kettle on,
We'll all have tea."

He is sing-songy-singing. It is contagious. It is infectious. I cannot help myself. I join in.

"Sukey take it off again,
Sukey take it off again,
Sukey take it off again,
They've all gone away."

"That was lovely. Even Frankie Sinatra and that Mister Bing Crosby couldn't have done a finer job singing in such harmony. Here, take one of these." A plate of biscuits is offered.

What's our Minister doing wearing a brown smock and that crucifix?

"It's too early for that most royal of biscuits, the chocolate Bourbon. Hmm, perhaps not the most appropriate of biscuits anyway; them Bourbons didn't have a happy ending.

"The Rich Tea is the right one for such a special moment. For making peace with oneself, it has to be the Rich Tea. The Rich Tea it is. The Rich Tea. Understated. Does the job. Pure Orkney.

"Here, take one. Have a good dunk. You cannot beat a good dunk. And if you slurp before you dunk, don't you worry now. This is not afternoon tea at the Ritz. This is not the ladies' finishing school at Cheltenham, though there are some fine fillies at Cheltenham." He speaks. Soft, compassionate.

What's our Minister doing carrying out this ritual from the other side, the Catholic side?

"An execution is not going to be a complete full stop for you. Regard it as a comma; a change of trains; a putting-back of the clocks for winter; a folding of a financial institution; the pangs of birth of a new nation.

"True, the trap door will be opened. True, the body will convulse. True, the head will twitch all over the place as the neck has a long holiday.

"Like a biscuit being dunked, there may be a difference in the texture of the body corporate before and after dunking, but we are still talking about the one basic entity." The Minister winks at me.

"A Rich Tea is as a Rich Tea does. The soul remains intact..."

Never mind your fucking soul, ask him where I end up.

"'........ and will leave to commence its journey, the most important journey of its life."

Sergeant Tulloch stands up. He looks like a man who can't wait to be off. He is waiting for the right moment.

The Minister continues. "This journey will take your soul to the northern tip of the Orkney Mainland at Birsay. The tides will part. Your soul will cross over to the Brough in the same floating casket as sweet baby Moses, to be found in the seaweedy bulrushes there.

"My son, you will find peace amongst the Neolithic ones, the Viking ones, and yes, the Ancient Egyptian ones."

He is painting such an inviting picture of what awaits me. You know what? I want it to happen as soon as possible. He is weaving a spell over me.

"Go on, help yourself to a second Rich Tea."

The sergeant yawns. He has heard it all before. His Rich Tea biscuit has been dunked for far too long and the soggy half has fallen into the tea. Detached. The biscuit like some sodden weight becomes stuck at the bottom. Unpleasant to scrape out.

Doesn't help the taste of the tea. Dregs steeped in dregs.

Back to the bitterness of reality.

I want this to be over with as soon as possible.

I am ready to meet my Maker.

"Sergeant Tulloch, can you switch the wireless on? It's over there – don't make it too loud. I must ask you to leave me alone with my friend so that I can hear his confession and deliver the final rites in private."

"I will be waiting just outside. If you need me, just give me a shout." Sergeant Tulloch closes the door behind him on his way out.

The Minister and myself are left alone.

"Alexander, my beuy, you're no doubt puzzled to see me in this Roman Catholic garb, but we all have to be seen to be doing our bit, going the whole hog in reaching out to those poor unfortunates who have every right to follow a different faith, but it just happens to be a lesser faith to our own.

"It can't be easy, mind, for my poor counterpart who has swapped with me. Delivering my standard Sabbath sermon at what critics would call a fire-and-brimstone volume has damaged his vocal cords. He can't even say boo to a goose now.

"It's one of these initiatives. What they call ecumenism. Do I believe in any of this? Of course not. Thank God there are still large swathes of the fine land of Scotland where Protestants hate the sight of Catholics and vice versa. You're always going to get a top dog. It just always happens to be us." The Minister is pleased with himself. It shows.

I nod.

"Another Rich Tea? No? Well, let's get back to the business in hand."

I am alone with the Minister. I feel unprepared. My life soon to be over. Maybe I will be asked to atone for my sins.

Maybe not. Maybe I have an hour or so left. Maybe not.

I feel this calmness. I know that I should speak about my life in a tense, not the present.

That was that.

The sergeant did not forget, as he was leaving, to turn the wireless on. The room fills with gentle, soothing music. Celestial and holy. Frankie Sinatra will never let you down. *My Way.* Only he, with that voice and phrasing, can capture the moment. *My Way.* I hum the song to myself. No outward sign of doing so. Lips not moving. My secret. *My Way.* My final prayer. *My Way.*

The Minister blesses me. His right leg starts to shake uncontrollably.

"Listen to me, my son." The Minister is smiling broadly. "You can see by the convulsions in my right leg where my real loyalty lies. The one-eyed lawyer has made contact with *our* leader on your behalf.

"Billy Fury apologises for the delay in coming to your rescue. He's been away, at the annual conference of All the Right-Leg-Shakers in Ireland. With Ireland, we're talking about the twenty-six counties plus the six at the top. That makes thirty-two in all.

"They've turned this association into a real money-spinner. On tour. Worldwide. Continuous. Folk just lap it up. Feet and ankles in an uncontrollable state of twitchiness and flux. Moving irrespective of the music. Irrespective. Possessed, they are. Possessed. Through the pain barrier, gritted teeth and all. It certainly knocks the spots off the do-si-do, and will give Scottish country dancing more than a good run for its money. That St Vitus, gold top.

"Billy Fury is sponsoring the Scottish leg of the tour. I don't know where he gets the money from; him just a piano tuner. You wouldn't think there'd be much money in that. Billed as *Waterdance – We Let our Feet do the Talking*. One can only marvel at the generosity of folk here. A wad of pound notes in the collection plate.

"*Waterdance* has reached the Mainland of Orkney, and with today's matinee performance being cancelled – some problem over there not being enough seats – we are here in numbers to come to the aid of a member of our brother- and sisterhood."

"Minister, bless you," I cry out with relief.

There is a tremendous noise outside, not of workmen hammering but of singing, a hundred voices in perfect pitch and harmony, putting to the sword those in the way of all that's good. Celestial.

"This power will defeat anything that stands in its way. The policemen will have fled for their lives by now if they've any sense. Three men against a hundred of the good. Sergeant Tulloch, Constable Mowat and Superintendent Glue are no fools. They will recognise that the odds are well and truly stacked against them.

"A Massey Ferguson is parked just beyond the gate. I give you its keys. May the tractor and trailer of life be with you."

I am near to tears. I hug the Minister and look up to the heavens.

Isn't the neck an anatomical wonder?! Its astonishing range of movement and all. I will never take my neck for granted again.

With head held high, I make my escape.

Today is my day. Bring out the Daddies!

CHAPTER 29

HOMEWARD BOUND

Early '60s

The Massey Ferguson greets me as an old friend, as a well-worn pair of slippers. Key turned in the ignition and away we go, me singing away at the top of my voice and the tractor providing the accompaniment.

I am as regal-looking as King Farouk on his throne. Homeward bound. We are as one as we build up speed along the country road, heading for the parish of Birsay, the West Mainland of Orkney. Leading the way, a flock of lapwings in V-formation acting as a guard of honour. There is no other traffic on the Stromness-to-Birsay road.

I look up and marvel at the Big Sky. It is South Sea island blue. No apology of a blue here. Cloudless. The sun is shining. There is no wind.

A show is being performed in my honour. Lapwings. White doves, cooing away. The corncrakes don't want to miss out on the fun, crex-crexing. And there, displaying, are hen harriers looking for a partner, and there's a chiffchaff or two, that modest little wonder, and those starlings looping the loop

– a bit early in the day, aren't they? All the birdies greeting me.

Hypnotic, must keep my eyes on the road.

I look in the side-view mirror… the left… the right… the left again.

I look back to check that no one is in pursuit.

I look straight in front, concentrating on the road ahead.

I repeat.

The neck is a holy wonder. The neck will always have an importance beyond the infinite.

The neck this. The neck that. What about me?

What the fuck about you?

I am looking forward to seeing Ephraim and the late Mister Flett again. Ephraim is a make-do faether figure for me, and the late Mister Flett is like a grandfaether figure who chimes on the hour, as all good grandfaether clocks do. I am sure they will be worried about me. The last time we'd have seen each other is on our outing to the Broch of Birsay in the middle of the night. How that ended, I am unclear.

Over a wee dram of whisky sitting by the peat fire, I will tell them about how I saw Gracie Fields and how I was befriended by Billy Fury, and what about my new haircut, and yes, how I was stitched up, about to hang, and am now on the run. Yes, I, Alexander A. Alexander, have lots of news to tell.

I nearly forget to turn left at the Quoyloo crossroads. I mustn't forget to celebrate my freedom with a quick salute to Kitchener's Memorial. If my luck is in, and it is, it will be low tide, making the Brough of Birsay and the rest of Birsay one entity.

Before I know it, I am back home.

I leave the Massey Ferguson at the top gate and start the short walk down to the bu.

After that final bend in the winding track, I am on the home stretch. There's my bu. It's so exciting. Now less than a hop, step and jump away. The farmstead looks different, though, freshened up. The strong sunlight must be playing tricks on me. I raise my right hand to shield my eyes, but no, I am not mistaken, Ephraim has given the outside of the bu a new lick of paint.

A postman freewheels past me, doing wheelies on his bike. A few minutes later, there he is again. This time, he is having to pedal furiously uphill.

"It's… a… fine… day." He huffs and puffs.

"Aye, aye." I don't recognise the postman. He must be the holiday relief.

The postman stops his bike. He seems quite happy to be passing the time of day. "I hear the *Waterdance* people are in town. I'm only going to see them out of sympathy. Indeed, they come from a strange land."

He looks around him to make sure no one is listening in.

"How in the hell can the *Waterdance* people say that they come from a civilised country. We don't have traffic lights here, but at least all of us in Orkney have been given postcodes."

Off he cycles to continue his morning round.

I hear a vehicle behind me. I look round to see a large white van coming my way, slowly reversing down the track. I stand to one side to let the van pass.

Outside the bu, two men get out. I see an elderly lady open the door of the farmstead. I cannot make out her features clearly. A three-piece suite is being delivered, not collected.

Maybe there is more to this than meets the eye.

A few minutes later, I have to get out of the way again as the white van is on the way back up.

The driver winds down the window.

"Fine day."

"Aye, aye."

"You from these parts?"

"I could very well ask the same of you."

"Is there a police station nearby?"

"That's a good question." I grin, rictus-like. The last place I need to be reminded of is a police station. "Continue into Stromness, just a few miles down the road, and you'll find it there, just as you come into town."

"I need to report the theft of—"

"Can't help you." I am sharp with him.

Without any further ado, the driver winds up his window and drives off.

Back on my own doorstep. At last. It is good to be back home. I take in a good gulp of fresh air. Me being so close to death, but safe at last. My senses on overdrive. I am a very lucky man. I have waited for this moment.

And then this rumbling sound starts up from inside the bu. I can't make head nor tail of what it might be. A fanciful thought – perhaps the furniture indoors is readying itself for a breakout? The throbbing increases.

I don't knock. Why should I? It's my bu. The front door is always open. I walk in. I have to shout to make myself heard.

"Aye, aye. It's me, I'm back." The noise is ear-splitting. Where is it coming from? "Aye, aye," I yell above the din. Then all goes quiet.

An old lady emerges from the oot-by; takes one look at me, mouth open in disbelief.

"And who might you be?" A presumptuous question for a visitor to ask, but this is my home after all. I have every right.

The old lady just stares back at me. She recognises me. She looks shocked.

"Michael, get your dad in here... fast," the old lady shouts at this lad who can't be more than sixteen years old. He still has puppy fat on him. He is wearing a watch.

"Can't it wait?" the youngster answers back.

"No, it cannot. Do, as you're told.

"Come in. Some tea? Ephraim's working in the yard. He won't be long." I recognise Gail's voice. I try hard to hide the shock. Time has not been kind to the girl of my dreams. Her long, flowing blonde hair now cropped short, her face deeply lined. That's Gail, the Gail of my dreams, there in front of me.

And me just yesterday (or was it the day before?) sitting on a wooden plank, looking at my face in the barber's mirror, asking for a DA but knowing full well that I'd be getting a short back and sides. The mirror is, as it always was in the oot-by, on the far wall. I do not want to look in it. I don't know what face I will find.

I will not look in it.

Gail's voice still has that power to send shivers through me. So Gail lives here.

A large, stout man with a bloated face comes into the room, takes one look at me and screams in horror. "What are you doing here? You should be..." This large, stout man is Ephraim. He starts to foam at the mouth, falls to the ground... a thudding noise on impact. Mouth open... a war dance of a tongue... a rattling sound... barely a twitch.

"Call the doctor, Michael. Be quick about it while I administer first aid to your dad."

Her Ephraim.

She looks down at this brute of a man on the floor and then up at me, pure hatred in her eyes. This, from my sweetheart. Only yesterday I picked out the gold ring to go on the fourth finger of her left hand. She and me as one.

What is happening now to Ephraim is not my fault. I haven't even had the chance to speak to him, my pretendy faether. What with him in his death throes and Gail, my sweetheart... I

271

decide that it is better for all concerned if I leave the bu straight away. A quick look at my ben, my bedroom, then I'll be off.

My conscience is clear.

I will walk through into the in-by.

I don't remember a door being there.

I push open the door.

Ding-a-ling. Ding-a-ling.

CHAPTER 30

THE LATE MISTER FLETT

Ding-a-ling. Ding-a-ling.

Sitting by the hearth in front of the peat fire is the late Mister Flett. He's in his usual place. He hasn't changed one iota. His neck is still his most distinguishing feature, a drainpipe with wobbly flab in the middle, stuck there until something annoys him.

The late Mister Flett is in the rocking chair.

He is motionless in the rocking chair.

I expect him to be motionless in the rocking chair.

Everything in its time and place.

I expect the late Mister Flett to be still life, a tableau like the Suffolk sheep in the distant fields.

I expect.

I want him to be so.

I need him to be so.

There is movement, imperceptible at first. A flicker of movement, the rocking chair forwards and backwards, backwards and forwards. It is the late Mister Flett's rocking chair, and it is the rocking chair's late Mister Flett.

The late Mister Flett proceeds to look me up and down. He then looks out of the window. It is now pitch-black outside. Something has caught his eye. He sits forward. The rocking chair, no longer forwards and backwards, returns to a tableau once more.

"Up there." The late Mister Flett points with his first finger, Kitchener-style, at something that has caught his attention. He repeats, "Look up there." Quietly spoken. His Adam's apple on the move. Doesn't get out of his rocking chair.

An enormous green object up there in the night sky, neon light glowing, a Merry Dancer of not one but three enormous human heads. Green is the colour. Orkney's Merry Dancer. Aurora Borealis. The Northern Lights.

This head is a distorted conjoining of the heads of the three policemen, Constable Mowat, Sergeant Tulloch and Superintendent Glue. An egg that un-luck has fertilised. These three swimmers, truncheons in hand, fighting for space on the one chair. Musical chairs without any music. Green. Green against the black night sky.

A fourth figure makes his entrance. Full-length, not just head. It is a *he*, Nureyev-build, ballet-slender, graceful, dressed in black from top to toe. A bright white, not green, light shines down on him. He has a thin face; one black trouser leg is tucked into the flap of his black boot. Oh yes, oh yes, this fourth figure has a tail and cloven feet. An important detail.

This figure walks in front of the three policemen, still fighting, and takes a deep bow. You can see his oink-oink curl as he does so, an oink-oink curl at the back of his clean-shaven head.

He fully extends both arms out in front of him. He is holding something with the thumb and forefinger of each hand, arms still out wide. Both arms are slowly brought back into the centre. You cannot see the fighting policemen.

As sure as eggs are eggs, he has drawn the curtains over the night's performance.

The late Mister Flett sits upright in his rocking chair, his chin on his left hand, supported by his right elbow tucked in midriff-high. A smile on his face; his expression straight out of the wrapper of a Fry's Five Boys chocolate bar. *Acclamation.*

His supported head moves from side to side, then stops. *Realisation.*

His supported head no longer moves from side to side, but now goes forwards, not once but twice, like a hen pecking at seed.

He knows something. He has found what to say. He will choose the right moment. The late Mister Flett is infirm and very old.

I don't know what's got into me. My teeth are chattering away loudly.

Since my return to Orkney, the only people to recognise me have been Gail, Ephraim and the late Mister Flett.

The late Mister Fleet returns his left hand to his side. The late Mister Flett returns his right elbow to his side. The late Mister Flett is still sitting upright. He is pinching his own cheek with the thumb and forefinger of his right hand.

He gets out of *his* chair.

I am taken by surprise. The rocking chair and the late Mister Flett, and the late Mister Flett and the rocking chair, no longer one the extension of the other. The late Mister Flett is standing up. I am just a cow's spit away.

The late Mister Flett speaks. A quiet, deliberate voice.

"The Lord giveth and the Lord taketh away. In the eyes of the Lord, we are all equal. All of us, equal. All of us, with our walk on part.

"We are all one and the same; no better, no worse. We are all equal and go round and round, in life and death until the winds take us out of our..."

Your mither and Ephraim. My-son-the-Minister and yours truly: Gail and her mither. The one-eyed lawyer and the world-famous hypnotist. Missus Linklater and Missus Mainland. The Lord and the Devil. Superintendent Glue, Sergeant Tulloch and Constable Mowat. Your good self and let's for once put royalty last – His Excellency, King Farouk.

The late Mister Flett is staring. He looks right into me, and is inside me. I will show no fear. I will step forward and fill the space between us. My teeth are chattering away. I have no say over my actions. I am primed, my hands raised. I am ready.

The moment has come. I am about to make the move.

"What is your name?" he whispers.

I don't reply. I am aware of his breath.

"You know full well your name is Alexander A. Alexander."

The late Mister Flett's voice is still soft to the ear, but there is an edge to it.

"I will ask again. What is your name?"

"I don't know." I am being wilful.

"Your name is Alexander A. Alexander. Why do you deny something that is as certain as the wind, the Big Sky, the sea and the Green Land? Repeat after me. Alexan..."

I want to believe that we are both playing a part. This is nothing more serious than a game. One of us the interrogator, the other the interrogated. Seek and hide. Hide and seek.

This is just a lot of *knick-knack-paddywhack-give-the-dog-a-bone*. This is just a lot of chiffchaff.

"I refuse to give people my name," I say, a smugness in my voice and smile. But underneath...

"Why, Alexander A. Alexander, do you refuse to give people your name?" A menacing quality now. Still softly spoken.

I have got it wrong. This is not a game. I take a step back.

"I always wanted to be... someone else... you see..."

It is a confession of sorts, an admission never made before, hesitant but out there now.

"Alexander, listen to me. Orkney folk can see things as they are and ask, 'Why?' Orkney folk can dream about things that never were and say, 'Why not?' Orkney folk have the gift of being both the narrators and actors in their own stories. We are special. We are the entitled. We can make happen the dreams that come to us wrapped up in a peaty ball of smoke every night."

He has the power. The initiative lies with this infirm and elderly man.

"What did I do to deserve this? Did your dreams give you the right, Alexander A. Alexander? What dreams now accompany your every...?"

I try to answer, but cannot find the words to do so.

"Did you think that returning would make you feel better about yourself... after what you did to me?"

There are tears in his eyes.

"What gives you the right to go away, come back and expect everything here to stand still? Did you think that Orkney was waiting for you?"

There is a long pause, a silence. I try to but cannot look the late Mister Flett in the eye. I try to.

"My valuable watch would have been yours anyway."

I don't know what to say. I don't know what to say.

"Alexander A. Alexander, the watch would have been yours. Do you hear me?" The late Mister Flett raises his voice and jabs his finger at me. "Yours." He is shouting. "You would have inherited it. You, after all, are my own flesh and..."

He takes a step forward. He is uncomfortably close to me. Nothing friendly or forgiving in his features. He is about to deliver the *coup de grâce*.

"I am the man whose seed brought you..."

CHAPTER 31

BARBERS

I am blessed to come from Orkney, with its wind and Big Sky and Green Land and sea. I always wanted to return home, and here I am.

But what I have just been told is too much for me to take in, far too much.

I must get away. I must get away immediately.

There is one thing I must do before I leave Orkney. I must pay a visit to the police station but need to look neat and tidy.

Over there is a building with a neon sign. *Paraffin – Esso Blue.*

The large white card on the door says, *Open.*

I push the door open.

Ding-a-ling. Ding-a-ling.

"Hello, boychik. Good to see you again. Where's your faether?"

The man asks me, clippers in hand.

He takes out a clean white handkerchief (free of snot).